"You're seeing me at ⟨...⟩ father...

"Burns, pet escapes, bathroom emergencies." Mike didn't want to see the disappointment in Georgie's eyes.

Georgie smiled. "I see a little girl who loves her father. Rachel is intelligent and independent."

"Thank you."

She picked up the nearby clipboard. "Any questions about the car restoration process?"

"Can I do any of this work myself? Save a few pennies?"

"Actually, yes." Coming over, she pointed to a couple of the steps. "It'll all come back to you when the time is right."

This close, her sweet scent tickled his nose.

Just tell her.

He moved closer. Opening his mouth, he wanted to find the right words to set her straight. Instead, the light of the shop reflected off her, cascading over her in a golden glow, her beauty striking him. Here she was...finally, after all these years. Why had he resisted her for so long?

Dear Reader,

Welcome to Hollydale!

On vacation a couple of summers ago, my family picnicked at a park near a classic-car show. During that week, I couldn't let go the idea of a heroine who drives a classic car, and that segued into someone who fixes cars, but not her own life. With that came a glimmer of Mike, who owns a Ford Thunderbird in need of repairs, the same as his rusty heart. As the Thunderbird is gutted for another day in the sun, Georgie and Mike discover the power of second chances. Mike's opportunity comes with a push from his daughter after Rachel and her pink purse make quite an impression on Georgie. Rachel kept me laughing as I wrote this, and I hope you find her as delightful as her dad and Georgie do.

Second chances have played an important role in my life and provide Georgie and Mike with a way to confront their pasts and accept the redemptive power of love.

I hope you love Hollydale as much as I do. You can reach out to me at Facebook.com/authortanyaagler or at tanyaagler.com. I hope to hear from you.

Tanya

HEARTWARMING

The Sheriff's Second Chance

———

Tanya Agler

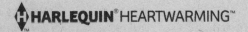

Recycling programs
for this product may
not exist in your area.

ISBN-13: 978-1-335-88956-0

The Sheriff's Second Chance

Copyright © 2020 by Tanya Agler

Printed in U.S.A.

Tanya Agler remembers the first set of Harlequin books her grandmother gifted her, and she's been in love with romance novels ever since. An award-winning author, Tanya makes her home in Georgia with her wonderful husband, their four children and a lovable basset, who really rules the roost. When she's not writing, Tanya loves classic movies and a good cup of tea. Visit her at tanyaagler.com or email her at tanyaagler@gmail.com.

To Jamie, who believed in me as an author before I did.

And thank you to my agent, Dawn Dowdle, for sticking by me and to my editor, Kathryn Lye, for taking a chance on me.

CHAPTER ONE

"BREAKING AND ENTERING reported at Max's Auto Repair. Not in progress."

Two robberies in one morning? A new record for Hollydale. One Mike Harrison would have loved not breaking.

"That makes five this month." Mike didn't flick on the siren. Instead, he turned onto Maple Drive and caught sight of the street's namesakes breaking into glorious shades of red and orange. "Anything else before I arrive?"

"Stay safe. We're down a patrol team of two officers as it is." Crackling came over the system, and Mike pulled into Max's.

Understaffed was an understatement with eleven people doing the work of thirteen. When the tourists flooded his small town in the Smokies, snapping pictures of every tree and ridge in sight, it would make even more work for the department, which was already running on a shoestring frayed on both ends. Mike wanted these burglaries solved, and fast. It was getting so bad that he and his daughter, Rachel, couldn't even wait for their favorite booth at the Holly Days Diner in peace. Not with the locals coming up and jabbing him in the ribs, asking when he was entering the sheriff's race. Shrugging, Mike always smiled and set the record straight. Hollydale already had a fine sheriff in Rick Donahue.

The sun's rays crept over the horizon, the promise of a warm day dampening the chill permeating the September air. Mike parked his squad car near a rusted Ford Taurus and a newer model red Toyota Prius. Using caution, he emerged with his hand on his utility belt and scanned the area. Not a soul greeted him. The hairs on the back of his neck bristled. From the corner of the long brick building, a colossal brown shaggy mutt bounded over. A couple of feet behind, a woman held on to a bright blue leash for dear life.

Mike's gaze met the woman's too-familiar green eyes. His heart rate accelerated.

Georgie Bennett was back in town.

Her shiny cap of chestnut hair, a slight curl at the ends, was shorter now, highlighting the cheekbones of her heart-shaped face. His gaze flickered over her black T-shirt and dark jeans accentuating her curves, clearly acquired since high school. She'd been cute then, but eleven years after graduation? The girl next door was quite the stunner.

He stopped short of rushing over. For one, he was here on official police business. For another, their friendship had ended on a sour note. All thanks to him. In a split second, Georgie's eyes flashed warmth, and even forgiveness. Then her jaw clenched, and she tightened her grip on the leash of the massive animal lumbering toward him.

Georgie's dog loped over the rest of the way. With a soft whine, the mutt settled on his haunches and lolled out his tongue in a friendly greeting. At least someone was happy to see him. Mike relaxed.

"Welcome home, Georgie." Mike glanced up and cleared his throat. "There's been a report of a B&E at this location. You and your dog need to leave and come back later."

"I'm the one who called it in." Her honey voice hit him hard.

Focus, Michael. If the perp was still in the building, innocent people could get hurt. Not again. Never again.

"Stay out here with…" The animal was too small for a buffalo. "Your dog."

Wheezing came from off in the distance. A stooped elderly man rounded the corner. Mike did a double take. It'd been a couple of months since he'd last seen his old high school teacher, Mr. Reedy. Never could get used to calling him Fred. Almost seemed sacrilegious somehow.

Mr. Reedy crooked his cane on his arm and adjusted the plastic cannula near his nose before wheeling an oxygen canister toward Mike.

"About time you showed up, Officer Harrison. Georgie must have called you a good half hour ago." Mr. Reedy stomped his cane on the pavement, not five feet away.

"Thirty-two minutes, according to my phone." Georgie waved it under Mike's face, her hand shaking like the red leaves of the nearby maples. This close he didn't miss the quaver in her voice or the pallor of her ashen skin.

He couldn't blame her. The criminal violation of a person's private or business space was traumatizing.

Mike blew out a deep breath "You two stay out here. I'll be right back."

Raising his trusty old Smith & Wesson, Mike entered the garage's reception area. Truth be told, he didn't expect anyone in here. Not with two people and a colossal beast of a dog out front. Still, better safe than sorry.

Flipping on the light switch, he groaned. Copies of *Car and Driver* littered the concrete floor. Hard pink shells of chewed bubble gum were stuck on the bottom of the upended coffee table. This wasn't anything like the B&E at Carter's Sporting Goods, where the crime scene was as neat as his mother's immaculate kitchen.

A quick scan of the bays in the garage yielded

no evidence and looked as though they hadn't been disturbed. Mike holstered his weapon and went outside.

"All clear."

As soon as he called out, Georgie rushed over, Mr. Reedy several steps behind. Georgie's dog nudged him as if asking what Mike intended to do about the mess.

"Plenty."

"Excuse me?" Georgie's eyebrows furrowed into a worried line. "Is that some sort of police jargon?"

"No." Mike rubbed his temples. "How long until Max arrives? I have some questions for him."

"About three months, give or take a week."

"Who's in charge while he's gone?"

A flicker of annoyance flashed behind Georgie's eyes, always expressive to say the least. Her shoulders stiffened, and she lifted her chin. No reason for her to be upset with him now. He was just doing his job.

"I am."

He slipped on his own mask, controlling his surprise. Wasn't often the town grapevine failed at its job. But if Georgie was back as a mechanic here? Georgie, a whiz with anything mechanical... Grandpa Ted's Thunderbird, now his, might have a second chance after all.

No. There were no second chances in life.

Why he hadn't sold the car yet, he didn't know. Stalling, most likely. Best change that as soon as possible. Tonight, even. Money from the sale would pay for those dance lessons Rachel had been begging for. He steeled himself. He had a duty to the citizens of this town. Investigating the scene would serve them better than wispy daydreams.

"Congratulations." He removed his notepad and pencil from his shirt pocket. "Mind if I ask you some questions?"

"Can I go inside and get Beau some water first?" Her pleading tone helped Mike stifle his laughter. Georgie still had her sense of humor if she named that homely mutt Beau. "I won't touch anything. The poor dog hasn't had anything to drink since he arrived. He and Mr. Reedy have been here for a while."

Georgie always had been a sucker for anything with four legs, although anything with four wheels pushed her over the moon.

Mike held up his hand. "Wait here."

Remembering the layout, Mike hurried back with a bowl filled with water. Best he could do under the circumstances. Georgie and Mr. Reedy had made their way over to a wrought iron bench. Mike bent and held the bowl out to Beau. The dog lapped up every drop.

Half of small-town police work centered on public relations as much as investigating crimes.

"I'm going to perform a more thorough investigation and take notes. Then I'll be back to ask you some further questions. I'll also want to take a look at the surveillance footage before I leave." Mike waited for Georgie's nod and then walked away.

Entering, he stopped and examined the lock on the front door. No scratches or other sign of forced entry. Unlike Carter's Sporting Goods, where the burglars had jimmied open the door, most likely with a crowbar, tripping the alarm. The security company had then contacted the police. A complete one-eighty from everything at this location.

He walked over to the windows. No marks of any kind there or on the locked back door, either. He huffed out a sigh and took out his fingerprinting kit. Dusting proved as futile here as it had at Carter's. There were simply too many smears to narrow any full prints down to one suspect.

The thieves knew what they were doing. Mike would give them that much. They'd make a mistake, though. When they did, he would solve the string of B&Es and get his dependable life back. The one that didn't involve people asking him pesky questions about running for sheriff. The one he'd scrabbled together the day Caitlyn sashayed into his dorm room announcing his impending fatherhood and he'd had to grow up quick.

As soon as Georgie provided an inventory of what was missing, he'd write up the report. Back at the station, without her. With the adrenaline of seeing her again wearing off, he needed to step back. Whenever he ran on emotion rather than logic, he ended up in a heap of trouble.

Rachel was more than enough proof of that.

SOME HOMECOMING. ONLY eighty-five days until her mentor, Max O'Hara, came back, and not an hour too soon. In the past five days, she'd survived her mother's stent procedure, a burglary and now Mike Harrison.

Of the three, Mike was the worst of the lot.

Georgie Bennett crossed her arms and settled next to Mr. Reedy. Beau, the big brown mutt, ambled over, pawed Georgie's steel-toed boot and whined. He nudged his wet snout against her hand. Then a huge pink tongue flicked out at her fingers. Glancing down, she gulped. Beau's brown eyes expressed his desire for something, but what? Georgie didn't speak dog. Did he want her attention? Did he want to go home? Follow him to a well and rescue a child?

"Keep a strong grip on his leash. Don't want him to get loose. He could get hurt on the road."

She lifted a brow. More likely Beau would wreak havoc upon the unsuspecting car and not get so much as his fur ruffled. How a man with a portable oxygen canister could take care of a dog who probably ate a pound of steak a day was beyond her. Where had this hulk of a dog been when the burglar struck? Formidable in size and weight, he'd be a great watchdog. She wiped her hand against her jeans. Either that or he'd lick the criminal until the police arrived.

"Let me take you and Beau home."

"Need a mechanic to look at my car." Mr. Reedy's tinny voice drew Georgie's attention away from Beau. "It's screeching something awful whenever I slow down for a red light. Good thing Hollydale only has three of them." He rubbed his chin with one hand while gripping his cane with his other. "Bad smell, too, after I park the car. Like burnt eggs. Course, I can't rightly tell if that's the car or Beau. He likes his hot dogs with a healthy helping of chili on top."

Beau's ears perked up. Figured a dog the size of a kid's bicycle would comprehend the words *hot dog* and *chili*.

"Mind if I take a look at it?" Fixing Mr. Reedy's car would help steady her nerves, rather shot from discovering a burglary first thing on a Tuesday morning.

"Didn't expect to see you back in these parts again. Especially with Mike Harrison settled down."

At Mike's name she jumped off the bench. "I'll be back." She tugged at Beau's leash. Mr. Reedy followed behind, the oxygen canister slowing him down. "No oval rear window. I'd say it was a '95 model."

"Not bad."

"Max trained me well." She smiled at the memory of the knobby-kneed teenager who had taken advantage of her late father's godfather, demanding he take her under his wing. "Taught me everything I knew about engines until I became ASE certified. Since then I've kept steady hours as a mechanic or an auto-body repair specialist." And, with luck and a good interview, she'd add pit crew member to the list in three months—if Brett Cullinan hired her for the racing newcomer's team. Until she heard from the veteran crew boss, she worked for Max and would take as much weight off his shoulders as possible during his medical tests. "What about it, Mr. Reedy? I'll drop you and Beau at home and come back and run diagnostics."

He frowned and shot her the same glare he had in high school whenever he caught her studying an engine schematic or sharing a laugh with Mike rather than paying attention to his teaching. "How much will that cost? Can't afford much. Not with Beau's nightly hot dog."

Mr. Reedy put up a good front, always hiding his big heart under that gruff exterior. If it weren't for him, she'd still be at her high school desk, taking history for the twelfth year in a row. Nudging her grade up two points, he might as well have signed her high school diploma. It was way past time for her to return the favor.

"The cost of the diagnostic test is free if you get your car repaired on premises." Based on what he'd described, the repair wouldn't be cheap. Brakes and maybe a new catalytic converter. She wouldn't know for certain until the results were in. "And today's senior citizen special is twelve months, no interest."

So she was bending the rules to their breaking point. Max would do the same.

"Might not be anything bad. Might be something a quart of oil can fix."

Not likely. Georgie bit her tongue, holding her response in check. "Only one way to know for sure."

"Fine. Run the test." His lips pursed into a straight line, too blue for Georgie's comfort. "If the cost is too much, I'll lose my car. Lose my independence." He shuffled away, Beau following him. He stopped and looked back. "Don't mind me. Once I get a strong cup of coffee inside me, I'll be my usual geezer self instead of this miserly grinch."

Independence. That was one word Georgie understood well. She caught up with him at the bench. "I'll need your keys."

Mike Harrison strode out of the repair shop. Way back in high school, he was the last person she'd expected to become a cop. After all, they'd spent quite a few Friday nights toilet papering yards. Still, his shoulders, husky and broad, filled his navy uniform well. His cropped hair was slightly darker, almost a dirty blond now. Those chocolate-brown eyes of his held more responsibility, more authority.

"Georgie." He approached, his tone lacking the laughing cadence of the past. "Have you worked here long enough to determine what's missing?"

"Of course." She turned and patted Mr. Reedy's arm. "You wait right here. I'll be back."

"Will you be okay with Georgie's dog?" Mike's tone was as cautious as his gaze.

Mr. Reedy yanked at the leash. "Beau's mine."

Mike glanced at Beau, then at her.

Georgie shrugged. "I kill houseplants."

"Follow me."

Her stomach roiled at entering the place someone had robbed earlier. The thieves wouldn't take her peace of mind. She wouldn't let them. Lifting her chin, she went inside and cleared her throat. "Is it okay to touch everything again?"

"Sure. No usable prints on the windows, knobs or any other surface. If I didn't know better, I'd say this was an inside job."

All the oxygen escaped her lungs. Had he just accused her of breaking into Max's Auto Repair? Max was the closest person she had to a father. She popped her hands onto her hips. "Is that your professional opinion?"

"It wasn't directed at you. Any new hires besides you? I'm assuming the Crowes still work here."

"No one else. And Travis and Heidi love this place. Surely you know them. Everyone does." She waited until he nodded.

"Older couple. He's tall and skinny? She's short and round?" Hand gestures accompanied the descriptions.

"You make them sound like Jack Sprat and his wife." Georgie chuckled. "It's just me and them." If Max was like a father, they were her honorary aunt and uncle. "They just celebrated their fortieth wedding anniversary. She's the office manager while Travis is about the best diesel mechanic I've ever met. Considering how many places I've worked, that's saying something."

She'd lost count of the number of cities and towns where she'd made pit stops. Boston, Atlanta and Seattle were a few of the places she'd called home for a brief time, with her current address technically being her apartment in Nashville. Until Kevin Doherty proposed, she hadn't wanted to settle down. After Kevin left, she especially didn't want to settle down.

"When are they supposed to get here?" Mike asked.

"Any minute now. I arrived early to read the operation manual for Max's diagnostic scanner. It's an older model, almost a relic compared to the newer ones."

"Since Travis is familiar with the equipment and customers, why didn't Max leave him in charge?"

Really?

He held up his hands, so her patented glare must have worked. "I hadn't heard about Max leaving or your return. They've worked here forever, and it's a logical question."

Okay, he had a point. Besides, she'd asked Max the same question. "They like to travel and don't want the responsibility." She hesitated. "Anyway, Max wanted to give me a shot at buying him out."

"Why now? Why didn't you come back to Hollydale a year ago or a year from now?"

Another long pause filled the air, laden with tension. "Last Friday my mother had a stent procedure in Asheville. I promised I'd stay with her while she recovered. When I called Max to see if he had an opening, he went one further." She paused. While her mother's condition was out in the open, Max's wasn't. A stickler for honesty, she chose her words with caution. "When I asked to rejoin his staff, he said it was about time he visited his sister in Florida. And this would be a trial run so I could decide if I wanted to buy the business or not. I started back yesterday."

"What are you keeping from me?"

He knew. He could always tell when she held something back. "Why do you ask?"

"Your face is ashen."

"It's been quite a morning." Her shaky smile wasn't convincing him or herself, but it was the best she could manage. Mike was here about the burglary, not to jump-start their friendship colder than a junkyard battery. She glanced around and headed for the door marked Closet.

"Georgie, I'm not worried about cleaning supplies and toilet paper."

"That's Max's idea of a joke." She pulled keys out of her pocket and jingled them. "This is his private office. Despite the closeness of this town, not many people know that."

She unlocked the door, and her jaw dropped. Someone knew this was Max's office. Pink and yellow invoices lay scattered over the floor like confetti. The file cabinet's metal drawers hung open, with manila folders in disarray. Exhaling, she collapsed onto the floor. It would take her and Heidi all morning to clean up this mess.

Mike picked up an invoice and studied it. "Doesn't Max believe in computers?"

Shrugging, she pulled herself together. "Different mechanics have different methods of remembering customers." The blood drained out of her face. "Max's folder."

She rifled through the filing cabinet. The familiar yellow binder was nowhere in sight. Neither were his comic books. Thank goodness he'd taken those with him. Her legs wobbled with the rubbery consistency of a Michelin. Max had taken his collection, hadn't he?

"Can I make a phone call?"

Mike laughed. "I usually mention phone calls after a Miranda warning." Her face must have given him pause, and he handed her his phone. "Who are you calling and why?"

"Max." She gulped, and her shoulders slumped.

"Use the speaker function."

She pressed oh-so-familiar numbers on the screen. Three rings, four, five. Finally someone answered.

"Hello, Max?"

"Georgie? Why did the number for the sheriff's office pop up on my screen?" Max's scraggly deep voice, fresh from slumber, made her stomach roil worse than the break-in. She refused to meet Mike's gaze. This was hard enough without looking at him.

"You took your comic books with you to Florida, right?" She crossed her fingers for luck. Something had to go her way today.

"No. I left them at the shop. It's got a security system. Didn't see the need in paying for one for my home when they charge me enough to guard my shop." A loud yawn came over the line. "What's wrong?"

Her mouth opened, but no words came out. Waking him up only to deliver bad news upon bad news was harder than she'd expected. That growing dread in her throat became downright metallic.

"This is Officer Michael Harrison." Mike saved her from having to speak. "I'm investigating a reported burglary at your repair shop."

"Georgie? Are you okay?" Alarm came out of Max's voice, and she loved him for it. "Are Travis and Heidi there? Are they safe?"

"No one was here when the burglary happened."

"That's good, very good." Max cleared his throat. "I'll be back in twelve to fourteen hours."

"No!" Georgie raised her voice, and Mike's eyes narrowed. "You told me you haven't seen your sister in years. Surely she wants to introduce you to her friends and other people."

If only Max would read between the lines. Scans of a tumor suspected of being malignant were more important than comic books. His life was worth way more. His sister had agreed, insisting Max consult with her oncologist in Florida rather than one closer to home.

"Max, what type of comic books are we talking about?" Mike held up his hand before she could start talking again.

"Golden Age, mint condition, all in protective covers."

Mike rubbed his hand over his chin and whistled. "Have you had them appraised?"

"Uh…yeah. Five years ago. They were worth thirty-five thousand dollars."

"Let the police investigate." Georgie's words tumbled out.

Comic books could be replaced. Max couldn't. Sometimes he was too rash for his own good. A Vietnam vet and one tough customer, he wouldn't take any of this lying down. Eleven years ago she'd lost her best friend, Mike. Friday her mother had undergone serious surgery. She couldn't lose her mentor. "Stay in Florida. You can't do anything here."

Max's sigh ripped through her. "I should stay. Would I be able to help or would I get in the way, Officer Harrison?"

"We'll investigate the best we can." Mike met her gaze. As if he read her concern, he held out his palms and his eyes widened. "I can't decide for him."

She threw him a grateful smile. "Please, Max. Give the police a little time."

"The doctor my sister recommended canceled and rescheduled my appointment for a week from today."

Some good news at last. If the doctor post-poned Max's scans, Max's case might not be that urgent. He might make a full recovery and maybe even come back to Hollydale. She'd grab that hope and run with it.

"If the police solve the case in the meantime, you'd lose that appointment and valuable days with it. I've got everything under control. I'll call you tonight with the latest update." She said goodbye and ended the call.

Mike crossed his arms and leveled a stern gaze. "I was about to ask Max for more infor-mation."

She stood, stretched and shook her head. "Let the poor man have a cup of coffee first. Please finish up so Heidi and I can open sometime today." Weighing her options made her pause. There was a lot for her to get her head around. "And Mr. Reedy will be frozen if we dawdle much longer."

"The police department will use all its re-sources to solve this and help Mr. O'Hara." He glanced out the window. "And I might have a solution to the other part of the puzzle. Excuse me for a minute."

He strode outside. This Mike spoke and acted with authority, unlike the gawky kid she'd known years ago. She took stock of the messy reception area. Burglaries, surgeries and Michael Harrison. She hadn't changed her mind one bit.

Of the three, Mike was the one who'd keep her awake at night.

CHAPTER TWO

THE THEFT OF the comic books bumped this case up to a high priority. Mike shook his head. Thirty-five thousand dollars? Who kept thirty-five thousand dollars' worth of comic books at a car repair shop? Between the upcoming tourist season and the B&Es, spending time with Rachel would be a luxury. One more quick look around Max's Auto Repair and he'd go back to the station and file his report.

Each of the four patrol teams, one short of the normal five covering Hollydale, would comb through his written findings for anything he might have missed. In no time they'd find the person, or persons, responsible.

He studied the reception area, chaos at work. Yet the flat-screen plasma television sat on an end table, not damaged in the least. Walking over to the reception, he spotted a desktop computer. The thief who broke into Carter's Sporting Goods had picked the manager's office clean of all the petty cash and electronic devices. A real professional job with surfaces wiped down. Same as the previous B&Es.

The MO was different here. It was almost as if two different burglars had struck on the same night.

He pulled open a drawer. A Kindle lay nestled snug above a black laptop. Instead of answers, more and more questions kept popping up. The sweet scent of lemons filled him. A shadow crossed over his shoulder. He didn't have to look back. Georgie smelled the same now as she had in high school.

"Why did the burglar take the comic books and Max's company folder but not Heidi's Kindle or laptop?" Georgie asked. "That doesn't make any sense."

"There's another question I'd like answered first. Did the security company call you to report the break-in? They sure didn't call the station."

Georgie moved away and tucked a strand of hair behind her ear. Despair flickered behind those green eyes. The sense she wasn't telling him everything was strong. Funny, he hadn't seen her in years, yet he already remembered her signals.

"Are you hiding something?"

She leaned against the nearby wall and shrugged. "My mother called at the end of the day as I was collecting the day's receipts."

"What does your mother have to do with the security system?"

Her gaze met his. A slight pink flush came over her cheeks.

Not good. Mike closed the drawer and gritted his teeth.

Too often in the past he'd heard stories about Mrs. Bennett. How proper young ladies never went out of the house without looking their best, including a demure smile. How young ladies didn't have oil and grease under their fingernails. How jeans should never grace the closet of a Southern lady, especially those attending cotillion.

"I deposited yesterday's money in the bank." She folded her arms, her fists visible. Everything about her demeanor screamed defense. "But I can't remember setting the alarm, which means I didn't. I'm not usually the last mechanic out for the night."

He exhaled slowly and jotted notes on his pad. "No alarm, then. What about video surveillance?"

Georgie shook her head and pointed to the corner. "That's a fake camera so customers will think there's extra security."

Great, just great. A working video camera might have had a time stamp. That would have given him some idea if the burglar struck here before or after Carter's. Or if different perps had struck at the same time.

"So thousands of dollars of comic books plus a proprietary folder are missing and there was little security at the time of the break-in. Earlier you mentioned Max wanted you to buy him out. Did he quote you a certain amount?"

Georgie blinked. "Mr. Reedy's probably wondering where we are."

"I sent him and Beau across the street to the Holly Days Diner for coffee. Why don't you want Max coming back?"

Conflict warred on her pretty face. She let out a deep breath and looked left and right, as if making sure no one was around.

"This stays in this room. Max had a colonoscopy last month. They found something. His sister, who lives in Florida, pulled through thyroid cancer and insisted her big brother consult her oncologist and not one around here. They've always been close, and he wanted to make her happy." She shook her head and sighed. "I shouldn't even have told you that much."

"How much does he want for the repair shop?"

Georgie winced. Maybe his voice did come out brisk and blunt. This was an official police investigation, not one of Rachel's tea parties with her stuffed animals. Still, part of him sought redemption from what he'd done to hurt the feelings of his former best friend all those years ago. The other part of him knew Georgie was the one who could restore the Thunderbird. Arresting her would make both those possibilities disappear.

"Thirty-five thousand, but…"

He held up his hand. As much as he hated to ask the next question, the sheriff and the state required it of him. "Where were you last night until this morning?"

"Wh-what?" The question sputtered out, and that doe-eyed gaze flew to his, shock registering in its depths. Mike repeated his question.

The shock in her eyes turned to pure anger. "I was at home, asleep."

"Can anyone verify that?"

Extending her hands in front of her, she cracked her knuckles. It was his turn to wince. Without a doubt she remembered how much that sound had grated on his last nerve.

"My mother." Pure satisfaction lightened her features.

He drew in a deep breath. "Georgie, I've always appreciated how honest and open you are, but now is not the time for equivocating."

"Your eyes, your tone, your little tic at the side of your eye." Taking a step back while facing him, she gasped. "You think I have something to do with this."

While Georgie Bennett was as likely a criminal as his own mother, who didn't even take the tags off her mattresses and pillows for fear the pillow police would come after her, a thorough investigation required looking at Georgie as a suspect. The fact she called this in was a point in her favor.

"I have to follow up on every possibility. You just admitted motive, and you yourself acknowledged you were the last to leave and didn't turn on the security system."

"You genuinely believe I'm a common thief?" Spittle escaped from between her clenched teeth and landed on his hand.

"I'll keep you informed of any progress on the B&Es, but don't leave town."

If the same perps didn't commit both burglaries, that left him with a short suspect list for the Max's Auto Repair B&E, with one name at the top in big, bold letters.

Georgie.

GEORGIE HELD UP the disposable cup from the diner while Mike walked Mr. Reedy to the bench under the lone tree shading the front entrance to Max's. So her former best friend now believed she was capable of theft, yet he'd made sure she had her morning coffee, a habit since their senior year. She couldn't figure him out. But once she moved on, she'd never have to lay eyes on the infuriating Mike Harrison again.

A black Ford F-150 pulled in to the parking lot. Before the engine stopped, Heidi Crowe, holding a familiar Tupperware container, disembarked from the passenger's side.

"Bless your heart." Heidi's Southern twang was as familiar as corn bread dunked in milk. "Tell me you didn't walk in on the robbery."

That might have made life easier.

Georgie shrugged and shook her head. "No one was here when I arrived. Mr. Reedy pulled up when I called the police." She pointed toward Mike's squad car, where Mr. Reedy and Mike were discussing something.

"Oh, darlin', have one of my peach blossom muffins." Heidi opened the lid, and Georgie inhaled the inviting aroma of peaches and sugar. "You're too skinny. Have two."

Georgie picked one and removed the wrapper. "There's more. Max knows." She bit into the muffin, the warm goodness calming her frayed nerves. "It was all I could do to talk him out of coming back."

"He's staying in Florida, right?" Heidi's brows furrowed. "He has to. His life might depend on it."

"I think I convinced him. You might want to call him later and back me up." Georgie demolished the rest of the muffin with a vengeance.

Heidi gave her a side hug. "Of course, darlin'.

I just thank the good stars above you weren't hurt."

Georgie sighed and wiped her hands, crumbs falling to the ground. Keeping the repair shop running was key to Max staying in Florida until he knew the extent of his condition. "We won't be able to open for a couple of hours. The mess will take a while to clean up."

"Honey, that's the least of my worries. If you'd walked in…" Heidi shuddered. "They might have hurt you. Or worse still, they could have…" She narrowed her eyes. "Good thing I didn't walk in. The doctors would still be picking buckshot out of the robber's backside."

Heidi's husband, Travis, came up behind Heidi and started massaging his wife's shoulders. "Now, honey, give Georgie some room. She's had a shock."

A shock that could cost her dearly. If Brett Cullinan heard of her negligence, she could kiss her chances on the pit crew goodbye. She glanced over at Mike near his squad car. A lost job might be the least of her worries.

"Nonsense." Heidi shooed her husband away. "She needs TLC. Have another muffin."

Travis pulled at Heidi's arm. "We'll ask Harrison if we can go inside."

They skedaddled, and Georgie furrowed her brows. Why the sudden rush to get away? Oh. A new model cream Mercedes convertible pulled up alongside her, and the answer became obvious. Her mother had arrived, her hazel eyes twitching just as they always did when she was determined to get her way.

No one who valued peace argued with Beverly Bennett.

"Georgianna Victoria! Is the news I heard from Harriet the dispatcher true? Was there a burglary here?" Beverly fanned herself with her hand.

"Yes, Mom. Hi, Kitty." Georgie whooshed out a breath, causing the bangs on her forehead to fly about before settling again. "But, Mom, you should be in bed instead of driving around with Kitty. No offense."

Georgie waved at her mother's best friend. Kitty waved back and switched off the car's ignition. Her sympathetic look was a sight friendlier than her mother's disapproving frown.

"None taken. I was more worried your mother's blood pressure would go up until she saw you were safe and sound." People often underestimated Kitty with her soft voice, but the slender reed of a woman possessed a backbone of steel. Had to, being married to the local district attorney and staying close to Beverly all these years.

"Don't talk about me as though I'm not here." Beverly's chin went up. "You should have called me, Georgianna. Imagine how I felt when someone else delivered the frightful news. Get in the car. We'll go straight to cousin Odalie's dress shop. Working at a dress shop is much more respectable than this repair shop." Beverly sniffed, her nose scrunched up with disdain.

Georgie's back stiffened as it always did whenever her mother went off on a similar tangent, which was near close to every day.

"I love being a mechanic." Then again, was her mother onto something? Kevin had spat out her lack of feminine wiles as his rear had collided with her front door. Georgie disagreed. She liked herself and wouldn't change for anyone. "Besides, the thief is long gone. I doubt he'll be back. All of this activity can't be good for your recovery. You need to go home and rest."

"Surely the doctor didn't perform my stent surgery last Friday so I could stay in bed while you're toiling in a hotbed of criminal activity." Beverly placed one hand over her heart and her other hand over her forehead.

"The officer investigating the breaking and entering is still here, talking to Mr. Reedy." Georgie pointed toward the bench. "What's safer than police on the premises? Not to mention Beau, Mr. Reedy's dog."

"Oh, goodness mercy," exclaimed Beverly. "You call that a dog? That's a monstrosity on legs. No self-respecting female would be caught dead with that beast. A poodle or Maltese, yes, but that?" She shuddered.

Georgie drew in another breath, knowing what her mother was about to say as well as she knew who manufactured the best spark plugs for this Mercedes.

"Thank goodness I'm allergic to animals and cannot have anything like that in my house."

Beads of sweat popped out on her mother's pale face. Beverly shouldn't even be out of bed yet, let alone traveling all over Hollydale. Georgie stepped toward the car.

"Are you okay? Do you need to see your doctor?" Georgie pulled out her smartphone from her jeans at the same time Kitty whipped hers out of her Coach handbag.

"I'm fine." Beverly sure didn't sound fine, the mere whisper most unlike her normal full bluster.

Georgie hovered, not buying her mother's easy brush-off. Beverly squinted, and Georgie bristled at the question she could predict was coming.

"Is Michael Harrison the officer assigned to this case?"

And there it is.

Beverly had been the only person to ever call Mike by his given first name rather than *Mike*, a gesture which he'd often rewarded with an eye roll.

"Yes, Mom." Georgie sighed and flicked imaginary muffin crumbs off her T-shirt. "Why didn't you tell me Mike was a cop?"

"I don't like to talk about men who don't keep promises. Mike broke my little girl's heart." Iciness marked Beverly's tone.

"What happened on prom night is water under the bridge. Ancient history, to say the least."

If her mother was going to be mad at anyone for breaking her heart, Georgie's ex-fiancé, Kevin Doherty, had much more claim to that anger. Beverly rubbed her chest and moaned. Georgie sent a pleading glance toward Kitty.

"I think I am tired, after all. Kitty, dear, please be a darling and drive me home."

"Of course." Kitty restarted the car. In spite of everything, the purr of a strong, powerful engine made Georgie smile before it faded under her mother's glare.

"Mom…"

"We'll talk more about cousin Odalie's kind offer of employment later." Beverly's piercing gaze didn't escape Georgie's notice.

With the recent stent implantation, Georgie wasn't about to argue here. She wouldn't do her mother's bidding, either, but her mother didn't have to know that this minute.

The convertible pulled out of the parking space, and Georgie was relieved. The feeling was short-lived as Mike made his way over, concern written in the fine etched lines on his forehead.

"Georgie, would you follow me to the bench?" Mike's voice was distant, almost hollow.

Cold water went through her veins before she shook off her worry. If he'd meant to arrest her, he'd be reading her Miranda rights rather than walking her over to Mr. Reedy.

"Actually, I need to help Travis and Heidi." Georgie jerked her thumb toward the garage. "Our first customers have bookings in less than fifteen minutes."

Mike cleared his throat and stood his ground. Same DNA, same voice, same deep brown eyes. But the lanky teenager had grown up, a virtual stranger in his place, a stranger unconvinced of her innocence.

"How long has it been since Mr. Reedy's eaten a substantial meal?" Mike lowered his voice enough so his words were for her ears only, a technique he'd perfected in the halls of Hollydale High.

"How should I know?" She spotted her former high school teacher being practically held up by Beau. Mr. Reedy's gasps and wheezes were more audible than ever. This wasn't good. Georgie sprinted over and she laid her hand on his arm. "What's wrong?"

Mr. Reedy sagged, and Mike rushed by her,

his hand reaching out to support the frail man. "Georgie, I'm taking him to the ER."

"Won't leave my dog." A coughing fit came over Mr. Reedy's frail body.

Georgie threw her arms around Mr. Reedy's shoulders, even thinner and bonier than she'd anticipated. Those blasted oxygen tubes were in the way, but they were sustaining him. She had to help.

"Say the word. I'll deliver Beau to whoever you want to take care of him for the next couple of days." Her gaze met Mike's. The comfort she sought that Mr. Reedy would be in and out of the hospital in no time wasn't there. "A neighbor? Anybody?"

"There's no one." Mr. Reedy spat out the admission like yesterday's bad news. More coughs racked his lungs, and Beau licked his owner's hand.

Georgie gestured at Beau and then at Mike. In the past he'd been good at reading her signals. Even now, a child would understand her signal, asking him to take care of Beau.

Mike shrugged and shook his head. "My daughter would have a fit if I brought Beau home. And I don't even want to think about Ginger's reaction to Beau."

Blood rushed around her ears. Mike was married and had a daughter? Her mother should have warned her. Then again, why would she? Georgie never brought up the subject of Mike, even in passing. And she and Kevin had been planning their wedding, the invitations addressed and waiting to be mailed, before he decided another woman would take care of his every need much better than Georgie. This was getting silly. If Mike wouldn't come to Beau's rescue, she would. Mr. Reedy's staggered breathing left her little choice.

"I'll take Beau home with me."

Beau's giant tail thumped on the pavement. Without further ado, the dog scooted around and licked her hand.

Mike raised an eyebrow. "Didn't you say you were staying at your mother's house?"

She nodded once.

"Isn't your mother allergic to dogs?"

"And cats. And guinea pigs. And hamsters." Georgie ticked off half a dozen animals on her fingers and huffed. "I'm in the garage apartment. She won't come in contact with Beau."

Mr. Reedy gasped out a breath. "I'm not going."

"Oh, yes, you are. Beau and I will get along fine," she assured him.

She glanced at Beau. With Mike eyeing her as a person of interest, her mother pleading with her to work elsewhere and Heidi peeking out the window taking in all the activity, the dog might be her only ally right now.

One she intended to keep on her side.

CHAPTER THREE

MIKE HUSTLED PAST the town square's gazebo, the new white paint glistening in the rays of the afternoon sun. Nearby two tourists posed for a selfie on the gazebo stairs while their golden retriever danced around them. The maples and oaks would provide a nice backsplash of red in that photo. Mike raised his hand in a friendly greeting while his gaze locked in on Sheriff Rick Donahue.

Heading toward his boss, Mike scanned the local shops as familiar as his daughter's smile. The Night Owl Bakery, Rachel's favorite, where they'd stop for red velvet cupcakes on the Sunday afternoons he didn't work. The Happy Paws Pet Shop, where he purchased Ginger's cat food. Neither of those owners had reported burglaries yet, and he checked for any signs of broken windows or anything else that might signal an opportunity for the thief. Not finding anything unusual, he closed the distance between himself and the sheriff.

"Almost done finalizing the traffic plan for

the art festival this weekend." Donahue's eyes never left his clipboard as he jotted notes. "Be with you in a sec."

One more sweep of the businesses and buildings satisfied Mike, his senses on full alert for anything out of the ordinary. Making sure there wasn't a sixth burglary was his top priority.

"Take your time." Mike noted the new security camera over John Cobb's real estate office. Good.

Donahue stopped writing and stuck his pencil stub into his pocket. Then he patted his stomach. "Melanie outdid herself last night with her lasagna for the whole family. Got to see our grandson for the first time since school started. Zachary's smart as a whip. Last night was a sight better than this morning with the news of two more break-ins."

"Yep." Mike frowned. "The suspects struck early."

"You said suspects, as in plural." Tucking his clipboard under his arm, Donahue jerked his thumb toward his squad car. "You think someone's working with a partner?"

Mike reviewed the two different cases and shook his head. "I'm not convinced the same person committed both of today's burglaries."

Donahue wiped the sweat off his forehead. "Any evidence of a copycat?"

A gut reaction wasn't enough. "Not necessarily. In my report I detailed the differences. The main thing was the haul. At Max's garage, the perp left behind electronics and anything that could be sold with relative ease."

"Maybe that one was an inside job." They reached Donahue's squad car, and the sheriff reached in for his water bottle. After a few sips he pressed the bottle to his forehead. "I read your report. If we find those comic books, we'll find the thief. Is Georgie Bennett back for good?"

Mike didn't like the way Donahue connected those two thoughts without so much as a pause. "She just returned to Hollydale. She couldn't have committed the other burglaries."

Donahue scratched his chin. "Travis Crowe and I rode bikes together way back when, and Heidi's the type that'll give you the shirt off her back. Georgie's been gone a long time. Real convenient someone knew where Max kept something valuable and stole his stash. Either this was part of the others and the burglar got sloppy, or it wasn't."

The hairs on the back of Mike's neck bristled. While Mike had doubted Georgie for all of two seconds, Donahue seemed ready to bring her in for formal questioning on the spot.

Mike would do well to call his mom and warn her he'd arrive home late, even though he hated missing another dinner with Rachel. Reviewing the evidence and photographs of the crime scenes might be the best way to prove Georgie's innocence and prevent another burglary.

A COLD BEER, a remote control and a comfortable bed. Three pieces of Mike's idea of sheer heaven.

Unlocking his door, Mike walked into his modest cottage and flicked off the porch lights. Snapping his fingers, he turned the lights on again for what would be his mom's short walk home, only two doors down. If it weren't for her tending to Rachel without pay, he'd be in a world of hurt. Too often he offered her a twenty. Her reply? Diane Harrison would push her nose in the air and stomp away, muttering how her ungrateful son didn't understand the bond between a grandmother and her granddaughter.

"Mom? Rachel?" Not even Ginger, princess kitty extraordinaire, was winding her furry orange body around his legs, as was her custom. "I'm home."

"We're in Rachel's room, honey," Mom's voice rang out.

Taking the stairs two at a time, he stopped at Rachel's doorway. Her legs crossed, Rachel sat on the floor with Mom behind her, her mouth full of bobby pins. His jaw slackened at Rachel's upswept hairdo. For the love of everything holy, his daughter was eight going on eighteen. Whether she was born an old soul or his ex-wife's desertion made her grow up too fast, he'd never know.

Rachel's lip jutted out. "You don't like my hair?"

"Of course I do." Mike composed himself. "You just reminded me I'm going to have to fight the boys away all too soon."

"Grandma painted my nails, too." She jumped up and wiggled her fingers in his face. "Purple and pink."

"We left you a bite of dinner." Mom rose from the floor, came over and hugged him. "Pimento cheese and fried okra."

"Thanks, Mom."

Hold on. Mom made her famous pimento cheese only when something was bothering her. One glance at her conflicted face confirmed his suspicions. "Spit it out."

"Why don't you both walk me home? Your father probably fell fast asleep on the couch while watching the Braves game."

In other words she was going to take her sweet time in telling him. After today's events he'd prefer for her to spit it out.

"We'd best hurry. School night."

Rachel skipped ahead while Mike closed the front door behind them. The male crickets chirped their hearts out to attract the females of their dreams. Speaking of females, should he wait to drop his own bombshell about Georgie Bennett or listen to Mom's news first?

Mike couldn't wait. "You'll never guess who's back in town." He'd drag it out, though. His love for a good guessing game often drove the other members of his family up Sully Creek, his favorite fishing spot.

"If you're talking about Georgie Bennett, I've known since last Friday." Gravel crunched under his mother's black loafers.

He scuffed the dirt under the gravel pebbles. Was he always the last to know everything?

"Why didn't you warn me?"

Rachel boomeranged back, hugged his side and skipped off again.

"Warn? That's an interesting choice of words. At one time you and Georgie were inseparable."

Until Mike had made a huge mistake. Then Georgie had not only called him out but declared their friendship over forever.

"I should have told you." Mom squeezed his hand. "With all the overtime you've been logging, I thought you had enough on your plate."

Little escaped Diane Harrison's line of sight, much to his sister Natalie's dismay. Mike often wondered if Mom's influence, more than any other, led him to become a cop, a job he loved so much. No argument about his plate being full. Maybe when Donahue hired more officers

would some of his workload begin to lessen.
Until then…

They reached his parents' home. Mom by-
passed the path to the front porch, perfect with
its view of the Great Smoky Mountains, and
headed toward the outbuilding in the back. The
structure was more of a barn than a shed. His
chest heaved. Of all the nights for her to bring
up the Thunderbird.

Rachel skipped ahead of him. Mom unlocked
the padlock and dragged the door open.

"Why tonight, Mom?"

Why'd she have to remind him of the travesty
he'd done to his grandpa Ted's '64 Ford Thunderbird when he was hungry and rather cranky?
Those pimento cheese sandwiches were calling
his name.

"Georgie Bennett. That's why." Mom traced
her finger along the car's built-up layer of dust
and frowned.

"Who's Georgie Bennett?" Rachel opened the
driver's door and pretended to drive, her whirring sounds tugging at Mike's heart.

"Your father's best friend growing up. She
knows a thing or two about cars."

Rachel stopped and gazed right at him. "So
she could make the car pretty again?"

Did he fall into this trap or what? An ambush
had more warning.

"It wouldn't be fair to ask her." Especially

since he gave her the order not to leave town, like some big-shot cop on television. He groaned. No cop in their right mind said that anymore.

"Rachel, why don't you go wake up Grandpa Carl? Otherwise he'll be up all night." His mom's soothing tone held an undercurrent of what was still to come. Mike's stomach took a nosedive.

"I like looking at cars, too, you know, and Grandpa Carl can be a bear to wake up." Rachel dragged one foot and then the other before walking backward toward the house she spent almost as many hours in as her own, if not more. Then she smiled that hundred-watt smile Mike loved so much. "He does give good bear hugs."

After his little pitcher was out of earshot, Mike turned to his mother. "So you knew about Georgie?"

Mom pointed to the dull finish, beginning to rust in spots. "Friendship is like this car. Too much rust can damage what was once shiny and new."

Yeah, yeah. Breaking his promise to Georgie about taking her to prom damaged their friendship beyond repair. And that was only the half of it. He hadn't had the courtesy to tell her face-to-face. No, he'd sent his sister Natalie with a note. Matters had flat-out nose-dived after that. Georgie had caught him and Wendy

MacNamara in the midst of some heavy-duty celebrating, if he wanted to put losing his virginity that way. The respect had drained away from Georgie's eyes in that split second. But that was eleven long years ago. Since then he'd made more than his fair share of mistakes. In a way, he owed his ex-wife, Caitlyn, a thank you. After she deserted her family, he sucked in his gut and swore he'd be the best father he could be to Rachel.

He could only hope he was fulfilling that promise.

He let out the deep breath pent up from within. "But a little elbow grease can buffer out rust."

His mother let loose a wide grin. "Exactly." Then she frowned. "Getting you to talk to Georgie about the Thunderbird is only part of my pimento cheese bribe. I have to leave you in the lurch."

"How could you ever do that?" He went over and side hugged her. "You and Rachel are my best girls."

"Ruthy and Don Abbott, my maid of honor and your father's best man, have a three-hour layover in Charlotte tomorrow before they fly home to LA."

"Go. You haven't seen Ruthy in a couple of years. I'll find someone else to watch Rachel after school. I'll call Natalie first." At least Natalie had recently moved back to Hollydale. He missed his other sister, Becks, who lived in California.

"I already tried your sister on the off chance she might be free after she's done teaching." She worried her lip. "Everyone's busy."

"I'll find somebody." A pounding throb pulsated between his earlobes. "Go rescue Dad before Rachel talks his ears off. You know how Dad is when he wakes up."

Mom laughed and started for the house. She stopped, rubbing her hand along his forearm. "Thanks for understanding."

He watched her walk away. This single-fatherhood gig wasn't easy. Not by a long shot. But Rachel's smiles and giggles made it all worthwhile. Combining fatherhood with work, though? That was the hard part, compounded with how many people kept asking him to run for sheriff. The administrative duties of that job? No thank you. He had to solve these burglaries and make sure Donahue received the credit.

He ran his hand over the Thunderbird insignia on the front hood. How many times had Grandpa Ted rattled the keys and Mike had come running? After he and Georgie became friends, his grandfather had let her tag along on their drives, where they'd often stop and hike along Timber River or throw in a line at Sully

Creek. He sure had loved this car. Mike deserved the tongue-lashing he'd get if Grandpa could see the condition of his beloved Miss Brittany, named for the Brittany-blue paint gracing her exterior.

Mom had been right about rust. He should never have let Georgie leave Hollydale without apologizing first.

Georgie. She'd grown up since she left Hollydale. In high school she'd stumbled like a newborn fawn, getting used to her height, a good three inches taller than all the other girls. And now? He'd have been blind not to notice her. She'd never looked better. Time had helped her grow into her, uh, skin. Confident and beautiful, she'd have turned his head if there wasn't a cloud of suspicion hanging over it.

He shook his head. Georgie had watched Grandpa Ted like a hawk whenever he worked on the car. If anyone could bring Miss Brittany back to her glory days, it was Georgie.

If he sold Miss Brittany as is, however, he'd still fetch a pretty penny. Enough so his mother would be off the hook for providing after-school care. Enough so he could afford to send Rachel to the Hollydale Dancing Academy, with its pickup service and group lessons. How perfect would that be for his little girl, who loved pink plastic purses, pink bows and pink nail polish.

He'd move heaven and earth to get things

right with the ladies in his life. He'd ruined his friendship with Georgie. His mom had sighed but supported him when he'd brought home a pregnant Caitlyn, his new fiancée. And Caitlyn? She'd just plain left him and Rachel.

Providing something special for Rachel? Surely Grandpa Ted would understand that type of legacy if Mike sold the Thunderbird.

After Rachel went to bed, he'd list the car. No, scratch that. Tonight he had to line up child care so he could work tomorrow afternoon. Something had to be done to solve this rash of burglaries, and soon. He'd list the car tomorrow night. Wouldn't get nearly as much for it in this condition, but something in the bank was better than nothing.

And Rachel's smile would be worth the pain of turning over the keys and registration to a total stranger.

CHAPTER FOUR

GEORGIE CURLED HER toes inside her steel-toed boots, while keeping her closed-lip smile frozen in place. Good thing the man in front of her couldn't register her blood boiling within her veins. Though he hid his chauvinism behind some veiled lies, she'd met his type before. Men who didn't want a woman repairing their cars, even if their lives depended on it.

Heidi clicked her heels behind Georgie. "What seems to be the problem, Mr. Crabtree?"

Take away the tree, and the last name fit the disagreeable man to a tee. No doubt he'd find some polite excuse and leave, without a properly serviced car.

"I have an appointment with Max." The man's dark gaze didn't meet Georgie's. Instead, he glared at Heidi. "She's not Max."

Mr. Crabtree jabbed a finger too close to her chest for Georgie's liking, and she opened her mouth to tell him so.

"Now, Dick." Heidi beat her to the punch, and Georgie counted to ten. "You had better watch yourself. You know Max is like a brother to me, but I have to say it's been a real pleasure working with Georgie again. Why, she's teaching Travis a couple of tricks he's been downright giddy to try out. Besides, Max left Georgie in charge. If he trusts her that much, shouldn't you?"

Turning around, Georgie softened her smile and mouthed a *thank you* to Heidi. Talk about a lifesaver over the past twenty-four hours. Sweet and caring, Heidi's maternal side roared in defense of her friends and family. Then Georgie faced Dick Crabtree again, his nostrils flaring.

"Don't matter none who Max left in charge." He removed his worn baseball cap and scratched his bald head before planting the cap back in place. "If Max isn't here, Travis can work on my truck. I trust Travis."

"Mr. Crabtree." Georgie took a deep breath and made her pitch. "I am most qualified to work on your Chevy. Once you drop off your key, I'll run the diagnostic test and let you know what I find out. You can relax in our comfortable waiting room or you can grab a cup of coffee at the Holly Days Diner across the street. Your choice."

"My choice is Travis."

Heidi cleared her throat. "My husband is servicing a fleet of diesel vehicles this week. It's Georgie or no one."

"Fine. Then it's no one." The man yanked his key ring off the counter. The front door rattled from the force of Crabtree's exit.

Georgie rubbed her forehead. Not a great way to wrap up a Wednesday morning, or any other morning.

"Have you had to deal with men like him before?"

Heidi's bluntness surprised her. She'd half expected Heidi to defend the customer, keeping in line with the old adage the customer was always right. Except when the customer couldn't accept the fact Georgie was every bit as capable as any male mechanic around.

"Yes, even in this day and age, I still run into people who cut me short like that. It won't be the last time, either."

A howl came from the direction of Max's closet office she'd confiscated for the time being. She hustled over to it.

"I'm taking Beau for a quick walk around the block. My calendar's empty until after lunch. Might as well make good use of the time."

"Aw, poor Beau. Do you think your mother will relent and let him stay at your place tomorrow?" Heidi's eyes oozed concern.

Georgie shrugged and grabbed her smartphone off the nearby desk. "Only as much as I think Dick Crabtree will bring back his car and let me service it."

Without another word she opened the door and greeted Beau, who wriggled happily all over. Gulping, she guarded her heart. Mr. Reedy wanted him back in a few days. No sense growing fond of Beau. Good thing the huge dog hogged the covers. Otherwise her heart would be toast.

She glanced around the small room, a pang of guilt threading through her. There must be a better solution than leaving him in this cramped space while she worked. She clicked on Beau's leash. Maybe the walk would help her come up with something.

Outside, Georgie glanced at Beau, his shaggy tail wagging faster than wipers in a thunderstorm. "East or west?" His tail kept wagging, seeming as if it would never stop. "West it is."

They hadn't taken two steps when Beau whined for the Holly Days Diner across the street. "While I could go for some pie myself, let's keep going."

The surrounding maples lent cool shade for their walk. A couple snapping photos next to Hollydale's largest oak took a picture of Beau. Georgie waved and progressed.

Turning right on Timber Road, Georgie soaked in Hollydale's ambience. Beau tugged on the leash, and Georgie kept a steady pace until she found herself face-to-face with the town square and the stately gazebo, a magnet for weddings and where generations of Hollydale High students posed for their prom pictures. She'd been set to declare her feelings for Mike on those steps.

"Georgie Bennett!" Miss Louise waved while handing out slips of paper in front of her ice cream parlor.

Georgie hurried over with Beau leading the way. How many times had she and Mike shared a banana split here? "Miss Louise. I've missed you."

The woman laughed. "Missed my sundaes, huh?"

Shrugging, Georgie wrapped Beau's leash around her hand. "I missed you. You gave the best advice on being yourself. I'll come back sometime without Beau."

"Wait here." Miss Louise shoved the rest of the coupons at Georgie and disappeared.

Georgie had no sooner handed out the last coupon when Miss Louise emerged with a cup and a cone, placing the cup on the sidewalk for Beau, who gobbled it up.

"Welcome back." Miss Louise handed her the cone. "I gave Beau vanilla. For you, rum raisin, your favorite. Eat it before it drips. Don't stay away so long next time."

After a quick thank you, Georgie was on her way, savoring the treat. What started out as a quick walk turned into a marathon as others also stopped to pass the time of day with her and Beau.

Eventually she returned to Max's, her heart feeling a good deal lighter.

Until Heidi broke the news that three other customers had canceled. She seethed and debated going another five miles with Beau.

"I'll be with Beau, catching up on the paperwork." Georgie escaped Heidi's bless-your-heart smile.

Someone knocked, and Georgie blinked at the hour that had passed without her even coming up for air. "Come in."

Heidi tilted her head toward the reception area. "Customer."

Georgie had never been so happy to see Kitty Everson.

"Oil change, please." Kitty smiled and threw the keys like a parent would to a newly licensed child.

Georgie caught them and returned her smile. "Thanks, Kitty."

Working on Kitty's Mercedes was sheer pleasure, almost as fun as the year Georgie had spent renovating classic cars, like the Thunderbird Mike's grandfather had owned. Ever since, she'd taken on similar restoration projects as a side business. She was finishing up the oil change for Kitty's car when Heidi came into the service area and waved her inside.

"Beau and I had ourselves a real nice time on a walk." Heidi patted her rather broad midsection and rang up Kitty, who departed with a wave and a blown kiss. Heidi turned back to Georgie. "My doctor, and my waistline, thank Beau for the exercise."

"I don't suppose…" Heidi and Travis' fenced-in yard had been the site of many delicious barbecues before she had left Hollydale.

Heidi shook her head, her gray curls flying every which way. "No, ma'am. I see that look." She cleared her throat, a sheepish smile spreading over her face. "Anyhow, I talked to Travis last night. I had a feeling your mother would look none too kindly to a big loveable mutt. Travis and Pretty Boy, his golden retriever, were like this for fifteen years." She crossed her middle and index fingers. "Travis took the loss real hard, and he's not ready for another dog in his life. Besides, on Saturday afternoons, we like to head out on our bikes. We explore the mountains. We go to the beach. Sometimes we head straight here on Monday mornings. Sorry, sweetie, but we can't leave on the spur of the minute with a dog."

Georgie nodded. Since she'd been home, nothing came easily. "It can't be good for him to be stuck inside a cramped room all day." A dog like Beau was meant to run free and be himself.

She stopped. She didn't want to pass Beau off on someone else. He was the best thing to happen to her since her return. If Mike Harrison hadn't believed she was a common criminal and if there weren't a female named Ginger in his life, she might have moved him to the top of her potential dogsitters list. Wasn't so long ago Mike was turning female heads in the high school hallway. Georgie, though, had considered it her personal responsibility to keep his head a reasonable size, making sure he didn't get overly cocky. Now, all these years later, he was all the more attractive, with his uniform showing off muscles that hadn't been there when she left. Not that she'd been looking at him. Not with him being married to Ginger.

"How about a compromise?" Heidi narrowed her eyes and blew out a deep breath. "On your way to work, you drop him off at our house. We haven't boarded up our dog door. When you're done, pick him up. If Travis agrees, that is."

"Agrees to what?" Travis walked in and winked at Heidi.

"Beau uses our yard while Georgie's at work."

Travis covered the distance to the desk, grabbing the cloth hanging off his pocket and wiping his hands. "Why the fuss? Fred Reedy will be out of the hospital soon. He'll pick up Beau then."

Georgie glanced at Heidi, who gave a slight

nod. They'd both seen Mr. Reedy before Mike accompanied him to the hospital. A strong wind would knock Mr. Reedy down.

"I talked to him last night," Georgie explained. "They want to send him to assisted living for rehab. But nothing's been decided yet."

"Oh." Heidi popped her arms on her hips, and Travis backed up.

"You can use our yard, but that's it." His Adam's apple bobbed, and he shrugged. "Don't think bad of me, Georgie. Pretty Boy meant the world to me."

"That's okay, Travis. I've never had a dog before. It's nice." There was something special about taking care of another being. Something new, something unexpected.

"Thanks, Georgie. Come on, Heidi. Time for a coffee break. Let's grab a cup at the diner." He and Heidi left with her waving a goodbye.

The cowbell on the front door jangled not long after, and in walked a little girl, no older than eight or nine, with brown ponytails. Georgie blinked. The girl had the biggest brown eyes, just like Mike Harrison. Was this his daughter?

"My name is Rachel, and I have a business prep—I mean, proposition." She stumbled over the big word before she broke out into a wide smile.

Georgie's emotions were all over the place. She hoped this wasn't Mike's daughter. Coming face-to-face with Mike Harrison's daughter would mean coming face-to-face with Mike Harrison's wife. She wasn't ready for that yet.

Georgie moved to the front of the desk, her gaze flying to the door. "Aren't you a little young to be here by yourself?"

"My babysitter, Emily, just finished having some test done to her car. Something that sounded like missions but wasn't." Rachel laid her book on the counter and reached into her pink purse. "Are you Georgie?"

"I am." Georgie wrinkled her brows. What purpose could a kid have with her?

"It's a pleasure to meet you," the girl said with a big grin on her face. She held out her hand to Georgie, who accepted her handshake. "My grandma always says it's much easier to get people to do your bidding if you butter them up first."

"Smart woman." Georgie moved until her back collided with the edge of the counter. "Oomph." She drank in the sight of this precocious girl, who liked to use big words and wasn't afraid to quote her family members. A scary combination, but likeable nonetheless. "Why do you think you have to butter me up? Do you have something hidden in your trunk that shouldn't be there?"

Rachel giggled for a full minute.

"How may I be of service, Miss Rachel?"

Georgie dipped her head and tried to make Rachel feel like she was the most important customer ever to grace Max's Auto Repair. For the moment, she was.

"I want to hire you." She opened her purse and pulled out a twenty-dollar bill. Then she plunked a plastic baggie of change onto the counter. "I have twenty-three dollars and fourteen cents. Is that enough?"

Georgie coughed away her laugh. At the memory of Mrs. Whittle, the laugh died, period. The way Mrs. Whittle patted Georgie's cheek, the overbearing scent of her cloying perfume hurting Georgie's nose, still elicited a shiver. Mrs. Whittle had dismissed her, insisting a child didn't know anything. Condescension at its worst. Georgie hated it then. She still hated it.

"For what?" Georgie folded her arms over her chest. Why wasn't Rachel's babysitter watching this woman in a girl's body?

"I want to hire you to fix my father."

Laughter exploded out of Georgie. Little pools of water condensed at the corners of her eyes. She dared to glance at Rachel, whose frown helped Georgie regain her composure.

"Rachel," Georgie said and cleared her throat. "You've come to the wrong place for that. I'm a mechanic. I fix cars, not people."

And, for the most part, twenty-three dollars

and some change wouldn't be enough to start fixing any man.

Rachel shook her head and crinkled her eyebrows. "My father's car is what I meant."

"Oh-hh-hh." Georgie drawled out the word, glad Rachel was starting to make some sense. What kind of father, though, hired a babysitter who didn't watch this child like a hawk? What kind of father depended on his young daughter to go around arranging repairs he should be in charge of?

Even though her own father died in a racing accident before she was born, Georgie was sure Stephen George Bennett wouldn't have been that type of derelict father.

"The car's in awful bad shape, and we can't go on car rides anymore. With his birthday coming up, I thought..." Rachel glanced at the stack of money. Her bottom lip jutted out. "That's not enough money, is it?"

Georgie's heart melted at Rachel's story. Even Georgie's throat was constricting the teensiest bit, not that she'd admit it.

"Lucky for you, we're running a special this afternoon." Georgie unfolded her arms and scooped Rachel's money into the bright pink purse, handing it back to its owner. "One free house call per customer. Only redeemable if your birthday is coming up. Parts and labor costs to be assessed at the scene."

"Huh? What's assessed?" Rachel narrowed her eyes while pushing her purse strap to the top of her shoulder.

"It means figuring out how much something will cost or how much something is worth. For instance, my assessment is you're priceless. Hope your father appreciates what you're doing for him."

"He does. Do you have a piece of paper?" Rachel glanced at the desk and latched onto the pen attached to the counter with a silver link chain.

Georgie handed her some scratch paper and waited.

"My father gets off work at seven. Is tonight good for you?"

Georgie nodded, admiring how Rachel was straight to the point, a girl after her own heart.

"You'll be a great surprise."

Somehow, Georgie doubted that.

As soon as Rachel had finished writing, she turned on her heel and headed for the door.

"Goodbye, Rachel. Very nice meeting you."

Rachel stopped, turned around and looked right at Georgie. "You won't forget. Tonight. After seven."

Georgie nodded and waved before the door closed. Beau barked, and Georgie pivoted toward Max's office. She stopped cold. She'd have to bring Beau along. It wouldn't be a long house call anyway. Most men didn't expect a mechanic as a birthday gift.

Then again, Rachel wasn't an ordinary girl. Maybe her father would be anything but ordinary, too. She shook her head. Most of the time, a house that came with an unusual father and daughter also came with an unusual mother.

Besides, the one man she'd have liked to spend time with while she stayed in Hollydale believed she was a common thief.

THE SIDEWALKS BUSTLED with people and activity this afternoon. More and more tourists were arriving in town for the display of color Hollydale was famous for. Mike nodded at a mother pushing a stroller, her husband behind her with a young girl riding on his shoulders. From the glee on the girl's face, there was no doubt where they were heading. A peek inside Miss Louise's Ice Cream Parlor showed they were in for a wait as a long line twisted around the iron tables and chairs. As much as he'd like to detour from his destination, Donahue and Officer Edwards were already almost finished processing the scene at Timber River Outfitters, the latest business targeted in the string of burglaries.

Mike entered the shop, his eyes adjusting to the dim lighting. Walls filled with kayaks and shelves with outdoor gear greeted him. While some came to Hollydale for a burst of color and relaxation, others took advantage of the wonders of the Timber River, with its hiking trails and Pine Falls promising adventure.

For Mike the burglaries themselves and Georgie's return were all he could handle at the moment.

The owner of the shop, a tall man in his thirties with thick brown hair, headed toward Mike, his hand extended. After a quick shake, Jeremy pointed to the back. "The sheriff and Officer Edwards are already in there, waiting for you."

Mike nodded. "Edwards filled me in. If you have a list of serial numbers, we'll need them to run a check on them. Also, we'll alert the local stores and the like."

Mike was about to move when Jeremy's voice stopped him. "Have a second?"

"Sure."

Jeremy went to a display of camping lanterns and picked one up. "These are our latest. One of these would be perfect for Rachel. Light enough for her to carry at night."

"I'll keep that in mind, but I need to be with Donahue and Edwards."

Stepping closer to Mike, Jeremy cleared his throat. "That's not the real reason I wanted to talk to you." He lowered his voice and glanced around. "Word on the street is you're going to run for sheriff."

Mike froze. "I'd prefer if the word on the

street had the name of the perp responsible for these burglaries."

"You'd be a great asset to this county. The deadline to register is coming up. Give it some thought. *Sheriff Harrison* has a great ring to it." Jeremy replaced the lantern on the shelf.

"I'll keep you apprised of any developments." Mike stifled a groan. That came out more ambiguous than he'd meant.

Rushing toward the door marked for employees only, Mike entered the back and found Donahue and Edwards hovered over a desk.

"We were examining the lock once more." Sam Edwards rose and shrugged. "This time it wasn't forced."

"Same as the MO at Max's Garage." Donahue took his time getting to his feet, his gaze going to the security camera. "Harrison, you're in charge of getting ahold of the footage and reviewing it back at the station." He met Mike's gaze. "What about the company? What did you find out about them?"

"No red flags." Mike joined them and tapped the desk. "They've been doing this for years, but they've had some glitches around the time of the first burglaries that they insist are now worked out. They want us to catch the thieves so nothing else happens on their watch."

Donahue scrubbed his face. "Keep an eye out. Edwards, every spare moment I want you combing thrift stores and garage sales for the missing electronics, although they're probably selling them online. Don't want to close these cases without an arrest. Staff meeting on Friday to detail more overtime shifts and how we're dealing being two officers short. Might have a lead on a new hire. You'll be pulling a double today, Mike."

More work and less time with Rachel. Those new hires couldn't come soon enough.

MIKE OPENED THE refrigerator and groaned. Some father he was. Overtime was running him ragged, and it was only Wednesday night. Tomorrow he'd have to find time to go grocery shopping. He reached for the gallon of milk, removed the cap and sniffed. Only three days past the expiration date. It was still drinkable.

"Daddy?" Rachel came up from behind, and she circled her arms around his waist. He smiled at how loving his daughter was, even though there were times he fell far short of deserving it.

Rachel released him, and he faced her.

Reaching for her waist, he picked her up and whirled her around the small kitchen. "Hey, kiddo. Spaghetti okay for dinner?"

"Yum, yum. My favorite." She giggled as he returned her to a standing position. "I have a question."

"And I'll do my best to answer it, but I have to

know what it is first." He bent down and pulled the big pot out of the lower cabinet.

As he walked to the pantry, she followed. He smiled at his little shadow. After Caitlyn left and filed for a quickie divorce, granting him full custody in the process, he'd worried something fierce about letting this little one down. Same as he did on nights like tonight when the refrigerator was rather bare and overtime kept him from spending as much time as he'd like with her. Thank goodness Rachel didn't seem to share his fears but threw herself into everything with her lovable self.

He had to sell the Thunderbird. As soon as he did so, he'd sign her up for those dance lessons, complete with an after-school program that would take care of the need for the occasional babysitter like this afternoon and free his mother for more time for herself, a rare luxury she hadn't had since Caitlyn left and she started caring for Rachel frequently.

"I was thinking…"

"That's a good thing to do, kiddo." He smiled and ruffled her hair. "I encourage that to the fullest." He filled the pot with water.

She giggled, and he reached for a jar of sauce. Ginger wandered into the kitchen, entangling herself in his legs. He popped open the sauce with too much force, and a streak of red plopped onto his favorite gray Hollydale Police Department T-shirt. Rachel laughed, and he searched for the roll of paper towels.

The doorbell rang. Could he catch a break ever? Or at least find the paper towels. He huffed. "Rachel, please get Ginger, while I go see who's at the door."

Rachel picked up Ginger, who meowed her displeasure at not having the person she wanted paying attention to her.

"Sorry, Ginge, you know I'll spoil you rotten later." He looked around for a dish towel, but the bell rang again. No time to clean up if somebody was that impatient.

He strode to the entranceway, still chastising himself about the sauce on his shirt.

"Daddy?" Rachel called out. Her "I did something wrong" voice gave him pause, but no time for that now. Not when he had to get rid of whoever was at the door and make dinner.

"Tell me during dinner, okay, kiddo."

He threw open the door. His jaw slackened at Georgie's presence. Georgie, even more beautiful in the glow of the porch light.

Her green eyes widened for a millisecond before a small smile crossed her lovely face. "I'm your early birthday present. One mechanic here to check out your car."

What with pursuing leads on the burglaries and trying to arrange childcare for Rachel, he'd forgotten about his upcoming birthday. Rather obviously, though, his mother hadn't, unless Ginger had found a new method to communicate, which he highly doubted.

"My mother is so going to regret this," Mike muttered under his breath. Rather than wait for him to contact Georgie, Mom had forged ahead and hired a mechanic. And did it have to be Georgie? He stood there, the cool night breeze coming in, along with the soft chirps of the crickets. Should he offer Georgie something to drink before he sent her on her way?

"Is this a bad time? She assured me this was a good time."

Why was Georgie looking behind him?

"Do you like her, Daddy?" Rachel clapped her hands, and he turned around. His daughter's wide smile stood in stark contrast to Ginger's discomfort.

The cat wriggled out of Rachel's hands and headed over to Georgie.

Georgie scooped up Ginger before she could run out. "Glad I kept Beau in the car. I believe this is yours."

"The cat would have gone straight to my mother's house, which is where I will be heading in a minute." Why couldn't she have bought him a tie for his birthday? Or a gift certificate for his favorite restaurant? Why did she have to play matchmaker at his age?

He accepted the cat.

Rachel yanked on his T-shirt. "Daddy?"

"Not now, Rache. Our visitor won't be staying. Once she leaves, I'll get dinner started." He held a wriggling cat in his arms. Walking purposely to the living room, he bent down and released Ginger before rushing back.

"Georgie, I can give you a quick update about what we've gathered about the breaking and entering while I walk you to your car. As for the birthday nonsense…"

"It's not nonsense, Daddy," Rachel interrupted. Mike flinched. His daughter knew better than to talk back like that. Dismissing it, he chalked it up to hunger.

At that exact second his stomach growled in empathy. Then he froze, his police instinct trilling. Rachel had been trying to get his attention for several minutes now. He glanced at his beloved daughter, her brightest smile kicking those bells and whistles into high gear.

"Rachel Diana Harrison, is there something you'd like to tell me?"

Her smile widened even more, and he was afraid at what was coming.

"I hired Miss Georgie. Great idea, huh? One free house call to customers who have birthdays coming up." She jumped up and down. "That's today's special."

He met Georgie's look. Eleven years was long enough to move past prom. At least it was enough time on his part. Once she glimpsed the Thunderbird, though? Any chance of true forgiveness would disappear. No doubt Georgie would blame him for the damage to Miss Brittany.

He sighed and shrugged. "You obviously didn't know I'm Rachel's father."

Georgie shook her head and darted a glance toward the empty driveway. "Is your squad car acting up? I can take a quick look at it and tell you if you need to bring it into the shop tomorrow."

"It's at my parents' house. The squad car's not the problem."

It suddenly dawned on him how much Georgie had missed over the past years. She had no idea about Grandpa Ted or anything else that had happened in his family. How would she? Beverly never even looked at him, let alone would she pass along details about his family.

"Then what is?"

He started at her husky voice. He'd missed it as soon as he'd given his sister Natalie the infamous note. He'd missed it more over the two years she stayed in Hollydale without speaking to him.

"Beau's waiting in the car, and I don't want to find a hole in the back seat."

Now or never. He could either show her the Thunderbird or make a quick sale without Georgie ever knowing how he'd let the car slip into a state of disrepair.

The latter was the easy choice. He glanced at his daughter. What sort of a role model would he be if he always traveled the easy road? Grandpa Ted hadn't taken the safe roads, preferring the twisty turns of the mountain parkways that led to sweeping vistas of mountaintops and valleys. Mike had loved riding shotgun, the wind ruffling through his hair, longer then than the shorter style he favored now.

"Why don't you get Beau? Then we'll all take a walk."

His stomach growled again, louder this time. Rachel giggled at the outburst. Even Georgie slipped her hand over her mouth. Their gazes connected, and Mike glimpsed laughter, and something else, in Georgie's green eyes. Something sizzled. Georgie broke the connection first.

She glanced around the yard. "Didn't your parents used to live on this street?"

"Still do." Mike gave a slight push on Rachel's shoulders. She skipped out onto the porch next to Georgie. He closed the door. "They live two houses down where my squad car is."

"You couldn't pay me to live that close to my mother." Georgie shuddered and started for the stairs.

"Wait a minute. I thought you were living

with her." Mike furrowed his brows and laid an arm around Rachel's shoulder.

If Georgie had lied to him, what else might she have lied to him about at the repair shop yesterday?

Georgie chuckled and continued along the path. "Temporarily. Only while she's recovering, that's all."

They arrived at her Prius. Georgie unraveled Beau's leash from the bar on the back of the passenger seat. Beau jumped out and shook his whole body, presumably enjoying the freedom after being cramped in the back seat.

Rachel jumped behind Mike. "He's big. Does he bite? Can I pet him?"

Mike blinked at how such contradictory sentences could come out of someone at the same time. Of course, he'd heard worse when perps pleaded their innocence in one breath before confessing in the next. Not that Hollydale was a den of criminal activity. The rash of B&Es was the worst wave since Sheriff Donahue had hired him eight years ago.

Georgie looked unsure. "I don't really know. I've never seen him around kids. I'm just taking care of him until his owner is better. Then he'll go back to his real home." She stuck her hand in front of Beau's nose. The dog sniffed and sat on his haunches. When Georgie stroked his head, his tongue lolled out. "I'll bet he'll love you, considering how much spunk and go-getter attitude you have."

Sure enough, the dog loved his daughter, the puppy expression endearing but futile. Beau wasn't going to be part of Rachel's life, and she'd be disappointed with someone else not becoming a permanent fixture in her life. He should have put an end to this inside the house. Later he'd have a long talk with Rachel about birthday presents, along with a lecture about asking strangers for favors.

Was Georgie a stranger? After such a long time away, could he count their teenage friendship as a basis for something real, something to build a lasting relationship on? Yesterday's break-in delivered a cold shock to his system. Every time he examined the evidence and compared it to the other crime scenes, something didn't add up. All the circumstantial evidence pointed to Georgie. She had motive, means and opportunity. The perfect trifecta.

He and Georgie locked gazes before he averted his. The sad truth crept into him. He didn't know Georgie Bennett anymore.

CHAPTER FIVE

CURIOSITY BIT INTO Georgie while she stared at the old dilapidated barn in Mike's parents' backyard. The peeling red paint had faded to a dull brick color, even darker in the dusky gray of early evening. What was so important here that Mike's daughter would approach a total stranger?

Tapping her foot, she waited on Beau, sniffing each and every one of Mrs. Harrison's chrysanthemums. Where were Mike and Rachel?

Her phone buzzed, and she extracted it from her pocket. Brett Cullinan's name brought a coil of tension to her stomach. If it was good news, he'd have called. Steeling herself, she read his text.

Financing issue delays. You're still in running for pit crew. Will contact after sponsor confirms deal. Cullinan.

Footsteps came from the upper path. Grinning, she pocketed her phone. Rachel bounded toward her. Mike held up a remote with his free hand, the other locked in Rachel's.

"Let there be light."

Brightness flooded the area, and Georgie shielded her eyes. Beau nudged Rachel with his nose. Rachel bent down and scratched him behind his ears.

"He likes me." Her high-pitched squeal gave away her delight. "I like him, too."

"Of course. Beau seems to like everyone and everything."

While Rachel and Beau were getting along, too bad she couldn't say the same about her and Mike.

Best cut this short and find out why she was here. "What's in the barn?"

Mike sighed and let go of Rachel, pulling on the barn door. "You're not going to like it."

She didn't like him believing she was a thief, either. Stealing from Max? No way. She owed him so much for giving her a job in high school and all the support he'd given her over the years. Tonight was about Rachel's request, not her.

"Why don't I be the judge of that?" She tightened her hold on Beau's leash.

Mike grimaced from over his shoulder. "Do you want to hear the whole explanation now or later?"

"Later." No use having her opinion clouded by mere words. Besides, his wife, Ginger, was lurking somewhere in the shadows. She might not like Mike explaining anything to Georgie.

Opening the door, he waved her inside. Goose bumps pricked her arms as she caught sight of something familiar yet not at the same time. She stopped and swallowed the lump in her throat. Ted Harrison's beloved Thunderbird, once in pristine condition, only two owners ever laying claim to its registration papers, was now the worse for wear.

"I can't believe your grandfather let this happen to his car." She ran her hand slowly over the paint, noting the rust in spots, her stomach sinking at the deterioration. A chill shivered its way through her, and a small moan escaped for the dear old man who'd treated her like a member of his own family. "He didn't, did he?"

Mike's gaze, and a single quick shake of his head, confirmed her fears. "How? When?" she asked.

"Heart attack. Middle of the night. Almost nine years ago." His jaw clicked, and Georgie didn't press the subject.

"Sorry. I didn't know." It must have happened soon after she left town. Her gaze flew over to Rachel, who appeared to be around eight or nine. She must also have happened soon after Georgie left.

Sadness at how much she'd missed ebbed through her. Beau whimpered before coming and sitting in front of her, his head tilting. She scratched behind his ear. Both Beau and this Thunderbird deserved some TLC. For the first time, regret she wouldn't be sticking around Hollydale for long shimmied through her.

"Miss Georgie, will my twenty-three dollars and fourteen cents be enough?"

"For what?"

"Fixing the car for my daddy's birthday present."

"Rachel, a repair job of this magnitude would cost a little more than that." Georgie shrugged.

Rachel leveled a wise-beyond-her-years look at her, and Georgie turned away.

"Okay, a lot more."

"How much more?" Mike made his presence known with his question. "After all, if anyone in the world knows the engine and exterior of this car, it's you."

Georgie's lips quirked downward. She could hear her mother from clear across town reminding her of the awful impact a frown had on the skin around her mouth. Might as well check the car out a little while she was here.

She walked over to the front grille and located the flat handle. Pulling once, she propped open the hood and jumped back. Her pulse raced and she threw her hand over her heart before she laughed. An old bird's nest wasn't that much cause for alarm.

"How long has it been since anyone's driven Miss Brittany?" All the mirth escaped her while she tallied a running list of repairs.

"You remember what Grandpa Ted called her." Mike came over, and his breath grazed the back of her neck.

Shivers cascaded down her spine, and she steeled herself against any reaction to the man she no longer knew, the man who believed she could commit a crime.

"Apparently you didn't remember to take care of this car." Straightening to her full height, she imitated her mother's best glare, the one that could make ice melt.

He offered a weak smile and petted Beau, as if the dog were a magic barrier that would protect him from her wrath. Animals and cars. Her two biggest weaknesses.

"Apparently," he replied, his stress on the word not escaping her. "You haven't been around. There might be good reasons for letting this happen."

"Not going to buy that, Mike." The crash of metal from the hood snapping down emphasized her point. "While my mother hasn't kept me up-to-date with your life story, there is no excuse for this, this…"

"Travesty," Rachel piped up.

Georgie stared at the girl before tilting her head up to meet Mike's gaze. "Where did you find her? Does her mother have a three hundred IQ or something?"

"When Daddy works late, I read. I've finished all seven Harry Potter books. Now I'm halfway through all of his old Hardy Boys stories." Rachel crooked her finger, and Georgie leaned over. "I like Nancy Drew better. I want to be a detective when I grow up."

Same as her father, who investigated crimes with the county sheriff.

Georgie held her breath as she backed away, but her rear came in contact with the Thunderbird. "I don't think this is a good idea."

Rattled, she looked back at the car and then at its current owner. To see the car in this shape hurt more than the accusation about her character. If Mike had let the car deteriorate like this, just like he'd sacrificed their friendship with an easy excuse on his lips, she had to leave. "Beau and I won't keep you from your dinner any longer."

She hurried out. Dusk was fading fast, the night sky taking over. Unlike in Salem or Boston or Nashville, stars twinkled in the firmament here, no light pollution blocking them from view. Georgie's teenage self would have found this romantic. What had she been thinking before prom, hoping Mike might also be sensing a shift in their relationship? She should have known someone like Wendy, with her lustrous hair and feminine hourglass figure, would appeal to Mike. Not a tall clumsy girl without any curves to speak of.

Honesty. She valued it. If she was being honest, it wasn't so much the last-minute cancellation that had set off her temper when she found the two of them together. It was losing the chance to tell him how she went all quivery around him.

She tugged on Beau's leash, kicking herself for not making some excuse to leave when Mike answered the door. Mike had moved on and was married with a daughter. Holding a grudge was pointless, especially after Kevin's betrayal.

The familiar itch acted up. After residing in seven states over the last nine years, she always listened to that itch, the one the led her to her next adventure waiting around the corner.

With any luck that adventure would come thanks to a brand-new career on the racing circuit.

"Wait a minute." Mike jogged over with Rachel in hand. "Hey, kiddo, run ahead, but stay in my sight while I talk to Miss Georgie."

Georgie withstood the urge to stand behind Beau. Instead, she jerked her thumb toward her Prius. "My mother is expecting me."

"Uh-oh. I'm in big trouble if you're invoking your mother." Laughter crinkled the edges around his eyes before a serious expression overtook his handsome face. "Is there any hope?"

Chills shot down her spine at Mike's question.

"For the Thunderbird?" he asked.

That breath she'd been holding wiggled out, along with a chuckle. What had she expected? That he'd pined for her all these years? That her return would make him confront feelings so deep he'd need a chisel to release them? Rachel skipping ahead in the distance was proof he'd moved on, and how.

It didn't take a rocket scientist to see the bond between Mike and Rachel. This Ginger, the same one who didn't want Beau around, was one lucky woman. The years had changed Mike, and for the better.

Mike touched her arm. "Does your silence mean Miss Brittany's too far gone or you don't want to help me? There's more to the story than meets the eye."

Georgie stilled, the slight wind picking up and going straight to her bones. How did Mike do that so well? Read her mind and be on the same wavelength?

"It means nine years is a long time. Long enough for a beautiful Thunderbird to obtain the equivalent of dry rot. Long enough for you to doubt my integrity." Long enough for her not to have a hometown anymore. Long enough for

Kevin Doherty to pin his cheating ways and their breakup on her.

Suddenly, the weight she'd been feeling on her shoulders felt heavy and burdensome. Relationships should be based on equality and mutual respect. Things lacking here tonight, as well.

"Give me a reason to believe in you again," she said. He winced and held up his hands in surrender. A wry smile enveloped him.

Her breath caught in her chest at the sight of how his face lightened and became—dare she even think it?—more handsome.

"That was wrong of me, Georgie. Besides, if either of us has a reason to be skeptical, it's you. I'm not perfect, and you have no reason to believe in me."

Rachel ran into the house, and Georgie turned her full attention to Mike. "This talk might have done some good before I left town nine years ago. But now? Why?"

"I should have apologized for the way I treated you when it happened." Mike stared down and scuffled the dirt with his sneaker. "I stayed away out of guilt. And the kicker was I lost my best friend."

"Finding you with Wendy MacNamara wasn't easy."

"I should have run after you then."

"Hard to do with your pants around your ankles." Thank goodness Rachel hadn't heard that. She stopped and exhaled. Guess that grudge went deeper after all. The past was in the past, she told herself. It deserved to stay there.

Mike faced her. "All those years ago, I made you cry. I'd never seen you cry before. I hated myself for that. It took all of my willpower to listen to you and stay away."

"You certainly listened well enough. Why didn't you ever try to talk to me after that?"

He frowned and stepped back. "Didn't your mother tell you?"

She shook her head. "Tell me what?"

"I came to your house twice. Both times your mother took great pleasure in telling me to go away. The first time she said you didn't want to speak to me. The other time she scowled and told me I was the reason you left Hollydale. Then she slammed the door in my face." His jaw clenched, and then he blinked. "Can we start over? Be friends?"

Did friendship die? Or did it just sit in a dusty barn waiting for ignition one day?

"Do friends think friends commit burglaries?"

He groaned and ran his hand through his short hair, highlighting his high, angular cheekbones. "I'm doing my job, Georgie, but the burglaries started before you returned to Hollydale, so that's a point in your favor." His facial muscles softened with his sigh. "Where have you kept yourself all these years?"

"When my mother called, I was living in Nashville." Where a friend of a friend had connected her with Brett Cullinan. With any luck, a move to Charlotte, North Carolina, would be in her future. "Before that, I spent two years in Atlanta." She couldn't leave that town soon enough after the Kevin debacle. "Before that was Boston. Couldn't handle the winter. Didn't even make it a whole year. Spent some time on the West Coast, too."

"You've moved quite often."

She shrugged. Not everyone had parents like Diane and Carl Harrison. Moving suited her. She stood in front of Mike's house, his home. Something she didn't have. Something she wasn't sure she could have.

"It's past Beau's bedtime. I have to go." She tugged on Beau's leash and started off at a clipped pace. "See you around, Officer Harrison."

Best to remind herself of his official capacity and distance herself now before she found herself wanting to do something stupid, like put down roots in Hollydale, where she'd lose her sense of herself forever.

Mike dashed by and halted smack-dab in front of her. She couldn't keep her forward momentum without running into him, so she applied the brakes hard. He reached his arm out, placing his hand on her forearm. Shivers of awareness rocketed to her fingertips, and she glared at the traitorous spot where her skin sold her out for his warm touch.

"Mike. Just plain Mike." Only the right side of his mouth quirked up, and for the briefest of seconds, she glimpsed the teenager who'd opened the door and scooted past her for the first soft serve cone of the season from the Dairy Shack, a literal shack on the side of the road. "No one has ever kept me from getting too big for my britches like you did. I miss that. Between being a cop and a single dad, it's hard to find someone who will keep me in line."

A single dad? She licked her lips, trying for any moisture to wet her parched mouth.

"Wait a second. Who is Ginger? Isn't she your wife? You mentioned her yesterday and how you were worried about her reaction to Beau. I just assumed…"

The left side of his mouth lifted, and that full smile threatened to stop her heart, right now, in front of his house. "Ginger has a hold on my heart, that's for sure. She's my cat." His grin widened, and he moved closer. "So you were hanging on my every word, huh?"

Mike was single? She had to wind this up before she did something stupid, like drown in those brown eyes dancing with mirth.

"Don't you wish." She pretended to scoff while backing up to the Prius. "My job involves more listening than you might think. I have to get an idea of what's wrong based on people imitating their engines with whistles and clicks."

Meanwhile warning bells clanged all around her. "Cars can be tricky machines to fix, you know. And if you don't operate them, they break down, and they're no use to anyone. But you know all that... Did I mention that I spent a year restoring cars at a great body shop and then kept that up as a side business? Give me a classic car show, and I'm in heaven." She sent a backward glance toward his parents' house, the barn no longer in sight. She was rambling, but she couldn't stop. "So many put their hearts into restoring a car down on its luck, and you should see the pride on people's faces when the cars are finished. For those folks it's about bringing cars back to life."

Beau circled his leash around her legs. Georgie twisted and flailed.

Mike landed his hand on her elbow. "Careful, now." His strong voice shouldn't be that comforting, but it was. "Want to come inside? Talk about the Thunderbird. Catch up on each other's lives. Let's bury the hatchet. I won't play bad cop, I promise."

He made an *X* over his heart.

Tempting didn't even begin to describe his

invitation. But the last thing she needed was another person hurting her heart, another machine that could get rusty all too quickly.

"My mother is still recovering. I… I need to check on her, relieve Kitty."

"Running away from a challenge that fast?" He shook his head and planted one hand on her Prius. "Tsk, tsk. That's not the Georgie Bennett I remember."

She arched her eyebrow. "What challenge?"

Her smartphone buzzed, and she dug it out of her pocket. The text from Kitty was short and sweet.

Your mother would like you to stop for chamomile tea. She'd like it delivered within the hour.

Georgie's fingers flew across the screen as she typed in an affirmative reply. "Duty calls as my mother is in desperate need of her favorite bedtime drink."

She went and opened the back door of her car for Beau, stopping to glance over her shoulder. Mike now stood on the edge of his driveway, his grin all the wider, as if he'd never doubted she'd look back.

"WHAT'S BEHIND THE DINER?" Mike approached Donahue, whose thick gloves nearly came up to his elbows.

"Received an anonymous tip about electronics in the dumpster. Since you're the lead, I waited for you." Donahue stepped toward the receptacle.

Mike donned his protective gloves and grabbed his flashlight. Peering inside, he found, among banana peels and chunks of chicken-fried steak, a couple of tablets and placed them in an evidence bag. "This seems almost too convenient. Why now?"

"More important, who has access to this dumpster?" Donahue jotted something on his notepad.

"The diner, Farr's Hardware and Max's garage, although they also use another for environmental purposes."

"Georgie Bennett enters the picture again."

Shaking his head, Mike sealed the evidence bags. "Georgie didn't live here when the crimes began, and she wouldn't throw these away in plain sight."

Donahue tilted his head toward downtown. "I'll meet you in my office after you dust for prints and log them into the evidence area."

Before Mike could say anything else, Donahue was gone.

Back at the station, Mike finished logging in the stolen items. When Donahue hired the two officers whose vacancies had thrown more work his way, his load might become manageable again.

Keeping Donahue in place was his top priority, along with solving the burglaries and clearing Georgie's name.

Donahue strode by, his shoes thumping along the gray epoxy floor. "It's Hollydale Florists. Let's go."

Mike followed and slid into the passenger seat. "What's happened?"

"Another B&E." Exasperation laced Donahue's voice. He started the car. "Door jimmied. Petty cash and small electronics taken. The security company alerted us."

Mike flipped through his notebook. "This makes six that follow the same pattern."

"It's the seventh overall." Donahue pulled out of the lot. "And ever since Georgie Bennett came back to town, they're increasing in frequency."

"I'm not sure whether to count Max's Auto Repair with the others, and Georgie wasn't in town for the first thefts," said Mike, returning his notebook to his pocket.

Arriving at the scene, Mike greeted the owner and processed the evidence, not that he found much. Dusting for fingerprints yielded nothing. If it weren't for the petty cash jar being empty and the back door ajar, there wouldn't be any signs of a theft.

Promising the owner to keep her updated, Mike and the sheriff exited the business. Once outside, Mike took a deep breath and released it, wondering what had happened to his town. The sheriff looked up and down Main Street as if trying to figure out where he was.

"Community heat is building, you know," said Donahue.

His boss's message came through loud and clear. Mike had to figure this out and soon.

"Any word on new recruits? They'd help with surveillance." Not to mention save Mike. He'd like to eat dinner with Rachel once in a blue moon. She was growing up so fast. Soon the days of tucking her in would come to a close.

"Talked to the head of the Tar Heel Recruit Academy yesterday. They're almost finished with a twenty-nine-week training session. Also had a résumé from an Atlanta officer this past week. I've arranged an interview and a ride through Daleford County." Donahue shrugged as he scratched the back of his neck. "Don't have much hopes for that one. City detective. He'd be taking quite a pay cut to work here."

"If your wife made him her pot roast and chocolate cake, he'd be convinced." Mike gave a half smile.

Donahue cracked a grin back as he patted his stomach. "Melanie does make a fine chocolate cake. Once we're not spread so thin, things will lighten up." He held up his hand. "I know. We need two someones, but who's counting? Until then don't make any vacation plans."

The sheriff brought up his chin, his usual manner of dismissal. Mike took a step toward the cruiser, and Donahue cleared his throat. "Wait. Talk to your mom about watching Rachel overnight sometime next week. The perps who're doing this might know we're down two officers. This way, they won't see us coming."

As much as he hated time away from Rachel, nipping this chain of B&Es was in everyone's best interests. "I'll arrange it today."

"Do it. While you're at it, set up the laser gun on the new stretch of State Road 41, heading out of town."

Groaning, Mike shook his head. "You sure about that? What if Evelyn Andrews is doing seventy in a forty-five again?"

Donahue scoffed and rolled his eyes. "When I hired her nephew, Billy, he had impeccable references from the academy. Didn't take into account the first speeding ticket he ever issued would be against his aunt."

"Or that his mother, who's won more than her fair share of blue ribbons for her pies, would threaten to cut him off if he didn't get that ticket dismissed." Mike laughed in spite of everything. More reasons not to throw his hat into the sheriff's ring. Donahue was much better suited for the politics of the job. "Guess peach pie is a good reason to quit when you're twenty-one and risk a lifetime expulsion from family gatherings."

"Yeah, but lousy for us." Donahue headed for their vehicle, and Mike followed. "You should be able to meet your quota for the year out there."

Returning to his desk, Mike grabbed his laser gun and stopped. Should he call his mother or wait until later? His key ring on the desk caught his attention. The triangular hole for the key of the Thunderbird stood out from the others.

He picked up the ring and tapped the older key against the edge of his desk. He still hadn't listed the car for sale. With Georgie's words echoing in his mind, he'd researched the difference in value. Her assessment proved correct. Cars in mint condition brought in almost double the amount as ones with a list of repairs a mile long. If he could restore the car, he'd fetch a whole lot more dollars, even after subtracting the price of parts and labor.

And it wouldn't happen right away. He'd be sure that he and Rachel could have one farewell ride in Miss Brittany. With the top down, she'd love the wind blowing through her hair. Rachel's giggles kept him motivated on his long days on the job.

But asking Georgie to do the work? He gulped

and blew out a deep breath. She'd knocked the equilibrium he'd found in the past eight years off kilter. After Georgie had left his house last night, he couldn't concentrate on anything else. The results hadn't been pretty. Splattering the sauce all over the cooktop. Pouring half a container of Parmesan cheese on top of his spaghetti. Reading the same page three times to Rachel. All thanks to Georgie's honest response to the indignity he'd done to Grandpa's car.

If she had only listened to his explanation…

Mike laughed, predicting what Georgie would do. She'd pop her hands onto her hips and send that gaze piercing into his forehead, reminding him excuses were regrets wrapped in fancy paper. She'd cut him down before he finished.

Grabbing his keys, he hurried out to his squad car, its utilitarian lines a far cry from the Thunderbird's classic ones. No sign of rust anywhere.

Unlike his heart.

CHAPTER SIX

"TWO MORE CANCELLATIONS, DARLIN'." Heidi banged down the phone and began doodling on the nearby notepad. "When I said Travis wasn't available, they didn't rebook."

As much as she wanted to pound her head into the wall after a week of pure frustration, Georgie stopped short and moved toward the reception desk instead. "What excuses did they use this time?"

Five cancellations in the past two days had really hit home. This reeked of being more personal than anything. Short of offering to work for free, she didn't know what to do. This Tuesday morning was going downhill fast.

"One person claimed the rash of robberies was making her ill and she was staying away from downtown until the police caught the thief. The other, though..." Heidi winced and shook her head. "Everyone knows Clyde Spratt is Dick Crabtree's only friend. Everyone in town avoids them like a pair of dead possums."

If customers didn't start returning soon, she'd

be giving back to Max the keys to a bankrupt business. She should tell Max about her shot at the pit crew position. At the least, she should tell Heidi and Travis. That way someone else could take her place.

No. Then it would look like she was hiding something. And she didn't have the position yet. She needed something to fall back on.

Georgie exhaled a long, deep breath and stuck her hands into her coverall pockets. "Thanks."

"Bless my heart. You look like a country music song. Is Beau okay? Your mama? You don't own a truck, so it's not that." Heidi came closer, so close her face was next to Georgie's. "You're whiter than clean sheets on a clothesline."

Georgie squirmed and moved back. Heidi's concern was downright maternal. Georgie smiled on the inside. It was nice having someone care. "Nothing like that."

"Cheer up, or Max will call me again like he did last night. Told me I wasn't doing a good enough job taking care of you."

Startled, Georgie blinked. "I do have a confession. He's asked me to buy him out. I'm worried about him."

"Don't fret none. He'll come back better than ever. Rosie wants him to stay awhile longer, and he has a hard time saying no to his sister." Heidi hugged her and broke away. "By the way, Max asked us to buy him out last year. We said no. Travis and I would like to retire sooner rather than later." She wiggled her finger toward Georgie. "I'll let you in on a secret. Missy and her husband, Bobby, are seeing a fertility specialist. We're helping with the cost of the IVF treatment. If it's successful, we'll be welcoming our first grandchild next year. That's why we're traveling now. Getting it out of our system so we can spend more time with the family later."

Family. In Hollydale, everyone seemed to help one another. If they trusted you, that is.

"I see."

"We just can't afford all of it. With the traveling and the IVF, we're stretched thinner than a cheap rubber band. Max said he understood."

Before Georgie could answer, the cowbell over the door jangled. A woman with blond hair tied back in a ponytail entered with two children, a boy tugging on one hand, while a girl held on to the other as if for dear life. The woman's haggard face gave Georgie pause, as if the woman was having an even worse day than she. The streaks of chocolate on her T-shirt only confirmed Georgie's suspicions.

"Is Max here?" Her soft drawl sounded familiar, as if Georgie had heard it before, but she couldn't place it.

"What you see is what you get." Georgie was fed up. It was about time people allowed her to do her job. "I'm fully trained and I'm a good mechanic." Georgie approached them. "How can I make your car run better today?"

The woman laughed and lifted the left side of her mouth in a wry, gut-wrenching half smile. "It would take a miracle and money I don't have in the bank to do that." She squinted at Georgie. "Oh, my goodness gracious. Georgie Bennett, is that you?"

Without further ado, the woman released the children's hands and ran to Georgie, hugging her with all her might.

Gasping at the stranger's hug, Georgie stiffened and tapped her on the shoulder. "Excuse me. You seem to know me, but I don't know you."

"Guess I have changed that much. I'm Lucie Decker—well, I used to be Lucie Appleby."

Georgie's eyes widened. This was Lucie, the most popular girl in school? Lucie's family had more money than Scrooge at one point, but something had changed. Georgie shook away her shock and gave a semblance of a smile, softening upon meeting the gazes of the two little ones, not more than six years old. "How can I be of service today?"

Lucie bit her lip and fingered the edge of her purse. Heidi cleared her throat, and Georgie felt like a yo-yo with her head going back and forth so much.

"Excuse me, darlin'." Heidi tapped Georgie's shoulder. "You remember that spill in the office. Let's clean it up." Heidi gestured toward Max's office, which seemed downright empty today without Beau.

Georgie smiled at Lucie, then followed Heidi.

Heidi made sure the door was shut. "Hasn't your mother kept you afloat of anything that's been going on in Hollydale?"

Georgie shook her head. "If it doesn't concern her health, her shopping sprees or her, pretty much the answer would be no."

"Lucie's parents died in a car accident while she was in college." Heidi wrung her hands. "She was so upset that she married the first guy who came along, and he ended up embezzling all her money, as well as the money of half the residents of Hollydale. As much as she wants to move, she can't afford to start over anywhere else."

Lucie Decker, broke and desperate, with two kids to support? A far cry from the effervescent teenager who could rally anyone to her cause and make it their own. "What does that have to do with Max?"

Rolling her eyes, Heidi sent her a look of pure exasperation. Georgie gave a weak smile in return. Engines and axles? She could fix those any day of the week. People? Not so much.

"She struck a chord with Max." Heidi fluffed

some lint off Georgie's shoulder. "He said she reminded him of his mother."

Georgie nodded. Max often spoke of his widowed mother, who'd endured and thrived while raising her son and daughter in the fifties and sixties but never remarried. "What can I do?"

"Max okayed Lucie to clean the office on Sundays, drop off casseroles and the like for the cost of labor. Then he allowed her to cover the cost of the parts through a payment plan. You should do the same."

"Now we're on the same wavelength." Relief stopped her squirming toes. "Gotcha."

Heidi pointed to the door. "Get out of here before she leaves in that clunker of hers."

That was enough time wasted gossiping. Georgie strode into the waiting area. "What's wrong with your car, Lucie?"

"Nothing too bad. I'm sure it can wait." Lucie glanced at each child, worry evident in her hazel eyes.

This wasn't the voice of the Lucie she'd known, that peppy assertiveness of someone breezing through life. Lucie turned and walked toward the door.

Huffing, Georgie hurried over, blocking the door before her former classmate could go. "You said your car needs servicing." She met Lucie's gaze and pointed to the two little ones, as it was obvious that was how to get through the shame written all over Lucie's face. "Come outside and tell me what's wrong. Heidi will take care of the little ones for a minute while we talk."

Lucie bit her lip and glanced over her shoulder. "Do you mind? Mattie and Ethan are usually good for other people."

"Not at all. It'll be excellent practice for when Missy has babies." Heidi held out her hands for the kids. "Come on, you two. You can sit behind the desk with me and be my helpers."

Georgie led the way outside, and Lucie pointed to a white PT Cruiser that had seen better days, years, decades. "This car is how old? Ten? Eleven?"

Lucie sighed, her eyes tentative. "Twelve. It's a clunker, but it's mine. It gets me to work and to the twins' day care."

Georgie wiggled her fingers. "Keys, please, along with a list of what's wrong."

"The car whines, and it takes a couple of times to turn over. When I was on the parkway last week, the car seemed to hesitate." Lucie paused before handing over her keys. "Is it something a simple oil change can fix?"

If only. "Sounds like a bad fuel pump. I'll take it into the garage and look it over."

"Are those cheap?" Lucie's shoulders dropped a couple of inches.

"Depends on your definition of cheap."

For the Lucie of old, a couple of hundred dollars hadn't been a big deal. In high school her designer shoes and purses had been proof of that. Georgie's gaze went to Lucie's handbag, falling apart at the seams. For this Lucie, the repair price might be exorbitant.

"I'd have to check the price of a new pump, but they run between two and four hundred dollars, plus labor."

Alarm registered on Lucie's face. She tried to pluck the keys out of Georgie's hand. "It'll have to wait."

"A bad fuel pump can't wait to be repaired."

"How bad could it be? I'll take my chances." Lucie tapped her foot and held out her hand.

Georgie shook her head and inserted the key in the ignition. Cranking it, she waited for the familiar sound of an engine igniting, but nothing came. Trying again produced the same result. The third time was finally the charm, but for how much longer? This car wasn't safe, and Georgie wasn't about to let Lucie on the road.

"Your fuel pump won't hold out much longer. I'm not feeding you a line, either. I don't have kids who need braces, and I don't have a vacation home in the Smokies that needs renovating. Pure and simple, this car won't start by week's end. Worse yet, it could stop all of a sudden, causing an accident, and your kids might be in the car."

"I can't let that happen, but I can't afford

this." She sounded horrified and planted her face in her hands. "I'm not the same Lucie from high school. Considering I never stopped to talk to you in the hallways, you might think that's a good thing."

Georgie's gaze lingered over Lucie's thin frame and her worn clothing, clean except for the chocolate smears. "Never." Taking pleasure in other's misfortunes had never been her style. "You really think I'm going to let someone who I've known almost all my life drive this car away in poor condition? My guess is your children are the same age we were when we met."

Lucie sniffled, a crooked smile coming out. "Yeah."

The first day of kindergarten flooded back like a bad engine. Georgie shuffled her feet. "You probably don't remember, but you introduced yourself to me. You were wearing a matching dress and headband…"

Lucie's smile became more genuine. "I loved that plaid jumper."

Georgie cleared her throat, and Lucie pretended to zip her lip. "You offered to be my friend." Here she had judged Lucie by her appearance, when she hated when people did the same. "And I turned you down flat. Hope that offer didn't come with an expiration date. Standing there, you look like you could use a friend."

"That obvious, huh?" asked Lucie.

Sighs came out of both of their mouths at the same time.

"Gosh, you have a good memory." Something in Lucie's eyes made Georgie give her a second glance.

There was something there Georgie could identify with. Lucie was a survivor.

"I always envied you, though," Lucie said.

Surprise flickered through Georgie. Since she'd come back to Hollydale, one surprise after another had greeted her. "Me? I wasn't popular or overly athletic, or the smartest."

Lucie smiled. "No, but you were sure of yourself. You always carried yourself with purpose."

Georgie pocketed the keys. Bluster and her friendship with Mike Harrison had gone a long way. Even with her independent streak, Mike had made everything better. Well, almost everything.

Georgie couldn't let Lucie drive away in this rattletrap. Besides, this was a true challenge, and she loved making an engine better again. "I'll make you a deal."

"I don't have any money to spare." Bitterness laced her words, and Lucie stopped short. "Sorry to be so blunt. My ex fleeced almost everyone in this town, me and our children most of all."

"Nothing shameful in a payment plan."

Lucie sent another wry smile her way. "Honesty. That's another quality I've long admired of yours. Never a desire to pretend like the rest of us."

"Here's the deal. Recommend me to your friends, and I'll reduce the cost of labor."

Lucie laughed and kicked the front tire. "My word doesn't mean much around here anymore."

Without references it would be a hard climb for other customers to trust her with their cars. "Any word of mouth is better than none."

"How much is the part you're talking about?"

"A few hundred."

Lucie whistled and shuffled away. "I'll be paying you and Max back when my kids attend Hollydale High." She frowned and extended her hand again. "Once the car goes kaput, we can walk until I save enough."

"Then I'll hire you." Where had that idea come from? And Lucie Decker, of all people? How many times had Beverly Bennett held up Lucie as a model of grace and charm? That didn't matter now. Keeping this car running did. Those kids mattered. Somehow, a part of her knew Lucie also counted for something, even if Lucie had forgotten that. "My mother recently had a stent procedure. Her best friend, Kitty, has helped her while I work."

"I'm not a nurse."

"No, but my mother has always liked you."

"I already have two jobs while they're at day care."

"They'll entertain my mother." An idea popped into Georgie's head. "She can also tell you about a fabulous job opening at my cousin's dress shop."

"It sounds too good to be true."

"Cost of labor in exchange for helping with my mother and…"

"A payment plan for the part."

"You have a deal."

They shook on it, and Georgie sighed. Another job she was practically doing for free. At least she was repairing something. A small start, but a start nonetheless.

MIKE SWUNG HIS duffel bag over his shoulder as he headed toward the Night Owl Bakery. He'd wanted one of their peach cobbler cookies all morning. After he bought two, one for him now and one for Rachel later, he'd head over to the gazebo and wolf down his lunch while reading over the police reports one more time. Maybe seeing the facades of the businesses while he ate would bring on fresh inspiration.

Mission accomplished. A warm cookie in hand and another in his bag, Mike made his way to the gazebo, the sidewalks less crowded with the art festival now in the annals of Hollydale history. Before he reached his destination, Donahue emerged from the courthouse and flagged Mike down.

"Just finalized getting my name on the ballot. Another unopposed election."

While more residents like Jeremy had asked Mike about running, Donahue had Mike's vote unless something changed.

"I'll be back at the station after lunch." Mike held up his cookie and duffel bag. "Thought a change of scenery might give me a fresh perspective on the crime scene reports."

Mike went to a bench, and Donahue sat down beside him. "Did you bring those reports with you?"

"Yep." Mike unzipped the duffel and pulled out the magazine on top. *Magazine?* He didn't put a magazine in there this morning. A closer inspection proved it wasn't a magazine but a comic book with a sticky note attached.

"What's that?" Donahue craned his neck.

"Rachel must have slipped it in for me." He read the note, which confirmed his guess.

Donahue grabbed the comic, his neck growing red near the collar. "A comic book, and it looks vintage. Where did Rachel get this?"

Mike's appetite deserted him, and he set aside the remaining cookie to give to Rachel later. "Georgie dropped off a box of books for Rachel. Could have been in there or it could have come from a friend at school. My dad might even have given it to her as a gift." Then an ad for a video game system on the back cover jumped out at him. This couldn't be one of Max's. "And looks can be deceiving. This is new."

"Georgie Bennett's name comes up again." Donahue jumped up and all but licked his lips. "I'll check with Max to see if he had any new comics mixed in with his older ones."

Mike tried to retrieve the comic book, but Donahue refused to hand it over.

"Until I find out if this is one of Max's, don't tell anyone about this."

"That's a far reach, isn't it?" A sliver of doubt burred its way into Mike's mind before he dismissed it. Georgie Bennett was innocent.

"She also had access to that dumpster." Donahue strode off in the direction of the police station.

While the comic book was circumstantial at best, Donahue seemed to take it as strong proof Georgie was responsible.

MIKE GRAZED THE back of his hand to Rachel's forehead. Burning hot. His daughter sniffled, and he handed her the box of tissues from her nightstand. A relapse of whatever she had two weeks ago. Mike headed for the bathroom for the children's pain reliever. Returning, he measured out a dose of the sticky pink stuff.

"Open up, kiddo." Mike held the capful of medicine under her nose.

"I like grape better." She sipped it slowly but eventually finished the liquid.

"While grape is the superior flavor to—" he held up the cap to read and winced "—whatever this is, it's the best we've got. You get the day off tomorrow."

"But tomorrow's Wednesday, our reward day. I'll miss out on popsicles." Rachel sneezed and wiped her hand on her shirtsleeve.

At times like this, he didn't know whether to miss Caitlyn or curse her for leaving.

"I'll step out while you change into pajamas, and I'll be back with a nice cup of…" He huffed out a deep breath. Decaf coffee wasn't a good solution here. "Tea or whatever Aunt Natalie drinks and leaves in the cabinet when she babysits."

Mike walked toward the hall, cap and bottle in hand. Glancing over his shoulder, he hated the misery on his little girl's face. "When I go to the store, I'll pick up banana popsicles. They're still your favorite, right?"

"It's not the same." Rachel dragged herself out of bed and went for the dresser.

Would a mother handle this better? He shrugged and hurried on. Doing the best with what he'd been given was his stock in trade.

Trouble now was finding someone to babysit a sick child while he went to work.

Picking up his smartphone, he called the first person on his list. "Hi, Mom."

"I was just about to call you. Smart minds think alike." Light laughter came over the line. "Guess what?"

"You had a great time with Ruthy and Don?" Safe guess, but he liked the safety of being right in this moment.

"Becks is pregnant! My second grandbaby. She's on the phone with Natalie now, and she's calling you next. Act surprised, okay?" Mom's excitement was palpable, and his mood elevated. So his little sister and her husband, Jack, were going to have a baby. He hustled back to Rachel's room, phone in hand.

He entered before a shriek stopped him cold. "Daddy, I'm changing."

He stepped back into the hallway. One of his little sisters was all grown up, and his daughter was growing up way too fast.

"Mike, are you there?" Mom's question gave him pause. He didn't want to ruin Becks's moment with the news Rachel was sick.

"That's great, Mom. And yes, I'll act surprised."

"There's more." Her tone changed from excitement to a hint of foreboding. "I know it's your birthday tomorrow, but I'm flying out to

LA. Ruthy and Don invited us, and they only live half an hour from Becks and Jack. Do you mind if I miss your birthday? After her miscarriage with the last baby, I want to help Becks stay off her feet."

"Good luck with that. Becks's idea of taking it easy is running a half triathlon."

"I know. Becks was born kicking a soccer ball while Natalie had a calculator in hand." Another giddy burst of laughter followed by a cheer. "We'll celebrate when I get back, okay? And I'll work out a deal with Natalie. She can pick Rachel up after she's done teaching for the day."

He couldn't stand in the way of his mother's happiness. Especially when Becks would be thrilled to see Mom. He'd talk to Natalie later. "Sounds good."

Rachel opened the door, exasperation clouding her brown eyes. "Daddy. I'm eight now. Please knock before you come in." She sniffled and shrugged, throwing her arms around him. "But I'm never too old to give you a hug. Love you."

"Time for bed." He tucked her in. Pressing a kiss to her hot forehead, he smiled. "By the way, you have to get better so you can Skype Aunt Becks tomorrow night."

Rachel's eyebrows wove together. "We don't call her until Sunday night."

"You'll want to suggest names for their new addition."

Ginger wandered into the room and jumped on Rachel's bed.

"Are they getting a kitten?" Rachel stroked Ginger's back and pressed her face to her side.

Ginger yowled and jumped off again.

"Or a dog?"

Trust his daughter to assume Becks and Jack were adding an animal to their family rather than a baby. "Actually, they won't be getting anything for about seven more months. Aunt Becks is pregnant."

Rachel clapped and sat straight up, her cheeks two bright beacons of pink. "I hope it's a girl."

She swung her legs, longer than this time last year, out of her bed.

Mike held up his hand. "Where are you going, young lady?"

"I want to talk to Aunt Becks today." She gazed at her father and climbed back into bed with a little huff. "I'll wait for tomorrow."

"Good answer." Mike brushed her damp hair off her forehead before grazing a kiss there. "Get some sleep."

He flicked off her bedroom light, then walked into the living room and went through his list of alternate babysitters. Forget it. Rachel needed rest and her father. Even though it was late, he called Sam Edwards, who couldn't switch shifts with him. That left Sheriff Donahue.

A few minutes later he pressed End Call on his phone and knocked his head against the wall. *That went well. Not at all.* Donahue made him pay through the nose. Two night shifts in exchange for staying home with Rachel tomorrow.

A sick child and laundry were a heck of a way to spend his thirtieth birthday.

If he had any luck at all, one of those night shifts better net the B&E perps.

Besides, Rachel was worth the trade. He settled on the couch and grabbed the remote. Ginger climbed onto his lap, and he stroked her soft fur, her purrs a great reward. Mike glanced at the ceiling, Rachel's room directly overhead. Hard to believe anything good came out of the first and only time he'd gotten stinking drunk. He'd gone to Bobby Joe's Bluegrass Bar in Asheville, looking for a temporary fix to all that was wrong with his life. He'd found that, and more, in the form of a shapely Caitlyn Anderson and a cheap motel. Six weeks later, she'd knocked on his door. Stunned, he'd knelt on one knee and didn't look back. Doing the honorable thing was never a question. He'd do the same all over again. Caitlyn, however, left after two months of motherhood, signing away all rights while claiming she was too young to settle down.

Shaking off the doldrums, he moved to the kitchen. Ginger wound herself around his ankles, reminding him, first and foremost, cats were the only necessary item on the list of life's blessings and he was her minion, existing to do her bidding. Laughing, he stroked her underbelly.

"So, Ginger. What should I get myself for my birthday?"

Georgie's offer ran through his mind. If he restored the Thunderbird, he and Rachel would have that long drive before he sold it. *Be honest, Mike.* Having Georgie in the front seat with him would be like old times.

A fresh start. That would be his birthday present to himself.

Despite Ginger's howls of protest when he stopped rubbing her tummy, Mike went over and picked up his smartphone. Frustration floated through him as he thumped the phone on the table. He didn't have Georgie's number. Getting her number off the police report for personal reasons crossed the line. And her old number from high school? Beverly Bennett found another aisle in the grocery store if she saw him coming. She sure wouldn't pass the phone to Georgie.

Tomorrow he'd call Max's Auto Repair and set this plan into motion.

Maybe it would be a happy birthday after all.

CHAPTER SEVEN

EVERY TIME GEORGIE passed Heidi's desk calendar, something pinged inside her like there was something important about this Wednesday she couldn't quite put her finger on. Seeing the date once more brought that same ache in her stomach. Again, nothing came to mind.

The phone rang, and Heidi moved to answer it.

"Max's Auto Repair. Heidi speaking. As a matter of fact, she is here." Heidi held out the receiver to Georgie. "Prospective client."

Finally. Georgie didn't care if it was a scooter or an electric skateboard. While she'd enjoyed handing Lucie the keys to her Cruiser this morning, she'd fix anything with wheels and a motor.

Georgie clenched her fist and pumped it toward her chest. "Georgie Bennett."

"Hi, it's Mike."

Her intake of breath gave away her surprise. *Mike.* How could she have forgotten, especially after proclaiming herself his present the other night? She bumped her forehead with her free hand. "Happy birthday to the bestest fella ever."

He laughed, a new wryness coming through. "I've missed that Georgie optimism."

She'd be a sight more optimistic once Mike solved the string of burglaries, the topic of many conversations around town, according to Heidi.

"How can Max's Auto Repair help you on this fine day?"

"You mentioned you'd spent time in different areas of the country. Boston and Atlanta among others, right?"

What she'd said meant something to him. He hadn't just filed it away with the report. Did she want him to pay attention? Her cheeks warmed, and she shifted the phone to her other ear.

"Yes, but what does that have to do with your birthday?"

"My birthday isn't why I called. Wait a minute, will you?" Silence came over his end of the line.

Then why was he calling? Was this personal or business? Did she care? Honesty time. The curve of his lips, the tiny scar under his forehead, the new wisdom in his demeanor. Something about him had knocked the wind out of her when he arrived to investigate the burglary. That wind still wasn't back.

The past eleven years had been kind to Mike. Downright generous, in fact. The lean, boyish figure matured into a muscular body. Those brown eyes held a hint of the world in them, but it would be too easy to lose herself in their depths.

And when he looked at her? It was as though he could pierce her soul and accept the real her, the woman who wanted to be loved for herself. Just plain Georgie.

Muffled words reached her ear, breaking her out of her reverie.

"Rachel, I'm on the phone. I know you're bored, but you can't have my phone if I'm on it."

"If this isn't a good time, maybe we can talk later." Georgie tried to interject a helpful note.

"Rachel has a cold, and I'm home with her. My mom flew out to Los Angeles today. And my dad promised to help out a buddy. Boredom has now set in, and Rachel would like to play her favorite app on my phone. Something where you can dress a ballerina and make her twirl and whirl. Girlie stuff."

Chuckling, Georgie doodled on a nearby notepad. "You're talking to the wrong girl about girlie stuff."

"Actually I'm talking to the right girl." He cleared his throat. For a second her heart fluttered. "I want to restore the Thunderbird. From what I saw at the barn, I know you're the only person to get it done. You and Grandpa Ted knew every inch of that car. I trust you."

The right girl for a business matter. Nothing more. Nothing personal.

Silence came over the line, and Georgie considered his offer. If people hadn't canceled their appointments, she wouldn't have had the time. As it was, this opportunity might be the best offer on her plate. More to the point, it might show the residents of the town her expertise when it came to cars.

"Well, I did work at a body shop for a year when I lived in Salem, Oregon, and have kept up my restoration skills ever since."

"Oregon?"

"I wanted to see the Pacific Ocean." A measure of defensiveness entered her tone, and she stiffened her shoulders. "There's nothing wrong with that."

"How many places have you lived since Hollydale?"

"Seven places in nine years." The only reason she'd stayed in one place for two years, rather than move on, was Kevin.

"I'm glad all roads led back to Hollydale for you, then." A muffled yell came through and he sighed. "Duty calls. Rachel's not sick often, but when she is, she can be a bear. Think about the Thunder—"

"I'll do it."

"You brighten my day like no one else."

"Wait, before you say that, I have some conditions." For one thing, she intended to document this restoration and post it on social media. Anything so the residents of this town could trust her with their cars.

She took a deep breath. She could also keep tabs on Mike. Find out if he had any leads on those comics. Clear her name.

"Rachel is calling. Gotta go."

The dial tone signaled he'd hung up. She glanced at the phone and then at Heidi. "Do you have Mike Harrison's phone number?"

"Yeah—911." Heidi wrinkled her brow. "When we service the fleet of police cars, I update Sheriff Donahue, not Mike."

A plan took shape. Towing the Thunderbird here was the first step. Easier to see the undercarriage and figure out the order of the repairs if Miss Brittany was in a service bay, rather than a dark and dusty barn.

Then she'd know how extensive this restoration would be and whether she could handle it by herself. She breathed in. If Mike had to help, would that be a blessing or not? There was no way she could keep this about business if he was near her all the time.

Somehow she'd have to find a way.

MIKE GLANCED AT the thermometer and stopped short of doing a victory dance. Happiness for Rachel's broken fever lightened his mood, already improved from this morning after Georgie agreed to look at the Thunderbird. Two excellent presents, if he did say so himself.

"Looks like you'll be well enough to go to school tomorrow."

"Can I call Lilah and find out my homework? I don't want to be behind tomorrow."

He rubbed his ear, then pressed the back of his hand to her forehead. "Excuse me. I thought I just heard someone asking for homework."

She giggled as Ginger jumped onto her bed. "I like school. Not as much as I love Ginger, but close." She met his gaze and smiled. "And you're my favorite daddy in the whole world."

He laughed and pulled her into a hug. "I'm your only father in the whole world."

For a second, he stiffened. At least to his knowledge he was. He'd never asked for a paternity test. Who was he kidding? Rachel had his eyes, his chin and his stubbornness.

Even if she didn't, he'd love her anyway. Parenthood wasn't about blood. It was about sweat and tears and joy. He was Rachel's father, in every true sense of the word.

Ginger inserted herself between them and snuggled close to his chest. This was a day for celebration. So there wasn't any cake or presents. Sam Edwards had called to wish him a happy birthday and update Mike on the progress, or lack thereof, on the burglaries. Rachel was feeling better, and that was all he needed. The tightness in his shoulders loosened.

"I'm going to fix dinner. Do you want chicken noodle soup or something more solid?"

"The soup with the stars in it." She reached for Ginger and smiled. "Please."

"Coming right up."

"Wait!" Urgency rang out in her voice. Alarmed, he stopped and ran back from the doorway. She wore a crooked smile. "I forgot to give you your card and present."

Blinking away the moisture in his eyes, he said, "I didn't expect you to get me anything, kiddo. Your recovery is all I want."

"It's not much." She reached under her bed and popped back up. "Here."

Rachel handed him a piece of folded construction paper with little hearts glued all over it. He opened it and smiled at her loopy writing proclaiming him the bestest dad ever. "Thank you. I love it."

"There's more."

She passed him a larger piece of rectangular paper. He gasped as he took in the charcoal sketch of Ginger and him on the couch. His daughter had talent. "Rache." Words lodged in his throat. This must have taken her hours, and his chest tightened.

"You don't like it." Her lips turned down in a

frown, and she slumped against her headboard. "It's not very good."

Reaching for it, she sighed.

He extended his arm, keeping it far from her. "I love it. I'm going to frame it and put it in my bedroom. This is much more special than a pack of bubble gum." Then again, for an eight-year-old, bubble gum was a big purchase for Father's Day, considering her allowance was only a dollar a week.

The frown stayed in place. He chucked her under the chin until she met his gaze. "Hey, kiddo. What's wrong?"

"I was hoping Miss Georgie would fix the Thunderbird." Rachel sneezed.

He handed her the box of Kleenex from her nightstand.

"I have some good news…"

The sound of the doorbell cut him off, and he wrinkled his forehead. He'd texted Dad and Natalie earlier, postponing his birthday celebration in case Rachel was contagious.

"Let me find out who this is, and then I'll be back to tell you the good news."

Hurrying out of the room, he closed the door and sent a silent apology to whoever was waiting for him. There was a good chance he'd infect him. At least his front door was no longer a revolving door like it was after his divorce. Every unattached female in a twenty-mile radius found a convenient excuse to stop by. Wincing, he remembered Mrs. Salinger, a fifty-something widow, who'd dropped by on the pretense of setting him up with her daughter. Mike shivered. That gleam in Mrs. Salinger's eye had left him wondering if she had, in fact, been the one interested in him.

Throwing open the door, he smiled at his most welcome birthday surprise.

"Georgie." He looked at the dog thumping his tail as if he didn't have a care in the world. "And Beau."

Unfortunately he had to send Georgie away. If there was one person in the world he didn't want to possibly catch Rachel's cold, it was her. He groaned and held up his hand.

"Don't come in." He stood his ground.

"Happy birthday to you." She picked up the handles of the huge brown bags and swept past him, along with Beau, who gazed at Georgie as if she was the best thing in the world, even better than a meaty bone from the butcher's.

Mike agreed with the sentiment.

"If you don't change that attitude, I'll sing to you."

Considering she was tone deaf, that wasn't an empty threat.

"I might be contagious. Rachel's been sick with a bad cold." His excuse sounded rather lame, yet the plain and simple truth sometimes did.

If anyone had taught him the importance of honesty, it was Georgie. He bit back the chuckle at how she'd pushed past the bullies surrounding him on the first day of middle school and asserted herself as his protector, standing in front of him, her arms outstretched.

No picking on him. It's not his fault he's the shortest boy in the whole school. Y'all leave him alone, do you hear?

"Miss Joanne's chicken noodle soup should make her right as rain again." She stopped and turned around. "How did that phrase get started anyway? Why is rain right? Usually it's a big old pain in the butt. Pretty good for the car repair business, though. People always bring their cars in after a good drenching rain."

"You brought Rachel soup?" Somehow Georgie bringing him food didn't drop an anvil on his shoulders like with those other women. Georgie did something only if she wanted to, not to get on anyone's good side.

Hmm, what would Donahue say? That she was buttering him up for info, or some such nonsense. If Georgie wanted information, she'd come right out and ask.

"And more. Where's your kitchen?"

He caught up to her and reached out.

She brought the bags close to her chest. "Uh-uh. My surprise, my big reveal."

Beau inched closer to Georgie, and Mike's

gaze darted toward the stairs. If that dog hadn't been fed today, he might eat Ginger for a snack. "My cat is with Rachel. Is Beau good with cats?"

"Don't know. We'll find out. He's good with people. I even introduced my mother to Beau. No hives, breakouts or any other signs of an allergic reaction." Georgie flashed a grin and strode away, craning her neck one way and the other. "My mother didn't sneeze or anything. Guess she was worried I'd bring home a me-nagerie. If every animal was as sweet as Beau, I would have. I'm sure he'll like your cat."

"Who's at the door?" Rachel's yell filled the air.

Before Mike could warn her to leave her door closed, he heard a squeak. An orange flash darted toward him. Beau thumped his tail again, and Ginger hissed and batted his nose. Beau whined and hid behind Georgie's legs.

"Guess I should have asked you if your cat was good with dogs." Georgie's bemused tone let him know she was okay.

He wasn't so sure about Beau, who seemed rather traumatized by Ginger's abrupt behavior.

"Ginger, behave around our guests." Mike shrugged and gave a half smile. "I need to check on Rachel. I'll be right back. Make yourself at home."

He rushed upstairs. Nick of time, too. Rachel was out of bed and almost at the door.

"Back to bed, young lady. I don't want you getting Miss Georgie sick. She brought you some chicken soup."

"From the Holly Days Diner." He hadn't even heard Georgie come up behind him. "Hi, Rachel. How are you feeling?"

"Better." Rachel's brown eyes lit up before the spark died. "Are you here for your twenty-three dollars?"

"And fourteen cents?" Georgie had a good memory, and Mike's spine straightened. "You know what—let's make a deal, shall we?"

Mike coiled tighter than an angry rattler.

"Depends." Rachel sat up against her pillows, folded her arms and sniffed. "What's the deal?"

"Your dad and I were great friends growing up. I bet the two of you went to the animal shelter and rescued Ginger."

"Daddy did."

He chuckled. Rachel had seen right through his elaborate story about finding Ginger at the grocery store between the cinnamon sugar and sage. He'd finally admitted he'd found her at the Humane Society, where she set eyes on him and yowled. While Ginger was a rescue cat, sometimes he could have sworn she rescued him at a low point and not the other way around.

"Rachel. Why don't you donate three dollars and fourteen cents to help out other cats in need and keep the rest?"

He turned, and Georgie wore a scrunched-up-nose smile that matched her tone.

"There's a rumor there may be a birthday cake in one of those bags downstairs. Is Rachel well enough to come down, sing to you and have a piece?"

"Please, Daddy." Rachel laced her fingers together and begged before gazing at Georgie with something akin to hero worship. "Thank you, Miss Georgie."

"Don't mention it."

Silence greeted him. For a second Mike cherished it after a day of Rachel's sniffles. Then alarm rocketed through him. "Ginger."

He sped to the kitchen, and his head jerked back. There on the linoleum floor next to Ginger's food dish were the two animals. Ginger lay snuggled up against Beau's curled tummy.

A few seconds later, Georgie followed. "See. Everything's fine."

How did she manage it? Within minutes of arriving, she'd lifted his spirits, as well as Rachel's. And she even threw in a lesson about charity. He didn't know whether to sit back and bask in the reflective glow of Georgie's kindness or bristle at how she did everything so much better than he did in ten short minutes.

Was there anything Georgie Bennett couldn't do?

THE NIGHT WAS almost over, but Mike didn't want it to end yet.

"Tell Rachel good-night for me. Beau and I should go." Georgie reached for Beau's leash.

"Ginger and Beau are still asleep." Mike touched Georgie's arm. "I'd like one more present to make my birthday complete."

"Dinner and cake not enough for you?"

"How about five minutes on my porch? I'll be close by if Rachel wakes up." Mike issued a dare, hoping that would entice Georgie.

"You're lucky I'm a sucker for a good porch swing." Georgie led the way outside.

Dusk had settled, but the glow from the porch light provided enough illumination. They sat in the swing, the metal chains clinking a sweet melody. With some people, silence was awkward. Never with Georgie, though.

"Any updates on the burglaries?"

The gentle rocking had lulled him into a false sense of security. "The stars are out and there's a good-looking guy next to you, and you want an update on the case?"

"Good-looking guy? Where?" Georgie laughed. "Are you any closer to the real thief?"

He'd love to know that, as well.

"There have been some developments I can't discuss. I believe in you, Georgie, and we're working on tracking the evidence to apprehend the real perp." Same as he was working on getting back in Georgie's good graces and getting the sheriff to believe in her.

"And we're friends again, aren't we?" Georgie scooted toward him.

Was that all they were? Friends and nothing more?

The air sparkled as something shifted in that moment. He leaned toward her, and she nodded. "I have one more birthday gift for you," she said.

Their lips almost touched, but the front door swung open.

"Daddy?"

Mike jumped away. If it weren't for Rachel, he would have kissed Georgie. While that would have been an unforgettable birthday present, Rachel was the best reminder of why he had to keep Georgie as a friend and nothing more.

CHAPTER EIGHT

GEORGIE WHISTLED AND entered her mother's front door. Successful evening. Mike had laughed and almost glowed while blowing out the candles on his cake. He had glowed when they almost kissed before Rachel interrupted them. When she left, his smile was back, and his shoulders no longer seemed to carry the weight of the world. Ten years were shaved off his appearance in the blink of an eye. Whether it was his favorite meatloaf platter from the Holly Days Diner or Rachel's rather bad mock-opera version of "Happy Birthday to You," she wasn't quite sure.

What if she was part of his megawatt smile? Did she want to be?

Beau trotted inside, and she closed the door. She'd miss the giant mutt once Mr. Reedy recovered.

"Georgie, is that you?" Her mother's brittle voice reached her.

She walked into the living room, the smile still on her lips. Beverly's pale skin stood out in the dim surroundings. Her tray held a plate full of food. If Georgie wasn't mistaken, her mother's cheeks were hollower than this morning. Georgie's exuberant mood fizzled like flat cola on a summer's day. She glanced at Kitty, who shrugged and kept knitting.

Beverly's eyes narrowed. "I thought you were coming home and eating with us." Her nose rose in the air, quivering like a bunny's. She pushed the tray away. "I'm not hungry."

"I brought dinner to a friend of mine whose daughter couldn't go to school today." While that was the truth, guilt rattled through Georgie at the omission of some details, like names.

"Was it that nice Lucie Decker? She and her lovely twins are coming tomorrow to keep me company after she finishes her shift at cousin Odalie's dress shop." Her mother's face lightened, although the dark circles still alarmed Georgie. "Feel free to invite your friends here anytime. After all, this is your home."

Georgie's mouth went dry. Her mother was trying. Perhaps the stent procedure might have done more than add years to her life. Perhaps it would bring them closer after all.

"I'll tell Mike you said that."

Beverly's expression changed faster than a pit crew could change a tire. "Mike? Are you talking about Mike Harrison? I don't like how he treated you in high school."

"Mike's changed. He stayed home tonight on his thirtieth birthday because his daughter was getting over a cold."

Beau whimpered.

She must have pinched her short nails into his fur. "Sorry about that, Beau."

"You can be sorry to that animal," Beverly's voice rose, "and for that man? What about me? What about an apology for not calling to tell me you were going to be late for dinner?"

"You're right. I should have let you know. That's common courtesy. But I reserve the right to disagree about Mike. He's changed." Georgie picked up her mother's fork and pushed around the dinner on the plate. It must be cold, having sat there for so long. "Do you want me to put this in the microwave?"

Beverly gurgled, and Georgie glanced up. "My *huuh*…"

Georgie strained to make out the words as her mother's voice was so weak.

"My *aaaht*…"

Kitty leapt to her feet, and Beau barked at the sudden movement. "I think it's her heart."

"Mom?" Alarm rose up in Georgie's chest. No matter what, her mother was her mother. Except for a few cousins, her mother was all the family she had left. She'd never known her father, and she wasn't ready to lose her mother. "Say something."

Beverly shook her head and clutched her chest. "My heart." Gasping for breath, she reached for the water next to her plate and drank greedy gulps. "My chest is on fire. Can't breathe."

Georgie whipped out her smartphone and dialed 911.

"I'M ADMITTING YOUR mother to the hospital." Dr. Nolan signed something on a chart and handed it to the nurse. "In the hour since the EMTs brought her in, her temperature has gone up a degree."

Georgie reached for Beverly's hand and squeezed. All her life she'd thought her mother was too strong willed for anything truly bad to happen to her. Yet streaks of gray lined Beverly's chestnut hair, tight in its bun. Her sallow skin added ten years to Beverly's age of fifty-four. The stent should have been a wake-up call, but whatever this was? This was a blaring alarm shrieking in Georgie's ears.

"It's that dog." The faintness of Beverly's voice didn't mask her anger.

Or her fear.

The doctor shook his head and pushed his glasses to the top of the bridge of his nose. "Your condition is not symptomatic of an allergic reaction. You most likely have an infection as a result of your stent implantation."

"So you prescribe some antibiotics, and I'll be in my bed in a couple of hours, right?"

"No. This is quite serious." The doctor pulled at the stethoscope around his neck. "I'm admitting you. We'll start you on an IV of antibiotics and draw some blood for tests. You'll have priority for imaging scans. We have to see what's going on around the stent site. If it's an infection, then as soon as it's safe to operate, your cardiologist will go back in and replace the stent from twelve days ago with a new one. Then we'll monitor you to make sure you have no signs of infection. My best estimate is three to four days in the hospital."

The doctor left, but Georgie continued to worry.

"Stop looking at me like I'm at death's door." Beverly released Georgie's hand. She nodded to the nurse. "Do I have enough time to say goodnight to my daughter before you move me to a room?"

"You'll have a little longer. I'll arrange for the blood work and give you a moment of privacy. If you need anything, press the nurse's button or call this number." She picked up a dry-erase marker and wrote on the whiteboard near the door. "And I'll come running."

Georgie pulled up a chair next to Beverly's bed. "What's this about good-night? I'm staying."

"No, you're not." Her mother's jaw clenched at the same time her left eyebrow arched up.

Georgie stared at the heart monitor. Beeps and numbers. The fact the high-pitched beeps were becoming more consistent couldn't be good. She held up her hands. "I won't argue with you in the hospital."

"Who argues? We have conversations that get rather heated, that's all." Her mother sighed and rested her head against the stark white pillow. "One of us should get some sleep tonight. Since it won't be me, it might as well be you."

Georgie leaned over the metal railing and grazed her mother's cheek with a kiss, the smell of Chanel overpowering the antiseptic for a mere second. "That's the sweetest thing you've said to me since I've been home."

Beverly gave a mere hint of a smile. "I do care, Georgie."

"Then I'll go. Kitty was a sweetheart to stay with Beau. I'll give her an update before she goes home." Georgie rose, but Beverly motioned for her to sit down again.

"What was this about you and Mike Harrison earlier?" Grit and determination laced those words. More beeps came out faster from the machine overhead.

"Concentrate on getting well and coming home. There will be plenty of time to talk about Mike later." Though what there was to talk about, she couldn't imagine. Sure, his shoulders filled out his uniform, and his whiskey voice penetrated deep to her heart. Not to mention the love in his eyes for his daughter and his cat shone through. Who wouldn't be attracted to all of that?

Georgie warned herself to not get involved with Mike. It couldn't be good for his job if she hung around him, considering he'd never told her she was cleared of all suspicion in Max's burglary. No, she couldn't get involved with him even if she was staying in Hollydale.

The jury was still out about that, as well. With no word from Cullinan and with a second chance with her mother, staying was becoming a distinct possibility.

"I don't want you to get hurt again." Tiredness crept into her mother's voice.

"I was eighteen. I recovered. I forgave Mike and moved on." From the set of her mother's jaw, Georgie wasn't so sure her mother had done the same. "Forgiveness is a good thing."

"Promise me you won't get involved with Mike Harrison." She reached for Georgie's hand. "I have no right to ask that of you, but when your father lost control of his car going into the final curve of the track, I watched and screamed, helpless to do anything. That's why I've never wanted you to have anything to do with cars or engines." She closed her eyes and shook her head. "I was pregnant with you, and I promised you, at that moment, you'd never feel that same helplessness, that same sense of utter loss."

Georgie's stomach churned, and a tear welled up in the corner of her eye. Her mother never talked about that fateful day or why she was so opposed to Georgie's choices. Yet cars and engines were in her blood.

"I am involved with Mike." She gulped. Her gaze flew to the monitor again, some of the numbers rising with every blip. "I promised to help restore his grandfather's car. We have a business relationship, that's all."

Her voice said otherwise, and she dismissed the notion. There was too much baggage for there to be anything more. If Brett Cullinan offered her the job, she'd leave in a second. And Sheriff Donahue probably wouldn't take kindly to Mike getting involved with a person of interest in a local crime. Even if Mike wanted more, which he'd given no signs of, she couldn't commit anyway. It wouldn't be fair to Rachel. Or Mike.

"Promise me you'll keep it that way." Her mother stared at her, a frail figure lying on the hospital bed. "Anything so you won't get hurt the way I was."

"No one can live their lives in a bubble."

The nurse entered, guiding a metal pole behind her. She went over to the monitor and clicked her tongue. "Time for your IV with a saline drip and the antibiotics the doctor ordered. The pharmacy staff is on the ball tonight." The nurse inserted a thermometer into her mother's mouth, waited for a beep and then removed it. "Enough excitement for now. Let's say goodnight and get these antibiotics into you."

"Georgie." Her mother reached out her hand, most likely her version of an olive branch.

Torn, Georgie struggled. She wanted her mother to get better, but she bristled at this kind of promise. "I'd like you to trust me, trust that I know what I'm doing."

Kevin had flung her independence at her when he left. The truth was sometimes the hardest medicine of all. Was she too independent to love someone else?

"I lived with you after Mike hurt you. Then you didn't come home after Kevin Doherty broke up with you. Why don't you ever listen to me and follow my advice?"

The nurse cleared her throat. "Tsk, tsk. We mustn't get anxious. Your heartbeat's accelerating."

An image of Mike's brown eyes danced in front of Georgie. Then his frown came into focus when he asked her not to leave town. "I'll keep this on a business level."

Georgie grabbed her purse from the hook on the wall and hurried away. Her heart squeezed tight in her chest. That vow hurt as much as Mike's letter had. Maybe even more. Running, she didn't stop until she reached her Prius. Her breaths came at a shallow rate. In the darkness of the night, all the emotion she'd been holding back poured out.

At the first chance to move, she'd bolted away from Hollydale, escaping without a look back. Guilt crashed down with all the broken relationships. Her mother. Lucie. Mike.

Her mother had a long road ahead of her, and Georgie's promise might make her recovery all the easier. But asking Georgie for that kind of promise, a promise no one should ask from anyone? That wasn't right.

What was best for Mike? In all of the night's events, she'd lost track of the most important aspects, namely him and Rachel. Tonight his radiant smile as he blew out the candles had warmed her heart like nothing else had in quite some time.

Yet she'd leave town in an instant if the call came, and she wouldn't ask him to jeopardize his job for her.

For his sake, and Rachel's, she'd keep the promise she just made to her mother.

That was for the best.

MIKE NAVIGATED HIS squad car into a parking spot at Max's Auto Repair. Nothing like a dose of Georgie to brighten an otherwise drab, not to mention hectic, Friday. Another burglary, another crestfallen storekeeper, another dead end.

"I didn't know you could whistle. Can you teach me?" Rachel blew air through her lips, wind coming out but not much else.

"Remind me later. You have your backpack, right?" He waited for her nod before he reached for the handle. "Good. You can start your homework so you won't have to worry about it this weekend while Miss Georgie and I discuss details about the Thunderbird."

Together they exited the cruiser, and he enveloped Rachel's hand in his. Pretty soon she'd be too old for that. Probably already was.

"Officer Harrison, is that you?" A dour-faced man scurried toward him from the direction of the nearby bank. "I closed up for the day and thought I recognized your squad car."

Mike kept from groaning and thanked his lucky stars the burglars had targeted only smaller businesses, like Timber River Outfitters and the Book Nook, rather than a bank. In that case, Sheriff Donahue would have had no choice but to call the FBI, likely sinking Donahue's chances of being reelected. Not that luck played into the equation, what with seven businesses plus Max's all getting hit.

"Mr. Garrity." If this went anything like he supposed it would, Mike would need an extra dose of Georgie's optimism. Hmm, interesting how she'd been back such a short time, yet she'd already become a mainstay in his mind. "What can I do for you?"

"Any leads on those burglaries? I don't mind telling you a couple of people were rather nervous at the Rotary Club meeting this morning." Mr. Garrity's lips stretched out in a thin line while he stood there, legs apart. "Heard your name floated as a candidate for sheriff. If you solved this crime spree, you'd be a shoo-in."

Mike bit back the sigh and pulled Rachel in front of him. Probably a bad father move, as it must have appeared he was using his daughter almost like a shield.

"The Hollydale Police Department is committed to bringing the thieves to justice. Once apprehended, they will be prosecuted to the fullest extent of the law. Sheriff Donahue is doing his job." That was as close to *no comment* as he could muster. With any luck, that would be enough for Mr. Garrity.

"Sounds like you're beating around the bush to me. Most people want advancement. You'd be a good sheriff. Donahue's done nothing." His narrowed gaze flew to the front of the repair shop. "Rumor around town is Georgie Bennett stole those comic books. Easy way to get enough money to buy Max out."

Rachel gasped, and Mike patted her shoulders. "Hey, kiddo, why don't you run inside and say hello to Miss Georgie while I finish this conversation with Mr. Garrity?"

Mike followed Rachel's movement until she reached the door. When she glanced at him over her shoulder, he waved and sent his friendliest father smile, the one he'd seen his dad wear often. After she was inside, Mike took a deep breath, checking the retort he longed to deliver.

"Georgie is one of the finest people I know. She's returned to Hollydale to take care of her mother." He paused before divulging the information about Max, since he wanted his medical condition kept under wraps until his prognosis was clear. "Since Georgie's been here, she's been helping Mr. Reedy take care of Beau and is assessing my grandfather's Thunderbird. I'd stake my reputation on Georgie's honesty."

Why Donahue wouldn't listen to him and remove Georgie from the suspect list, he didn't know.

Mr. Garrity folded his arms and shook his head. "Hope it doesn't come down to that. You catch those thieves so the business owners of Hollydale feel secure at night again. I'd say that should take top priority at the moment over your grandfather's car."

He stomped away, and Mike let out a slow, deep breath. *Good riddance.* He was entitled to a private life. Then again, police duties required total concentration. Getting involved with Georgie was a distraction of the highest magnitude.

His heart fluttered. *Getting involved with Georgie?* Her spark and fire had always balanced his cooler, more detached self. He'd been a fool not to appreciate their friendship. Heck, he'd been a bigger fool to ditch her for the privilege of consoling Wendy after the star quarterback had dumped her the day before prom.

Brushing off Mr. Garrity, Mike strode toward the shop's entrance. Defending Georgie was a no-brainer, as far as he was concerned. Even if he had screwed up in the past, he wasn't about to let his teenage stupidity hold him back anymore.

That was the worst part about living in a small town, though. Sometimes the past did stand in the way of the present. He believed in Georgie, but it was Georgie herself, along with Donahue, that he had to convince.

First things first. He stepped inside, eager to hit the ground running. With any luck, the Thunderbird would soon be running again, as well.

CHAPTER NINE

GEORGIE TAPPED THE index card on the reception desk and then glanced at Rachel, sitting with her gaze fixed on the window. Never before had the girl been so silent around her. What was wrong? Bad day at school? Relapse of her cold? Whatever it was couldn't be nearly as bad as the news she'd have to break to her and Mike.

When all was said and done, recommending a body shop in Asheville would be good for all concerned. And after her mother heard what she'd done, no doubt her recovery would take a giant leap forward. Choosing between a relationship with her mother and one with Mike tore her up inside. Living with her mother provided them common ground, a chance to get closer. But she and Mike? Without the Thunderbird, they had nothing binding them together. No business angle, no personal angle, nothing. Well, apart from his half-hearted belief that she could be the B&E culprit. Why else hadn't he told her everything on the porch?

Mike entered, setting off the cowbell hanging above the door. Rachel scurried over, hugging his legs with what pretty much looked like every ounce of strength in her.

"Daddy, please tell me that's not our bank." Rachel broke her silence, her rather harsh tone most un-Rachel-like. "Please tell me you can make that man be nice to Miss Georgie from now on. If not, you can arrest him, right?"

Stepping away from the desk, Georgie crossed over to them. This feeling of being the last one to the party didn't play well on her nerves, which were already shot due to the last twenty-four hours.

Mike's gaze met hers, and he frowned. Yep, she was late to the party.

"What's going on?" Georgie tapped her foot against the concrete with more certainty than she felt.

"Nothing for you to be worried about." Mike led Rachel to the seating area. "I set him straight. Don't worry. All settled?"

"Maybe I should be the judge of that." The hairs on the back of her neck stood on end. What was Mike holding back? It couldn't be worse than her news. The tension in her coiled like a cat ready to pounce on an unsuspecting mouse.

"Rachel's been subdued, and that's so unlike her, unless she's sick."

Even though they'd met only a few times,

Georgie was convinced Rachel was a happy soul. And gifted. And outgoing.

Georgie switched her gaze to Mike and drank in the sight of him. His jeans and black T-shirt contrasted nicely with his dirty-blond hair, darker than in high school. Unlike in high school, his maturity tempered his keen sense of humor like spring steel. Everything about him screamed boyfriend potential.

If she told him what was building inside her and he rejected her a second time? That had the potential of being more devastating than Kevin's last-minute bailout from their engagement. Yeah, she did have to recommend the other body shop.

She walked back to Heidi's desk and searched for the printout about Foreman's Classic Body Shop.

Before she could find it, Mike cleared his throat and said, "Mr. Garrity from the bank came over and asked me some questions about the burglaries." Mike evaded her gaze. Instead, he reached inside Rachel's backpack, pulled out a purple folder and examined its contents as though his life depended on it.

"And?" A chill swept over her as though Mr. Garrity's attitude could provide some insight into why some people were still canceling their repairs with her. Determined to get straight answers, Georgie placed her hand on

Mike's, pressing him on. "What else did Mr. Garrity have to say?"

"He wasn't nice." Rachel stomped her foot against the concrete.

Mike must have sensed Georgie was nearing her boiling point, for he tilted his head toward the hallway. She understood too well. If he couldn't say this in front of Rachel, this had the potential for disaster.

He pulled her aside and then glanced at Rachel. Georgie's gaze followed in that direction, only to find Rachel engrossed in a book.

To Mike she said, "Out with it."

"Mr. Garrity found out you're a suspect in the B&E here."

Her chest clenched at Mike's use of the present tense.

"I see." That explained the rather frosty reception at Holly Days Diner last night, until she had explained about Mike's birthday. "And how would that be common knowledge?"

"Police reports are public knowledge. Besides, this is Hollydale." Mike shrugged. "Rachel's teacher knew she was coming down with a cold before I did."

Georgie wondered. That might or might not explain those cancellations. Who wanted a thief working on their car?

What happened to looking past the obvious and not taking things at face value? Dwelling on this wouldn't help. She needed a plan. Somehow she had to make the town gossips work for her, instead of against her. Only then would there be a line of cars stretching onto Maple Street. More important, she might justify some of that faith Max had in her, enough faith to leave her in charge, enough to ask her to buy him out, enough to keep his legacy in the garage alive.

Mike reached out and stilled her fingers. "It'll be okay."

"Yeah, as long as I don't have to make any deposits." She gave a hollow laugh.

Max had kept his doctor's appointment and was awaiting the results. Georgie had asked him point-blank why he didn't consult with an oncologist in Asheville. Between his sister spoiling him and his interest in a local Hollydale widow who'd lost a husband to cancer, he wanted certainty before he came home. She didn't want to let him down. Still, her throat ached at how little the town's residents thought of her.

Mike lowered his head until his gaze met hers. "I set Mr. Garrity straight. The new Georgie has all the kind and honest qualities of high school Georgie, but more." His chest puffed out, and a determined gleam turned his brown eyes to dark chunks of amber. "If anyone says anything to you, let me know."

Their gazes met, and electricity sparked between them. No. She couldn't break her promise to her mother in less than twenty-four hours. Like Mike said, everyone in Hollydale knew everyone's business. Her mother would find out. This couldn't continue.

"I can take care of myself."

"No doubt you would have given Mr. Garrity a piece of your mind had we both been outside. But I was able to help. It's not bad to accept help, say thank you and move on." He sauntered back to the reception area.

Georgie appreciated the added space between them. Made it a whole lot easier to think.

"Now, what arrangements do I need to make for the tow truck to bring the Thunderbird here?"

Back to business. This she could handle.

Taking a quick peek at Rachel, scribbling away in a notebook, Georgie steeled herself against the rush of emotion. As much as she wanted a crack at the Thunderbird, she couldn't let herself stand in the way of what was best for her mother.

"I would strongly suggest calling Foreman's Classic Body Shop in Asheville." She returned to Heidi's desk and handed him the printout. "I've worked with Evan, the owner, before. They do solid work, and they won't rip you off. And they'll keep the Thunderbird as close to its original state as possible. Too many people lower the value of the car by adding modern features. Evan won't do that. He'll deliver a car you'll be able to drive for years to come."

Mike shook his head and pushed the paper back. "I trust you. Besides, didn't you say you've done this type of work before?"

Nodding, she used one finger to scoot the paper once more. "It's not fair to Travis, though, to take time away from the normal repair schedule to do this." As free as that was. She exhaled that breath she'd been holding. "And my mother is back in the hospital."

He gasped and reached for her hand. "Georgie, I hadn't heard about that." He glanced over his shoulder. "Wrap it up, Rache. Slight change of plans." Returning his attention to Georgie, he smiled. "We'll follow you home and get Beau so you can stay as long as you want at the hospital. I'll make you dinner. When you're done, come to my house. Then we'll talk about fixing the car." He met her gaze and rubbed her hand. "Or at least check it over to tell me what all needs to be done. Deal?"

His hand felt so good over hers, warm and strong. His taking charge of the situation should have chafed more. After all, she'd lived by herself as soon as she could afford paying for rent and utilities, preferring the freedom of no one looking over her shoulder. She waited for the resentment, but none came.

"I visited her once today. She practically ordered me to go to work." The shock of that still hadn't subsided. "I'll take you up on that offer, though. Thank you."

Besides, they'd be discussing business while Rachel would spoil Beau by preening over him. A friendly gesture on Mike's part since her mother was in the hospital would be rude to refuse. That was all it was, and nothing more.

This time a feeling did come over her.

An attraction that made her wonder whether she could limit this to business.

HE'LL DELIVER A car you'll be able to drive for years to come. Mike thought back to his conversations with Georgie about the Thunderbird. Hadn't he made it clear he had every intention of selling the car? As nice as it was to imagine a life with the restored classic, it was even nicer to have a cushion in the bank for Rachel. Dance lessons, art lessons, after-school programs, all of which weren't manageable with his current salary.

The sheriff's job paid more.

No. That was the last reason he'd consider the position. A sheriff had a duty to the community. Mike didn't shy away from that. He loved Hollydale and its residents. No, other reasons dug their claws in and took hold. Rachel was only young once. Donahue was good at his job. Let him deal with the politicians, the added stress, the extra paperwork.

He and Rachel had lived on what he made so far. They'd continue to do so.

His parents taught him a thing or two about stretching pennies. The Harrisons had sacrificed over the years. Three children cost more to raise than one.

They never stinted on love, though.

He blinked as that thought blindsided him. Had he been trying to buy Rachel's love?

"Daddy, please hand me the plates." Rachel tugged on his T-shirt. "I can't reach them."

The doorbell rang, and he dropped the plates onto the floor, the clattering sharp and unexpected. Thank goodness they were still intact.

"Can you pick those up for me, kiddo? I'll be right back." With Georgie, no doubt. On his way to the door, he stopped short. If he told Georgie the truth, she'd insist on taking the Thunderbird to Foreman's. Then he wouldn't have an excuse to spend time with her. He shook his head. As much as he wanted that, he had to be up front with her.

Hadn't he learned anything over the years?

He opened the door, and his jaw dropped. While Georgie was a knockout in whatever she wore, he liked how the dark green swirls on her shirt accented her bright eyes. Words deserted him with her so close.

Determined, he steeled himself to do the right thing and tell her about selling the Thunderbird. Maybe if he'd been more truthful with Caitlyn and the two of them had worked on an honest-to-goodness relationship before getting married, she wouldn't have been so quick to leave.

"Are you okay? You have the strangest expression on your face." She gave a wistful smile and plucked at her blouse. "I'm running late because showering and changing before I came over seemed like a no-brainer. Smelling antiseptic and bleach while I'm at the hospital? Okay. Same smell adhering to me the rest of the night?" She wrinkled her nose and waved her hand underneath. "Not my favorite perfume."

Her sweet lemon smell was fast becoming his favorite, though.

"Believe me, it's the host and not the company. You look great."

Before he could get anything off his chest, a bark and a blur of brown fur flashed by and jumped up on Georgie.

"There's my sweet boy." Georgie smiled before she winced. "Down, Beau. Your nails are sharp."

Mike noticed Ginger had wound her long body around his ankles. He reached down and scooped up the cat. "Come on in. I don't want Ginger darting outside."

"Something smells wonderful." Georgie entered, and Beau followed.

"Georgie, wait." He heaved a deep breath and exhaled. "Before dinner, I need to tell you the truth."

A loud crash from the direction of the kitchen came on the heels of an even louder scream. Mike dropped Ginger, ignoring her hiss of protest. In the kitchen Rachel howled, grasped her left hand and fell to the floor in obvious pain. Wet pasta stuck to the front of the stove and the sink. A silver pot lay on its side near Rachel's feet.

Beau barked, rushed in and began licking Rachel's face. Fear shot through Mike, and he sprinted forward.

"Rachel!" Adrenaline made his voice harsher than intended. He softened and knelt beside her. "I need to see your hand."

"No." Fresh tears exploded out of her. "I just wanted to be helpful."

He rubbed her shoulder. "Let me see your hand, kiddo."

"No." Sweat broke out on her forehead. Rachel pulled her hand close to her chest before letting loose with another howl of pain, an arrow straight to his heart.

Georgie stepped forward, concern clear in her green eyes. "Hey there, darling. You're not in trouble. Your dad loves you, and he has to see your hand to figure out if you need medical help."

Rachel sniffled, her bottom lip quivering. She held out her hand. Mike's stomach lurched. Ugly red blisters were already forming, and his daughter whimpered. A trip to urgent care wasn't even a question. It was a necessity.

"Hey, kiddo," Mike whispered, "time to go find someone who can take care of that."

She shook her head, her brown hair flying all over. Both Ginger and Beau seemed to sense the youngest human needed their support. Beau moved back and stood guard while Ginger nudged Rachel's knee. Mike understood too well their desire to make Rachel feel better. He'd accept Rachel's pain as his own in a second.

"No." Rachel pulled her hand toward her, hiding it from view.

"We have to leave now," he urged his daughter.

"I'll drive," said Georgie, flicking off the stove top and shutting off the running water in the sink.

He'd almost forgotten she was there. Turning, he opened his mouth in protest.

She held up her hand. "You're in shock and in no condition to drive a car. Hold on one second."

"Thank you." Humbled, he couldn't think of anything else to say. Instead, he held Rachel shivering under his touch, her whimpers of pain heartbreaking.

Georgie moved about, and he devoted his attention to Rachel. Stroking her hair, he brought her close, a giant ache spreading through his chest. Rachel knew better than to touch a boiling pot of water. Chiding wouldn't help, not with her sobs so raw and so open.

"Ready?" Georgie gave Beau a pat. "They'll be okay together while we're gone."

Mike nodded and scooted Rachel out to the foyer, grabbing his wallet along the way. He turned to Georgie. "You don't have to come with us. I'm sure the urgent care will smell like antiseptic."

She arched one eyebrow and pointed to the door. "I'll mark that pitiful excuse of a protest down to worry. Now scoot, or so help me, I'll take Rachel without you."

After eight years of single parenting, he wasn't used to having someone else to lean on, to take charge in an emergency. He liked having Georgie at his side. Too much.

CHAPTER TEN

"RACHEL! WHAT ARE you doing here?" Georgie slid off one work glove and then the other. She crossed the reception area and hugged the girl. "How are you feeling?"

Hard to believe this was Georgie's first glimpse of Rachel in almost a week. How had so long passed without her setting eyes on any member of the Harrison household? Her mother, life and work, which was picking up at last. That was why. Almost three weeks back in Hollydale had passed in a blink of an eye.

Georgie stepped away and studied Rachel. Her hand was bandaged, yet her face had some color in it today. So much better than the pasty white pallor of the other night.

"I didn't have to play dodgeball today. Hooray." Rachel lifted the left side of her mouth in a half smile, the same expression as Mike's. "My PE teacher let me sit out."

The front door opened, the cowbell jangling away. In walked a young woman with curly red hair and blue eyes. Georgie stared, and then her jaw dropped. Was this the little squirt who'd trailed her and Mike while reciting the periodic table?

"Natalie Harrison? Is that really you?"

"That's rich coming from someone who has made a total stranger of herself over the past couple of years." She laughed and removed her sunglasses, placing them in her purse. "Aw, this is too formal. Hug time."

Natalie rushed over and embraced Georgie. The squirt had a last-minute growth spurt, too. Georgie could have sworn she'd been taller than Natalie the last time she'd seen her.

"I don't think I've seen you since you delivered Mike's note."

Natalie gave her a sheepish look. "I should have read it first. If it's any consolation, I chastised Mike on your behalf for a couple of years."

Rachel stepped between them, her head turning from one to the other before she settled her gaze on Georgie. "My dad sent you notes? Did your teacher read them aloud to the whole class like mine does?"

Georgie laughed and tilted her head. "Hmm. I think your father is rather glad this one didn't go viral. As a matter of fact, I don't even have it anymore. I burned it a long time ago." Her eyes widened, and her hands flew over her mouth. "Oh, Rachel, I'm sorry. I shouldn't have mentioned burns."

Being spurned by Mike was in the past. It was time to look to the future. Sure, the whole prom disaster had caused heartache and embarrassment. In the grand scheme of things, though? She'd survived Kevin, and that was far worse.

"So, why are you both here?"

"Mike has to get some sleep for his stakeout tonight, so I'm spending time with my favorite niece."

"I forgot to say thank you," Rachel interrupted and threw her arms around Georgie's waist.

Georgie quelled a rising level of affection for the young girl, along with the questions about Mike's investigation. If she moved to Charlotte, she'd leave Mike and Rachel behind. Was working at the track where her father once lived and breathed worth losing out on relationships? She honestly didn't know.

"Thank you for what?" She hadn't done anything special.

"I love the stuffed cat you brought me. I named her Pollyanna after one of my favorite movies. You didn't stay and say hello. Why not?"

"Your grandfather said you were sleeping, and I didn't want him to wake you. Saturday was busy here at the shop, and on Sunday, my mother was released from the hospital."

Although, Georgie wished she could have spent some time with the two Harrisons. They were laying claim to a chunk of her heart.

"Oh, okay." Rachel reached for Georgie's hand with her free one. "Thank you for Pollyanna."

Natalie cleared her throat. Georgie winced. She'd forgotten Natalie was there.

"By the way, Rachel is an excellent saleswoman on your behalf."

Georgie was confused. "This isn't a social call?"

"Nope." Natalie shook her head and pointed out the window. "I can't hear anything, but Miss Rachel insists my tires are making a whirring sound."

Rachel nodded up and down in an exaggerated motion.

Hmm. This doesn't sound good.

Georgie ran through the list of possible problems and hid her frown.

"Let's go see what's wrong." Tilting her head toward the entrance, she squeezed Rachel's hand, the smaller fingers cool and soft against hers. She glanced down. "Can you imitate the noise you heard?"

Rachel roared like a pouncing tiger.

Within seconds Georgie knelt and examined Natalie's front tires. *Darn it.* Her suspicions were right.

"Come here, Natalie."

"It can't be the tires. I had them replaced a couple of months ago."

"Are you sure it wasn't two years ago?" Georgie waited for Natalie, while keeping Rachel in her sights. Once Natalie crouched on the pavement, Georgie pointed her short nail downward. "See these silver lines running down the edge of your tire? Your tread is shot." Scanning the ground, Georgie found a lost penny, retrieved it and hunkered down again. "You can do the penny test on your own. I insert it into the treads and—see how you can see all of Lincoln's head? This tire is almost bare."

"No way. The son of—" Natalie glanced at Rachel as a pink blush spread across her apple cheeks "—a sea biscuit. I'm positive I bought new tires a few months ago."

Natalie opened the passenger door, and Georgie straightened. Rolling her neck, she breathed in the mountain air, the clean linen smell of fall. This weekend had brought a dip in the temperature and fewer tourists.

"Aha!" Natalie's triumphant voice filled Georgie's ears with a blast. "I was right."

She shoved the receipt under Georgie's nose and waved it about. Rachel giggled from the sidelines, a beautiful sound after last week.

Georgie reached out for the receipt. A thousand dollars for four tires, and they weren't even high-grade tires. Retreads at best. Shaking her head, she handed the receipt back to Natalie. "You were ripped off."

"What?" The word exploded out of Natalie as the rosy pink changed into a dull red. Her shoulders slumped. "You're kidding."

Walking around the car, Georgie examined each tire. Sighing, she returned and folded her arms. "All four are in bad shape. The rear passenger's side is the worst. It's bare. That's the sound Rachel heard."

Natalie fisted her hands, the receipt crushing under the weight. Georgie couldn't say she blamed her. A thousand dollars for those pieces of rubber trash, not even fit for a junkyard? Con artists like that gave mechanics a bad name.

Natalie took several deep breaths, her hands loosening their grip and her knuckles returning to their normal color. "The worst part is I was visiting my old college roommate, who lives five hundred miles away, over the summer break. Between teaching and Mike's work schedule, I don't have the time to drive back there so they can replace them."

At the sound of Mike's name, Georgie's ears perked up. "Mike's work schedule?" Her attempt at nonchalance failed with a capital *F*. "Didn't you mention a stakeout earlier?"

"Oops. You didn't hear that from me. It's very hush-hush." A slight spark lit some life into Natalie's eyes. "Unless my ears deceive me, I think someone might like my brother. In which case, you might need your head examined."

She winked, but even so, Georgie's defenses were raised. After all, she had promised her mother she'd keep everything professional and aboveboard. "I was only asking because I had the Thunderbird towed here on Saturday, and I plan to do the inspection tomorrow morning before I start on my scheduled repairs."

"Uh-huh." Natalie clicked her tongue. "I believe you as much as I believe the owners who scammed me are going to give me a new set of tires out of the kindness of their hearts."

"It's not safe to drive anywhere on that set, let alone five hundred miles." Latching on to the obvious proved a good distraction technique, and Georgie ran with it. "If I were to call them right now, they'd give me a line about how they're under new management or how someone must have swapped out the tires."

"What do you recommend?"

A customer might have a hard time hearing about an expensive procedure, but she'd never get ahead by betraying a customer's trust.

"Four new tires." Georgie glanced at Rachel, who was pulling on her bandage and shifting her weight from one side to the other, sure signs of boredom. "Let's go in, and we'll talk."

Natalie threw her arm around Georgie.

"Where was someone like you when I got ripped off?" Sadness almost dripped from the words, and Natalie delivered a huge sigh. "Here I am, a summa cum laude graduate of Chapel Hill, and I don't even know a new tire from a clunker."

Hmm. Some of the men in town didn't trust Georgie yet. But there were single women like Natalie who needed someone honest, someone who wouldn't give them a line or the runaround. Someone who would explain the procedure in detail and help them not get ripped off in the future.

"You've just given me an idea."

The women of Hollydale needed a car care class.

And Georgie was the perfect teacher.

MIKE CAREFULLY POURED coffee into his travel cup. None of his usual sugar in this brew. He'd made it double strong for tonight's stakeout. Sheriff Donahue had nixed an electronic stakeout from the luxury of the station. Instead, Mike found himself in Melanie Donahue's pristine pine-scented automobile, binoculars in hand, coffee at his side.

Only the sheriff and he knew where he was— plus the sheriff's wife knew, and Natalie. He'd made his sister, who was spending the night with Rachel, promise under the threat of setting her up on a blind date not to leak any information about his whereabouts. With any luck he would arrive home in plenty of time to see Rachel off to school tomorrow morning.

He sent up a silent prayer for his daughter. A good night's sleep had eluded her since she'd burned herself. Every night for the past week, her screams reached him and tore out his heart. Even now her wails echoed through him, and his jaw clenched.

But duty called in the form of a sheriff, who reminded him, in no uncertain terms, Mike had missed three shifts last week. While all were family emergencies, Mike had no choice but to accept this assignment.

Hopefully it wouldn't be a wild-goose chase. Donahue had pinned the robberies on a map. Farr's Hardware hadn't fallen victim yet. Neither had the Holly Days Diner. Donahue's plan was simple. Mike would scope out the buildings with his binoculars from a block away, while Donahue covered the rears near the dumpsters.

Fatigue tore at Mike's limbs. Coffee might help. He sipped the brew strong enough to lift a couple of hundred-pound barbells without any trouble. The streetlights provided him enough light from this vantage point, close enough to catch anyone in the act, far enough away not to be easily spotted. He glanced at his phone—only five more hours until he could call it quits.

A shadow approached the front of his car. Any hint of sleepiness went away. Adrenaline jolted his body awake. He planted his hand on his Taser.

"Mike? Is that you?" Georgie's husky voice registered.

His breath of relief could probably be heard in Tennessee.

"Georgie Bennett." He switched on the car's ignition and used the door control, rolling down the shaded window enough for him to see most of her. "How did you know it was me?" This wasn't his normal police cruiser.

"You forget I'm a mechanic. Melanie Donahue brought the car in last week. A 2007 Hyundai Sonata, gray, tinted windows, dent in the back bumper, new Michelins." She ran her hand along the window's edge. "And Natalie told me this afternoon."

Oh, he was going to set his sister up with a doozy of a date.

"Well, your sneaking up on me like that could have caused me to do something rash."

She leaned over so her face was boxed in the open square. "Beau made enough noise to wake up an army. Didn't you hear him?"

Rolling down the window the rest of the way, Mike stared at the big friendly dog, who had settled on his haunches and was listening as if he knew they were talking about him.

"No, I didn't." He drained the rest of his coffee and shook off the last vestiges of his reverie. "What in the world are you doing walking a dog this late at night? It's past eleven."

She scoffed. "I'd never have walked Beau this late in Boston, but, for crying out loud, Mike, this is Hollydale." Her huff for emphasis didn't escape him. "And Beau is a pretty good companion. Would you attack me with him at my side?"

Mike glanced at the dog, his tongue lolling and his tail thumping away. Mike arched an eyebrow. "Ferocious guard dog there."

"When you have to go, you have to go." She shrugged and delivered an exaggerated sigh. "I'll take my chances out here rather than with my mother's reaction if Beau had an accident in the middle of the night."

He'd concede that point. "This is a bad time for a chat. I'm on a stakeout. I shouldn't be talking to anyone."

Georgie raised her hands, the leash flapping as she did so. "You're a hard man to track down. I just wanted to tell you I've done a preliminary inspection of the Thunderbird. When's a good time to talk to you about it?"

Guilt racked him. Since Rachel's accident, the car occupied the bottom rung of his priorities—just as it had the past eight years. To top everything off, he never had leveled with

Georgie about the Thunderbird's future. With the added expense of Rachel's urgent care visit, the special cream and other prescriptions, selling the car sooner rather than later still made selling the car the better route.

No matter what, though, a stakeout wasn't the time or place to bring it up.

"How's tomorrow night?"

"Shop closes at seven. If you and Rachel want to drop by around eight, I'll have had a chance to collect Beau and walk him." Georgie leaned over to the dog and gave him a good scratch around his ears.

Mike half envied Beau, having Georgie all to himself.

"As long as Rachel's up to it." He started to click the button and stopped as his gaze wandered over Georgie's clothing. That black T-shirt clung to her curves but wasn't the best color for walking in the dark, even with the bright streetlights flooding the area. "Next time wear something more appropriate for—"

"My T-shirt and jeans are comfortable. I like what I'm wearing."

"I like your clothes, too." And he liked the way she filled them out. There was nothing unfeminine about Georgie. "But the dark colors help you blend in with your surroundings, making it difficult to see you."

"Oh."

"For the record, your clothes become you. You've never tried to be something you're not." Something he didn't always appreciate. Now that Georgie was back in Hollydale, he was starting to. "But you know, black at night…"

His gaze swept over her. Black T-shirt, black jeans, dark sneakers. Not the usual attire for walking a dog late at night. No way. Georgie wouldn't be so dumb as to rob the hardware store with Beau, would she? Of course not. It was so late he'd lost any sense of reason.

Her eyes widened, and she backed away from the car. Her frostiness could have fogged up the window. "Don't tell me…"

But she knew. From the horror-filled expression on her face, she had as much as read his mind in the brief millisecond he'd imagined the worst.

"Georgie!" He groaned. His uniform had changed everything between them in a flash. Although he wanted to go after her, he couldn't give away his position. "Wait."

"I'm glad you're not coming until tomorrow night." She spat out the words, her gleaming green eyes pure weapons of destruction. "It will take me that long to cool down. You don't really believe I walked here and brought a dog with me so I could break into somewhere."

When she put it that way, it did sound ridiculous. Why had he presumed the worst about her? Ever since she'd returned, she'd done nothing but help him and others.

"Of course not." His denial sounded rather lame, even to his own ears.

"I am so glad I promised my mother I would keep our relationship strictly business."

She pivoted and stormed away.

Cold air bit into him, and he closed the window before banging his head against it. Relationship? He and Georgie were involved?

Satisfaction flowed through him, and he smiled.

When all was said and done, they made a good team.

But she'd promised her mother she'd keep whatever was simmering between him and her under the surface on a business level. Her mother? A month ago, he wasn't sure whether Georgie had ever forgiven him and moved past the prom. Now she was discussing him with her mother.

So their chemistry was off the charts enough so that they both were aware of it. For the first time in so long, he found himself believing he was good enough for a long-term relationship. There was something different about the Georgie who had returned. Always strong and decisive, she'd grown up while she was away, and it had turned her into a knockout. Her fieriness could thaw his cool exterior if he let her.

But what had he done? For the second time he'd stopped short of flat-out accusing her of being a criminal.

Hard to start a relationship if she was always wondering if he was going to arrest her any minute.

"Mike?" Donahue's voice crackled over the walkie-talkie. "Anything suspicious?"

Grabbing the radio receiver, Mike hesitated. When he didn't listen to his conscience, he always burned himself. First he had ditched Georgie for Wendy MacNamara and lost Georgie's friendship for years. Then he'd gone to the bar after his grandfather's funeral, got plastered to the wind and ended up marrying Caitlyn. His ex-wife hadn't been ready for motherhood, or adulthood, either. The divorce papers proved that.

Duty had to come first, and that compelled him to report what had just happened. "Made contact with a pedestrian walking her dog."

Donahue cleared his throat as more crackles came over the system. "Who was the pedestrian?"

Mike's stomach churned. He'd thrown Georgie under the bus all those years ago, but this? He felt like he was throwing her to the sharks this time. "Georgie Bennett."

"I don't like coincidences."

"She's watching Fred Reedy's dog, Beau. Her

mother isn't…" Sometimes being diplomatic late at night wasn't easy.

"I've met Beverly Bennett. Say no more. I'll check back later."

Mike traded the handset for his coffee. He didn't like coincidences, either. Once they apprehended the real burglars, so much the better. Not only would Hollydale's longest crime spree in ages come to an end, but he and Georgie could laugh about the misunderstanding.

If he could ever persuade her he believed in her.

CHAPTER ELEVEN

IF SOMEONE HAD told Georgie she'd be spending her Friday nights in Hollydale with a muscular male with the most incredible brown eyes, she'd still be on the floor laughing. After all, Kevin's farewell speech, the one where he'd harped on her independence, compelling him to find someone who devoted herself to him, had rung in her ears for over a year before she realized her worth.

There was no doubt Beau fit that description, though, his brown eyes second only to Mike's.

"What do you say? Five more minutes until we give up on Mike and Rachel?" She tapped her watch and glanced at Beau, who trotted over. "Thirty minutes is long enough."

If she'd known the pleasure of spending Friday nights with a dog, she'd have adopted one long ago. Then again, she should have visited Hollydale more often. There'd been times over the past years she'd thought about her hometown while missing Mike, her friend who threw his whole self into laughter, especially at his own corny jokes. She missed the way he brought her a Diet Coke and a Snickers with only a few grumbles about girl food.

She waited for that same sort of feeling about Kevin. None came. The truth was her ex-fiancé had never accepted her, tomboy ways and all. She was better off without him. Mike might accept her, but she didn't even merit a call with an explanation of why he was a no-show.

The other night he'd made it too clear he could think of her as a perpetrator. Was the robbery standing between them? She'd seen the flicker of doubt die in Mike's eyes. Heard his contrition, too. But, for that brief second, Mike had doubted her. Her breath caught. Not any simple wrongdoing, either. Breaking and entering. Theft of valuable comic books. A felony.

Sure, he trusted her with his grandfather's Thunderbird. At one point he and his grandfather counted it as one of their most cherished possessions. If he cared about the car, why wasn't he here? Was the car special, or was it an anchor dragging him down?

A half-hour extension was beyond generous. No call. No email. No text. Nothing to let her know he valued the Thunderbird.

Or her.

"That's enough time. Let's go home, Beau."

Mike's squad car pulled up into a parking spot, and her jaw clenched. It would serve him right if she handed him the Thunderbird keys and an order to have it towed to Foreman's in Asheville.

Mike and Rachel scurried out at the same time. Beau's welcome bark rang out loud, broken by the simultaneous slamming of the car doors. Rachel ran over and petted Beau. Mike stopped short of barreling into Georgie.

Showing her displeasure with a frown, she tapped her foot and her watch. "I can't work with someone who doesn't respect…"

"Please let me explain." His rushed words came with that grin she'd seen so often over the years, the grin that had always melted her heart.

Way back when, before dreams came with engagement rings and promises shattered with harsh words.

Now she limited her dreams to what she could make a reality without depending on anyone else.

"It was my fault, Miss Georgie." Rachel came over and wrapped her arms around Georgie's waist. "When I took out the recyclables, I left the door open. Ginger ran out."

"She climbed the tree right outside our back door." Mike stopped and gave an exaggerated huff, reeking of playfulness. "How would it look if one of Hollydale's finest had to call the fire department to get his cat out of a tree?"

"I'd pay to see it." She chuckled and rolled

her eyes. Hard to stay mad at someone who made you laugh.

"I fetched the ladder, climbed it and then wouldn't you know it?"

"Ginger jumped down all by herself." Rachel tugged on Georgie's T-shirt and roared with laughter, so much so she ended up doubling over. "It was so funny."

Mike winced. "Not really. My magic tricks are funny, but this? Possibly a four on a scale of ten."

He met Georgie's gaze. A sizzle of energy passed between them.

Georgie caught her breath and blinked first. "For Ginger's sake, we'll move forward. Next time call or something, okay?"

"Got it." Mike tapped his forehead with his index finger. "No note, no late excuse. A phone call, plain and simple."

"Better yet, don't get in trouble again." She glared at him, although she was smiling inside. Since she'd come back to Hollydale, Mike's serious side had been in the forefront. Glad to see he was still in touch with the boy who'd made her laugh.

He arched his eyebrows and chucked Georgie's chin. "I'm not the one you need to worry about. Trouble should have been your middle name."

"Hmm. Georgianna Trouble Bennett. Sounds

better than the mouthful that is Georgianna Victoria Bennett." She held up the leash and strode toward the repair shop entrance. "Enough chit-chat. I have a hot date tonight."

Mike cleared his throat, and she turned. He stood there, his arms folded, his chin higher in the air. "Hot date?"

Did she detect a note of jealousy in his tone? Her smile on the inside broadened to match the width of Mike's shoulders. He was jealous. "Yep."

"Scott from the bike store?" He wrinkled his forehead, and his lips formed a straight line. "Garrett McGee, the assistant principal at the middle school?"

"Groot, the *Guardians of the Galaxy* and my mother. She'll love Groot."

"You always did like superhero movies. Save a night for me."

Her insides gave a little dance. He remembered her favorite type of movie, and she'd detected a note of jealousy.

Friday nights in Hollydale might prove more interesting than she'd ever thought possible.

"I'D SAY WE'RE looking at a good month of steady work. If I get really busy on a project…"

Mike smiled and touched Georgie's arm, soft and muscular at the same time. She never failed to amaze him. Too bad his teenage self hadn't gotten that message.

Note to teenage self: you were so incredibly stupid.

"It's okay. I know you have customers who need their cars sooner rather than later."

"Business has picked up at last."

"I'll help as much as possible, as well."

A month of working with Georgie on a regular basis? He'd take it.

"Actually, I paused because of Max."

"Yeah, I've been in touch with Max. Hope the biopsy comes back benign." She startled, and he shrugged. "Police officers have to keep secrets."

Tension creased Georgie's forehead. Cursing inside, he blasted himself for bringing up the sensitive subject.

A flash of pain crossed her expressive face. "Actually, it came back malignant. His surgery is set for a week from now. The doctor's hopeful he might not even have to undergo chemo. It depends on what they find. Rosie is pushing him to stay longer." She snapped off her gloves and glanced over his shoulder. "Hey, Rachel, are you okay?"

"I really need to use the bathroom." His daughter's urgency made Mike turn.

Rachel had that look on her face, the one where she'd waited five minutes too long to speak up.

"There's one right inside the reception area." Georgie approached Rachel and held out her hand. "Do you want me to show you?"

"No, I can find it."

"Do you need help because of the bandages?"

"I'm good." Her high-pitched voice gave away too much, and Rachel scurried out of there faster than a mouse smelling cheese.

The door closed behind her before Mike sighed and walked back to the Thunderbird. "You're seeing me at my worst as a father. Burns, pet escapes, bathroom emergencies."

He looked away; he didn't want to see the disappointment in her eyes. Heck, he was disappointed in himself. Shuddering, he remembered all too well the cold, hard looks from his twin sisters after he'd conducted himself in a manner most unbecoming a Harrison by ditching Georgie. He hadn't missed the pitying looks from half the town after Caitlyn left him with a baby daughter. Those were bad enough. He didn't want to wake up at four in the morning with the memory of Georgie's green emeralds seared into his brain.

He jumped when fingers landed on his shoulder. "I see a little girl who loves her father. Rachel is intelligent and independent. Most fathers would be proud of those qualities rather than beating themselves up."

Turning, he didn't see judgment and harshness anywhere in the fine features of her face.

"Thank you."

Georgie shrugged and stepped away. Already he missed her touch.

Picking up the nearby clipboard, she scanned the paper before unclipping it and handing it over. "Any questions about the process?"

"Can I do any of this work myself? Save a few pennies?" He doubted it but figured he'd ask anyway.

"Actually, yes." Coming over, she pointed to a couple of the steps. "Way back when, we did some of this in your grandfather's driveway. It should be like riding a bike. It'll all come back when the time is right."

This close, her lemony smell tickled his nose. He'd never craved a cool, tall glass of lemonade more. Her short shiny brown hair caught his attention, and he longed to reach out and touch those silky strands so close and yet so far away. *Just tell her.* With all that had happened to Rachel and since, he never had told her his intentions regarding the Thunderbird.

Without warning, those bright green emeralds sparkled. "I'm glad you're keeping Miss Brittany. Your grandfather would be so proud."

He moved closer. Opening his mouth, he wanted to find the right words to set her straight. Instead, the light of the shop reflected off her, cascading her in a golden glow, her beauty striking him. Taking her in his arms, he pulled her toward him and lowered his head. Before he knew any better, his lips were tasting hers, tangier than even lemon meringue pie. He hesitated. At that second Georgie closed the gap between them and deepened the kiss. Here she was, after all these years, in his arms.

Nothing had ever felt so right.

Mike pressed his hand to the small of her back, the cotton of her T-shirt smooth and soft as the world spun around on its axis. Her slight moan let him know she was enjoying this as much as he was.

Bells started ringing.

Her hands pressed against his chest as her lips pulled away. "That's my mother on the phone."

Those were the only words that could pry him away from her in this moment. As Georgie answered, Rachel came skipping in, relief plastered all over her darling face. Mike blinked. What had he been thinking? Kissing Georgie when his daughter, who'd never seen him kissing a woman, could have walked in and started asking questions.

Georgie stepped away, her head nodding, no words coming from her side of the conversation, the light in her eyes fading with each passing second.

"Hi, Daddy." Rachel rushed in and tugged at his T-shirt. "Are you finished yet? I want to go home. My arm hurts."

One look at Rachel's exhausted face left him little choice. "We have to say goodbye to Miss Georgie first."

Georgie's lips, so soft and supple a mere whisper of seconds before, formed into a straight line. "I'm not avoiding you, Mom. We just finished. And no, picking up popcorn on the way home isn't a good idea. You're recovering from your second stent implantation."

He pointed to the exit. "Do you want us to go?" Mouthing the words, he backed up and reached for Rachel's good hand.

Georgie held up an index finger. "Mom, the sooner I say goodbye, the sooner I'll be home, okay? Goodbye."

She let out a deep huff and ended the call before giving him and Rachel a genuine smile.

He spoke up before she mentioned the kiss. "We have to go. It's time for Rachel's nightly doses of medicine."

That smile stayed on, but a tinge of sadness entered her eyes. Was he the cause? He hoped not. Her eyes should dance with happiness, not show such seriousness in their depths.

"Talk tomorrow?"

Mike took a deep breath. What had they just done? At the stakeout she'd been blunt about keeping their relationship on a business level. What was more, she had promised her mother she'd do so. Georgie breaking a promise was like him not fulfilling his sworn duty as a police officer. He couldn't go back on an oath. Not anymore.

He should have told her the truth about the Thunderbird. Instead, he'd thought of himself and missed the perfect opportunity for getting his reasons out into the open.

She'd asked him to keep this professional between them, and he'd failed her again. For her sake he needed to back away.

"You're right. We should keep this on a purely business level."

Hurt flickered in her expression. He had no choice. If she broke a promise for him? That would go against her ideals. Okay for a kiss, but not for a lifetime.

"Same time, then?"

Her gaze met his, and a look of understanding passed over her. His heart plummeted.

He squinted and searched for something else in her eyes. Something that said they weren't finished yet.

Grasping Rachel's hand, he broke away. No sense in reading too much into a kiss and a look.

That kiss represented everything he wanted out of life, though.

Everything he couldn't have.

CHAPTER TWELVE

GEORGIE HAD WARNED Mike that the Thunderbird restoration would get much worse before it got better. Two weeks to the day after they'd agreed to have her start the repairs, her prophecy was true.

She tilted her camera and snapped more pictures of the dash harness. The sheer number of wires demanded careful preparation for this step of the disassembly process. Not that there was much left of the car to take apart. Arriving for work before dawn every day for the past fourteen mornings had resulted in a skeleton rather than a recognizable automobile. Days were now filled with returning customers, and late evenings helped hurry the process along, too. Working this late on a Friday was par for the course.

Someday, though, Mike would have a good laugh about this stage of the process during a long Sunday drive with Rachel.

Would Georgie be welcome to accompany them?

Ever since he okayed the repairs and kissed

her, Mike had clammed up as silent as if she'd read him Miranda rights. Was that kiss really two weeks ago? Whenever Mike dropped by after work to help, he found some excuse not to be alone with Georgie. The excuse was mostly Rachel. Not that she minded the delightful girl. Georgie smiled at the interest Rachel had displayed in the engine block. Her great-grandfather would have loved that.

But every time Rachel headed for the bathroom, and Georgie had Mike alone for two minutes, he busied himself with some fine detail. A guilty shadow always passed over his face and then a mask hid it.

Concentrate, Georgie. The car wouldn't regenerate under its own power. Before she reached for the first wire, the door to the reception area opened.

"Isn't your first car care class tonight?" Heidi crossed over to the farthest of the three bays, the one occupied by the Thunderbird.

Cursing, Georgie yanked her hand back from the dash harness. How could she forget? In the little spare time that she'd had, she'd distributed flyers, posted the event on social media and told everyone she met.

"Thanks for reminding me." She checked her watch. Ten minutes to go. "Are you sure you can't stay? I'd love a familiar face in the crowd."

Heidi shook her head, her dress flowing

around her. "We're visiting Max in Florida this weekend."

"Give him a hug for me. Maybe the sunshine the meteorologist keeps promising is there. Bring it back with you, okay? Max, too, if he lets you." Georgie followed Heidi to the waiting area and stared out the window, gray clouds hanging overhead. Every passing day grew a bit nippier. She'd be trading her jacket for her coat soon enough. With the colder temps, some people might bring their cars by for a winter preparation check. Georgie wouldn't mind that.

"I talked to Rosie. She's happy he's staying put for the time being. The trip is our anniversary present to ourselves."

"Happy anniversary." Georgie made a mental note to pick up a cake tomorrow for a celebration before they left.

"Those folding chairs are still in my car. Can you help me bring them in?"

"Sure." Following Heidi outside, Georgie shivered and reached for two metal chairs. Hurrying back, she set them up near the couch area, along with the cookies and appetizers specially purchased for tonight.

"Do you need anything else?" Heidi hovered near the front door. "Travis is already home. He was hoping for one more night of grilled burgers before he put the cover on the gas grill. Think I'll broil them instead."

"Can you spare two minutes while I remove my coveralls?" She plucked at the dingy navy top, splattered with oil splotches, before sneaking another peek at her watch. "Welcome everyone and tell them I'll be right back."

Running into the bathroom, Georgie shucked off her coveralls in no time flat. With a quick glance in the mirror, she finger-combed her hair, a bit damp and frizzy after a day's work. She took a deep breath, ready to answer any questions about car repair from the people waiting out there. Fingers crossed she had enough cookies for everyone.

Back in the waiting room, she stopped short. Heidi was thumbing through an ancient magazine she must have read twenty times already. No one else was here. Where was everyone? This was Hollydale, so traffic wasn't an excuse. Panic scratched at her throat. Friday night was a bad idea for this type of activity after all.

Heidi laid the magazine down and stood, sympathy in her gray eyes. She came over and patted Georgie's shoulder. "Don't worry, honey. People will show up. They might be running late because they're buying Halloween candy." She scrunched up her cheeks and shrugged, her bright smile no doubt designed to lift Georgie's spirits.

With well over two weeks remaining until Halloween, Georgie didn't quite believe her, but she hugged Heidi anyway. "Thanks. You run on home and enjoy a hamburger for me."

"You sure, darlin'?" Heidi smiled. "I can stay for a while."

"Please go." Georgie wanted a few minutes of peace, her skin already itching for the new adventure around the bend.

Heidi waved goodbye with another flash of a smile. Georgie sank onto the ancient couch, faded to a dark tan from the sun. Maybe she should have targeted high school students learning how to drive instead.

Five more minutes passed, and Georgie's stomach roiled. She might as well stop by Mike's house and show him the newest batch of pictures before taking Beau on a long run. The thought of seeing Mike brightened her surly mood. Georgie rose from the couch, and the door opened, sending the cowbell jangling. In walked Lucie Decker, a harried expression on her face.

"Don't tell me I'm that late." She reached into her purse and pulled out her phone. "Ten minutes isn't bad for me. My babysitter's math-tutoring session lasted longer than she expected. I thought about bringing the twins, but..."

Georgie glanced at the three dozen cookies on the table. "Since I daresay there will be left-over cookies, please take as many as you want home with you. The twins deserve them for helping you with my mother. The car care program is officially DOA."

"But I've been looking forward to this." Lucie hugged her, and Georgie stiffened from the unexpected greeting. "I need this class."

"Why?"

Lucie's eyebrows veered downward, and she bit her lip. She dropped onto the couch. Georgie settled on one of the aluminum chairs. "You're so self-reliant and all. You won't understand."

"Try me."

Lucie gave a tentative smile, one that didn't light up her eyes. "My parents bought me an AAA membership in high school. Then after I married, my husband took care of the cars." She glanced up, her shoulders stiff as a spark plug. "I suppose you heard how my marriage turned out."

Georgie kept her gaze steady. She wasn't one to judge a failed relationship. "Heidi might have mentioned it."

"I don't know how to change a tire or how to connect bumper cables."

"You mean jumper cables."

Lucie popped off the couch, anger lurking in those hazel eyes. She strode toward the exit. "I didn't come here for you to make fun of me."

Georgie jumped up, rushed over and blocked the door. "I was correcting you, not making fun of you. There's a difference. If you're serious about this, you have to learn the proper terminology."

"I see the looks people give me. It's okay if you don't want to teach me."

"Hey, this is one of life's basic necessities. I came up with the idea, didn't I?" Even if Lucie was her only student, Georgie would consider this a success. It was her imprint on Max's Auto Repair. This place still bore his name. She lived in her mother's home. Even her dog wasn't hers. Mr. Reedy was supposed to leave the convalescence center in a mere two weeks.

"I hope some of your toughness rubs off on me."

"I've always been my own person." Letting others in, though? It wasn't as bad as she'd thought.

Mike flashed into her mind. In his living room with Ginger at his side. In the shop, his sandalwood smell mixing with coffee. At the urgent care with Rachel hugging him close. Warmth filled her chest.

Lucie's laugh brought her back. Lucie entwined her arm through Georgie's. "That you have. I envied that in high school."

"Don't be too envious, Lucie." Georgie led Lucie back to the couch. "Before we get down to business, we have an important matter to take care of."

"Isn't the class free?" Lucie's eyes widened. "I have to pay the babysitter. I can't afford—"

"Oatmeal raisin or chocolate chip." Georgie measured her deadpan delivery so Lucie wouldn't take off again. Those twins, while precocious, were important to Lucie. Keeping that family safe was Georgie's new pressing goal. Until Lucie graduated from this class, Georgie wouldn't let her off the hook. "Which type do you prefer? Since you and I are the only ones here..."

The front door cracked open, and the cowbell jangled. "Sorry I'm late. The student I was tutoring couldn't get the difference between an acute angle and an obtuse one. I swear, how she made it out of middle school, I don't know."

Natalie rushed in, out of breath, her sundress swishing all around her, showcasing a pair of blue leather boots. Not Georgie's style. But on Natalie it worked.

"Have I missed anything important?"

Georgie met Lucie's gaze, and the two of them burst out laughing.

"The most important lesson we've covered so far is whether you would prefer oatmeal raisin or chocolate chip." Georgie picked up the tray and waved it in front of Natalie's nose.

"Chocolate chip, of course. Anything is better with chocolate." Natalie smiled and flounced onto the couch.

"Oh, and of course—why are you here?"

Natalie glanced up, her mouth full of cookie, two crumbs hanging on the side of her mouth. Lucie also chose chocolate chip, and Georgie grabbed her favorite, oatmeal raisin, before sitting in one of the metal chairs.

Natalie wiped her mouth with the back of her hand, her curly red hair bouncing along. "Mike, for one thing." She squinted, and a smile came over her. "Georgie, you're definitely redder now than you were when I walked in. This is so exciting. He hasn't been involved with anyone…" She nibbled at her cookie, a determined glint in her eye. "Not with anyone seriously since Caitlyn walked out on him. I always had a feeling about you two, even back in high school."

Georgie shook her head and held her hands high. "This is about automotive maintenance, not me."

"You weren't that red when I was ready to leave," Lucie's blond ponytail bounced for emphasis.

"Let's get started." Wanting off the hot seat, Georgie grabbed her notes from the table and flipped through them, skipping the preliminary joke. "Car care is an important part of everyday life. When we take care of our cars, our cars can take us anywhere our hearts desire."

"I still say your heart desires my brother." Natalie reached for another cookie and bit into it for emphasis. "Sorry I'm scarfing these down. Didn't have time for dinner."

It was obvious nothing would get done until Georgie cleared the air. Best to get this over with and move on. So this was what women did when they gathered together. Come to think of it, she'd never belonged to a group of girlfriends chatting about boys, exchanging makeup tips and trying on one another's clothes. This was kind of nice.

"Okay, Mike kissed me."

A huge grin broke out over Natalie, and even Lucie leaned forward.

Georgie hurried to correct the misconception anything was going on between her and Mike. "Two weeks ago."

"What?" Natalie and Lucie said in unison.

Georgie frowned. "He hasn't tried to kiss me again. And I don't have time for a relationship." She grasped at straws, hesitant to share the deep reasons with these two. Old habits die hard. "My mother's been recovering. When I haven't been with her or Beau, I've been here working on the Thunderbird."

"Hmm." Natalie reached for a cookie and sat back. "Your voice sounds official, but your eyes say romance and dreams and second chances."

If anyone had moondust in her blue eyes, it was Natalie Harrison.

"Look, if Mike was interested in me, he'd

have said something. He doesn't beat around the bush."

"Are you interested in him?" Lucie reached for a chocolate chip cookie, bit into it and moaned with pleasure. Guilt came over her face. "I never get a second cookie at home. If I don't reach for what I want, I don't get it. Same thing goes for you. Tell him how you feel. Kiss him, but make sure he's a good guy first. Don't rush into anything. I learned that lesson the hard way."

Natalie nudged Lucie, her grin becoming broader. "I like how you think. By the way, if you don't remember who I am, name's Natalie Harrison. I'm Mike's sister."

"I'm Lucie—"

"Lucie Decker. You were a year ahead of me in school, and, truthfully," Natalie said, shrugging and wiping her hands free of crumbs, "everyone in Hollydale knows you."

Lucie sighed and shook her head, her ivory skin even paler. "The problem is everyone knows what my ex-husband did. Not many people know me. I should go."

Glaring at Natalie, Georgie rested her hand on Lucie's arm. "You're paying a babysitter, and I'll teach you how to change a tire even if it's the last thing I do. You're also helping my mother, and that's worth a great deal to me."

"I'm sorry." Natalie grasped Lucie's other

arm. "I wasn't trying to run you off. Mike says while I'm one of the smartest people he's ever met, I also tend to speak first and think after. No filter, I'm afraid. We both speak our minds, though, so we'll get along fine." She met Georgie's gaze. "And speaking of Mike…"

Mike underestimated Natalie. She wasn't the same pliable teenager who delivered a note without reading it. Instead, she was persistent and tenacious like a bulldog.

"Mike doesn't like me in any special way. We've only just become friends again. That's enough for the both of us."

Shaking her head, Natalie resumed her seat. "Mike has a strong sense of duty. To family, to work, to this community. He won't jeopardize his job, and he feels guilty about Rachel. She'll have a permanent scar, you know."

Her own sense of guilt shot through Georgie. "No, I didn't." After this, she'd walk Beau, and if they ended up over at the Harrisons', so be it. She and Mike had much to discuss. "I have a duty to each of you to make sure you both learn the ins and outs about cars over the next month. That way, no one takes advantage of you." She sent a pointed look Natalie's way. "And you can feel more in control of your life."

Control of her life.

A lesson she had best learn herself before she tried teaching it to others. Come to think of it, she was finding herself, too, at least the parts she'd kept hidden for too long. Getting everything out into the open with Mike would be the best place to start.

Control was a two-way street, though. It meant harnessing her feelings rather than jumping into any commitments without considering what was best for her and all involved. Before she could talk to Mike about any chance they might have, she had to speak with her mother and wriggle free of that promise from a while back. Control started with making her own decisions about whom she associated with, and how.

Control that she had every intention of wresting back for herself, and keeping.

CHAPTER THIRTEEN

THE SECOND THAT MIKE settled into his chair, Ginger made herself comfortable on his lap. Laughing, he admired the cat's forthrightness when someone rang the doorbell. He glanced at his watch and frowned. Rather late on a Monday night for the casual visitor. When he rose, Ginger slipped off his lap and meowed her displeasure at being displaced.

Checking the peephole, he found Georgie waiting outside, tapping her foot. A deep breath escaped his lips. How would he keep her distracted without the Thunderbird nearby and Rachel asleep? He opened the door, taking care not to let Ginger out this late. Beau bounded in first, with Georgie on his heels.

"Hi, Mike. Have a minute?" Georgie sped by him. "Long time no see."

"Not that long. Come on in." He stayed behind, waving at air, muttering to no one in particular. If she'd thought it was easy to stay away from her, she was wrong. "Make yourself comfortable. I'm doing well, thanks for asking."

There weren't enough deep breaths to contend with the loss of equilibrium whenever he was in Georgie's presence.

Mike walked into the living room, where Ginger was holding court, staring down a dog several times bigger than her small self. Didn't matter. A cat to her inner core, Ginger was quite independent, deigning to let others into her world. A little like Georgie. He'd never met such an independent soul, yet Georgie wasn't imperious. Unlike Ginger, Georgie never wanted to be queen. Instead, she just wanted to be herself.

Ginger rose and arched her back before snuggling against the dog's stomach. With a cute grin lightening her features, Georgie deposited herself on the armchair near his couch. Then she reached into her purse.

"I brought over the latest photos of the Thunderbird. It was totally dismantled. Over the weekend, I started putting everything back together."

Straight to the point. The arrow zinged him in his heart. If he let himself, he could fall for the beautiful, vibrant woman sitting so near. There were a thousand and one reasons why he shouldn't, but they all scattered away like the wind when she was nearby.

Still, those reasons existed. The B&E, her independence, his baggage. He bit back that dratted sigh. Best to get his intentions over selling the Thunderbird off his chest. If Georgie left town, that was her decision. Enough keeping his distance already.

Seeing the disappointment in her eyes, though, when he told her he'd be selling the Thunderbird?

It no longer mattered. He couldn't hold it in any longer. He cleared his throat and sat opposite her. "Georgie."

She held up her hand. "Business first, then we talk." She handed him her phone with a grin. "Isn't it beautiful?"

He gasped as the barest of car skeletons greeted him. "What is it?"

"That was the Thunderbird on Friday. I made faster progress than anticipated." She shrugged and reached for the phone. "This past weekend, Kitty and my mom decided to have a movie marathon." She shuddered. "I hate musicals. Whenever I wasn't with Beau, I dismantled."

A skeleton had more meat on its bones. His breath came in short spurts. His grandfather's Thunderbird was literally in thousands of pieces.

She waved her phone under his nose. "You did know this had to be done? In order to do it right, that is."

Knowing something and seeing it were two different things entirely. The stark reality of his grandfather's Thunderbird being reduced to a heap of wires and metal like that? He gulped down the emotion that kept him from talking. Even though Miss Brittany would shine soon, the present reality was hard to bear.

He handed her the phone back with a nod. "Reminds me of when Caitlyn left. Even though I sensed she wasn't happy, it was still a shock."

He didn't talk to his family about Caitlyn's desertion. But he'd never hidden much from Georgie. Talking with her seemed effortless, except when it came to the fate of the Thunderbird.

What if he brought it up and she turned the car, along with its myriad of pieces, over to Foreman's?

The time with Georgie and Rachel working on the Thunderbird kept him going, what with the increased pressure to run for sheriff and the medical bills mounting from Rachel's burns.

It was pure selfishness not to tell her. The silence stretched out before she rested her hand over his. "So Caitlyn just up and left you?"

He'd forgotten there was someone who didn't know about that bittersweet period. He should regret hooking up with Caitlyn the night of his grandfather's funeral. Yet he couldn't regret Rachel, his precious little girl.

"You haven't heard the story, have you?" He fidgeted with the remote. Might as well start with his past and work up to the present. Getting everything off his chest would help him sleep well tonight. Ginger jumped up onto his lap, and he took comfort in petting her, the rhythmic motions calming. "I was twenty-one when Grandpa Ted died. No one I'd ever cared about had died before. I was lucky, I suppose."

"Lucky? Odd choice of words."

His chest heaved, and he shook his head. "Not lucky for losing him, but for not experiencing death any sooner." Although, a previous lifelong separation before that he'd felt but had no control over. His birth mother's decision to give him up for adoption had ended up being a blessing for him. Parents didn't come better than the Harrisons.

"What does your grandfather's death have to do with Rachel's mother?"

"Something snapped after my grandfather died. I wanted to do something wild, something where I didn't have to think. I went to Asheville and ended up stinking drunk."

He glanced up. There was no condemnation in her green gaze.

"Sorry I wasn't your designated driver that night."

Lifting the left side of his mouth, he relaxed for the first time in a while. The protective side of Georgie was one of the many things he'd missed over the years.

"But then I wouldn' have Rachel so as

hard as the decision would be, I'd do it all over again."

Georgie reached over and squeezed his hand. Ginger jumped off his lap with a yowl.

"Georgie—"

"Mike—"

They laughed, and he pointed to her so she'd go first.

"Now that we know our names…" Georgie's green eyes twinkled again, and all seemed right with Mike's world. "What were you about to say?"

"You're my guest. Ladies first."

"According to my mother, I'm not a lady." Georgie gave a bright smile and winked. "But I think I have more fun my way."

His breath caught as the truth flooded over him. *Fun*. He'd lost touch with his lighter side. "Why'd you drop by?"

Georgie's gaze wandered over to Beau, Ginger now nestled at his side. Beau's snores filled the air. "I assure you it wasn't for Beau's nap time. I need to get something off my chest."

Speaking of holding back, this was as good a time as any to tell her about Donahue and his ongoing suspicions. "Let me go first."

Her eyes narrowed, meeting his gaze head on. His muscles stiffened, the mellowness seeping away.

"Hold on. Your breath has become shallow."

She squinted at his forehead. "Is that a bead of sweat?"

"Donahue and I found stolen tablets in a dumpster, one you have access to. But—" His voice came out garbled as if a jar of marbles had taken up residence in his cheeks.

He reached out for her, but she brushed away his hand.

Walking over to Beau, she hooked his leash back to his harness. "It was bad enough when you didn't have the heart to tell me in person you were ditching me the day of prom. I forgave you a long time ago. But thinking I'm a thief? For the record I would never, ever steal from anyone, especially Max. Come on, Beau, we're out of here."

Her swift intake of breath came with a quick shake of her head. Shutting him out dug deep to his core.

Beau whined in protest, and Ginger meowed at being displaced again. Georgie strode to the door, and Mike caught up with her. "Georgie, please wait."

"For what?" She turned, anger radiating out of those expressive green eyes. "For you to accuse me of something I didn't do? To stay in your house when you believe I'm a common criminal?"

"I know you're not a criminal. I've told Donahue that over and over. Please listen."

"Daddy?" A small voice caught his attention, and he looked toward the stairs. Rachel rubbed her eyes with her good hand. A smile lightened her sleepy features. "Miss Georgie! Beau!"

Beau gave a joyful bark and bounded toward Rachel before the leash yanked him back. Georgie dropped the leash. Beau closed the distance, sitting at Rachel's feet, waiting for his due attention. Ginger crept over and wound her body around Mike's ankles. Bending, he picked the cat up. At least he still had one relationship with a female that he hadn't messed up. Yet.

"Beau and I were just about to leave, sweetheart."

"Please stay." Rachel knelt and hugged Beau, her whole body leaning into the patient animal. "I…"

Mike deposited Ginger on the couch and rushed over. "Are you okay, kiddo? Is your hand hurting?"

He rubbed Rachel's shoulder, and she snuggled her face into the dog's fur.

On Rachel's other side, Georgie knelt and cleared her throat. "Rachel? What's wrong? Your dad is really concerned. I haven't seen that face on him since he failed two chemistry tests in a row."

A tiny chuckle set Mike's heart to beating again.

Rachel focused on Georgie. "Daddy failed tests?"

"Yep," he answered and took his latest trip down memory lane. "Even worse, I had to tell Grandma and Grandpa. They laid down the law and arranged a tutor for me."

Georgie laughed, some of that earlier sparkle returning to her green eyes. "I'd forgotten how mad you were about that."

"Daddy was angry?"

"Hmm, come to think of it, you're right, Rachel. He wasn't mad." Georgie scratched behind Beau's ears and didn't meet Mike's gaze. "He usually stays on an even keel. Even keeps me in check."

Rachel swiveled around, her fine brown hair mussed, circles under her eyes. "Were you mad at Grandma and Grandpa? You said I should respect them."

"Of course I always respected them. That wasn't the problem."

"Go ahead and tell her, Mike." A hint of laughter lay under Georgie's words. "Don't be shy."

He arched one eyebrow and huffed. "They hired Aunt Natalie."

"What's wrong with Aunt Natalie?" Rachel asked.

"Nothing, but for a high school student to have to accept help from his little sister?"

Mike blinked, remembering his parents sitting him down and telling him in no uncertain terms he had to shape up. It wasn't the talk that hurt. It was them not trusting him to study and shape up on his own.

Trust. Georgie always accepted him, to the point of protecting him, in fact, back when they were kids in middle school. Now she doubted his belief in her.

That was flat-out wrong. While Georgie had an independent soul, everyone needed someone sometime. With several people in town having silent accusations in their eyes, thinking Georgie stole the comic books, she needed someone to be there for her.

Needed was the wrong word—she *deserved* someone in her corner. He reached out and covered her hand.

"I believe in you, Georgie."

Their gazes met, and he stayed stock-still, despite the electricity that almost knocked him into the next county.

How had he been so blind all these years?

"Believing someone and believing *in* someone are two different things." She removed her hand, giving no sign of accepting his apology.

"I know you would never take something that didn't belong to you. I'm doing all I can to prove that."

Georgie tugged at Beau's leash until the dog,

with some reluctance, stretched his way into a standing position. "Call if you have time to help with the reassembly."

Mike stepped toward her, laying his arm on hers until her gaze lifted. "Let's start over."

"Why?"

"For one thing, there's Miss Brittany. She's stripped down to her barest bones and out there for all to see." He stopped and ran his hand through his hair.

"Keep going." Her voice didn't disguise the dare lurking in the shadows, almost like she was prodding him to reach deep inside and confront the romantic in him, the side he never gave in to.

"Then there's me. You've seen me at my worst, betraying what was right in my teenage world."

"You're being a bit harsh on yourself, don't you think?" She shifted her weight onto her other leg. Beau whined before nudging her hand with his snout. She began petting him, and the dog's protests faded away.

"You were my best friend. You deserved better."

"I have a best friend—Lilah," Rachel piped up. She came over to him, leaning her head into his side, seeking love and affection he was only too happy to deliver. "We always play together. She hugs me when my hand hurts." Rachel nodded. "It's important to be nice to your best friend."

In all those years no one had ever taken Georgie's place as his best friend. Between the police academy and single parenthood, he didn't have the time or the energy. Could he ever have replaced her? He bit back the sigh as honesty overtook him. Time and energy had nothing to do with it. Georgie was one of a kind. There would never be anyone like her.

"Rachel's right. We should be nicer to each other, beginning with me believing in you." He ruffled his daughter's hair and smiled over at Georgie. "What do you say? A fresh start." He caught his breath. A new relationship taking the place of the old one. "What were you going to say earlier?"

Georgie started and knelt next to Beau, kneading her fingers in his fur. "Um…"

His phone rang, and he checked the screen. "It's the station. I have to take this."

Getting everything into the open might let them take the bare bones of their relationship and build something new and meaningful, something classic and timeless. Most unlike what he'd shared with Caitlyn. He'd take the call, tuck Rachel in and move on with Georgie.

"Harrison."

"Need you at the station, stat."

His heart plummeted. "Can you get someone else? I'm home with Rachel."

"It's not a request." Donahue's voice was tight and unyielding.

Mike rubbed his forehead, the pressure in his temples excruciating. "Can't you call Edwards?"

"Already did. He has a 102-degree fever."

"Dad flew out to California to be with Mom and Becks today. There's no one to watch Rachel."

That pressure became downright unbearable. Headlines of "Cop Arrested for Leaving Daughter Alone" flashed before his eyes. Someone tapped his shoulder, and he jumped.

"I'll stay with Rachel."

He turned around and cupped the lower part of his smartphone. "I can't ask you to do that, Georgie."

"You're not asking. I'm offering." She dipped her head, that signal of determination he'd missed so much over the years.

"Thanks," he mouthed before lifting his hand and getting back to Donahue. "I'll be there as soon as possible."

Rachel gave a brave smile.

Georgie headed over and squeezed Rachel's shoulders. "Beau and I will stay with you in your room while you fall asleep."

The brief glimpse of what he could have if

he asked for a second chance was too much. He ran upstairs and reached for his uniform. The perfect opportunity for honesty had presented itself, and he'd dragged his feet once more.

The truth seared through him. What was he really afraid of? Her running away? Like his birth mother and Caitlyn? Heck, yeah. He leaned his head against the door to his closet. If he had another choice, he'd grab it. As things stood now, remaining silent was his only option, though. Rachel deserved a better life, one with dance lessons or art lessons.

Was he using money to make up for his failings? For Rachel living with a scar the rest of her life?

Did it matter? Lessons and some luxuries might make life better for Rachel. His skin crawled at using Georgie for Rachel's gain. Georgie was bound to be hurt once the truth about the Thunderbird came out.

No other options entered his mind, and he hurried to get ready for work.

HER NERVES ON EDGE, Georgie followed Rachel upstairs. Ginger rushed ahead while faithful Beau hovered at her side. Rachel clambered into her bed, flashing a tired smile.

"Thank you for staying with me, Miss Georgie." Rachel patted her bed and then pointed at a pile of books. "Will you read me a book? KitKat told me a story will help me fall asleep faster."

Georgie glanced around, her smile frozen in place, her gaze sweeping the room. Did Mike have another pet he hadn't told her about? "Who's KitKat?"

Ginger jumped onto the foot of the bed, and Rachel giggled. "KitKat's my teddy bear."

Georgie chuckled and sauntered over to pick the first book off the pile. A cover with a princess and a baby dragon stared back at her. It figured that a girl with enough gumption to approach a stranger about fixing her father's car would like something different.

Without further ado, Georgie settled on a spot near the corner, away from Rachel.

"KitKat doesn't mind if you come closer." Rachel picked up her teddy bear. "She likes hugs."

Okay, then. Sidling closer, Georgie slipped her arm around Rachel, gave her a quick squeeze and released her. A whiff of something clean and fresh tickled her nose. Baby shampoo wasn't that bad.

Had Kevin been wrong? Opening her heart for Rachel and her father was easy, too easy. Besides, they made it almost as effortless as a Maserati engine, except for the times when Mike doubted her. Then she wanted to pull out her hair or go fix a carburetor to offset his sheer stubbornness.

Slaying her own dragons was proving more difficult than she'd imagined. Exhaling, she opened the book and started reading. Georgie laughed at the picture of the baby dragon causing mayhem at dinner. Rachel giggled, too, and right there, she stole Georgie's heart.

Georgie kept reading, her eyes misting at the courage this little princess summoned when leaving the castle to raise the dragon by herself.

Rachel pulled on Georgie's sleeve. "Are you okay?"

Georgie laid the book on her lap, turned to Rachel and smiled. The princess didn't have anything on this little girl, who'd gone through so much physical pain over the past month. "I like your story. Thank you for letting me read to you."

"I like Princess Alixandra. She's doesn't think inside the box."

Georgie chuckled. She had a feeling Mike would hear that often about Rachel in the years ahead. Then the soft glow faded. Georgie wouldn't be around for those exchanges. Mike would tell some other woman all about Rachel's progress. Georgie's stomach knotted at the idea of another woman chatting with Mike, laughing with him, kissing him. Her jaw clenched, and she let the jealousy wash over her.

Blinking it away, Georgie nodded. "A lot like you."

Rachel shrugged. Ginger snuggled against her, and Rachel stroked the cat's fur. "I couldn't leave my daddy like Princess Alixandra does." Her voice was soft, almost hesitant. "My daddy thinks I want art lessons and dance lessons, but I just want to spend time with him."

If anything, Georgie was more convinced than ever she'd misjudged how intelligent Rachel was.

"A girl who knows what she likes. Nothing wrong with that. Definitely outside the box."

"Keep reading, please."

A few more pages later, Georgie glanced at Rachel, asleep, her mouth slightly ajar, her cheeks soft with slumber. With as much stealth as she could muster, Georgie closed the book and eased off the bed. The pets jumped down. Rachel moaned and turned over, her arms clutching KitKat. After Ginger and Beau slipped out, Georgie clicked off the light and shut the door behind her.

After kicking off her shoes, she curled up on the couch, checked her smartphone and winced. Three texts from her mother. Her fingers flew against the screen, letting her mother know an emergency came up and she was fine. After updating the repair shop's Facebook page to include the time for the next car care class,

Georgie checked on Beau. Chuckling, she found him asleep in the corner with Ginger cuddled up against him. Who'd have guessed a prickly independent cat would become best friends with a lovable furry dog?

Then again, she and Mike shouldn't have worked as best friends in high school. A prickly independent female hanging out with a popular family-driven guy. Yet they had worked.

For a while. Both of them had moved on since. Maybe it was time for her to move on once more. Getting attached to Mike and Rachel? Was that too inside the box for her?

The beep of an incoming text roiled her stomach. She'd already answered her mother. Whipping out her phone, she paused. It wasn't her mother. It was Max.

Surgery successful. No chemo. Next scan in 3 wks. Travis says you're bringing new customers in. Expected no less. Will sign contract & collect down payment upon return. Any word on comics? If not found, can't reduce asking price.

Georgie clutched her phone as tightly as Rachel had grasped KitKat. She didn't know what surprised her more, Travis's belief in her or Max's expectation of her buying him out. She had only said she might be interested. Then again, she hadn't expected Cullinan to keep stalling about the pit crew with texts of sponsors pulling out and other excuses. Bristling at all the changes and upcoming decisions, she curled up on the couch.

The biggest decision, though, revolved around Mike and his question. Would she give their friendship a fresh start? Her insides churned. Even she could tell the chemistry between them was mutual. Was friendship a precursor for something more? Something serious and mind-boggling and real?

She'd never stayed in one place long, except during her engagement. She'd never wanted to. Rising off the couch, she paced the room. Beau stirred, and both pets whined in protest over their disrupted sleep.

A relationship with Mike would change everything.

Mike would come in handy about now. His emotional steadiness calmed her, even more than assembling an engine, reading an owner's manual or attending a car show.

She missed Mike.

But could they start over? Not with the promise to her mother hanging over her head. With a harsh sigh, she picked up her phone and typed in her reply. She couldn't buy Max out. All weekend she could have interrupted her mother's musical fest with Kitty and talked to her. Yet she hadn't. That, in itself, spoke volumes. Leaving as soon as Max returned would be best for everyone. Her fingers stilled. She couldn't hit the Send arrow.

Instead, she deleted her answer.

The reasons she had for leaving were the same for staying.

MIKE OPENED THE creaky door and tiptoed into his house. This time the security company showed up and the robbers had fled. One of these days...

His breath whooshed out of his lungs at the sight of Georgie asleep on the couch, curled in a sweet ball. It wasn't often she wasn't moving at hurricane force. This was a rare opportunity, indeed. Without a doubt she was gorgeous, with those long full eyelashes and rosy cheeks. He almost hated to wake her.

She stirred and rubbed her eyes before noticing him. A smile brightened her sleepy features. Waking up to this face would be a blessing.

"You're back." Even with the tinge of sleep slightly slurring her words, that husky voice packed a punch.

"Yeah." *Stop sounding tongue-tied. It's Georgie.* He'd stayed up many a late night before, so he couldn't use that as an excuse, either, for the lightness spreading through his limbs. "It's close to two, so feel free to stay. My bed is comfortable." Her eyes widened, and she sat straight up. He hurried his explanation, "I'll sleep on the couch."

Georgie reached for her shoes and slipped them on. "I appreciate the offer, but I should be getting home. If Rachel saw us both here in the morning, she'd undoubtedly ask a lot of questions."

"She would."

Of course, Georgie was right. He'd never let a woman spend the night here. Between work and single fatherhood, he hadn't dated much. Hadn't wanted to. Until now.

Beau lifted his head and trotted over, wagging his tail. Mike bent down and scratched behind Beau's ear. Ginger peeked open one eye and carried herself upstairs with a regal air, as if the interruption to her sleep schedule was most intolerable.

Georgie met his gaze, a chuckle crossing her lips. "I guess Miss Ginger loves her beauty sleep."

She found Beau's leash and clicked it onto his collar. When she walked by, the sweet smell of her tingled his nose. She reached for the doorknob, but he held up his hand.

"You never told me why you came tonight."

"Like I said earlier, it doesn't matter." Her gaze lowered to the carpet. For once Georgie wasn't being entirely honest.

He reached out, his index finger caressing the soft skin under her chin. "Please tell me."

Gulping, she stepped back. He removed his finger, giving her the space she needed and clearly wanted.

"It's late. I'm not making sense. You get me all jumbled up."

His chest swelled, and a slight smirk came over him. Georgie was so independent, so together. "Yeah?"

"Yeah." She parroted his face, and he couldn't help but laugh, a strange feeling taking hold in his gut. Then a blank expression came over her. "You haven't tried to kiss me again."

He took a deep breath as he remembered why he hadn't tried to kiss her again. *Just tell her. I might be blowing this all out of proportion.* Letting her decide was the fair and honorable thing to do.

She moved toward the door. "Your silence says everything."

Forget silence. He wedged himself between her and Beau and leaned down, the sweet smell of her never sweeter. Her lips were sweet, too. He'd waited so long for another kiss. Intelligent, caring, sweet Georgie, part of his youth, part of his present. Most important, he wanted her as part of his future. Pulling her closer, he waited for any sign she didn't want him to kiss her. Instead, she kissed him, her lips warm and giving. All he knew was he didn't want to be anywhere else. For once he didn't have to second-guess himself. This was right.

Too soon, she broke off and blinked, her green eyes glittering.

Sizzling tension electrified the air.

"I've wanted to do that for two weeks," he admitted.

"Next time don't take so long." She escaped out the door faster than a Corvette on octane.

He watched her until she and Beau were safe in her car and her taillights faded from view.

The taste of Georgie lingered on his lips. By all rights, he should be floating. Why hadn't he told her the simple truth and let her decide if she wanted another kiss after he laid everything out on the table?

The truth was ugly. It wasn't just the Thunderbird, and he knew it. He'd been able to get over Caitlyn because she'd never gotten under his skin like Georgie. He wouldn't deny he'd loved Caitlyn. Devastated at her walking away without a backward glance, he'd had a reason to pick up the pieces and stay strong. Rachel had been a baby, starving for love, hungry for life, hungry, period.

But Georgie?

Georgie was one of a kind.

He cared. Caring, though, created a combustible combination, perhaps too dangerous, with his long record of women who had left him.

CHAPTER FOURTEEN

GEORGIE WHISTLED AS she made her way to the kitchen. Beau's dish was empty and so was Georgie's stomach. A quick breakfast and she'd be off to work, where Miss Louise would be waiting for her to repair her sedan.

She breathed in the aroma of cinnamon and vanilla but stopped short. Her mother stood in front of the stove. Georgie strode over and peeked in the black skillet. French toast?

"Mom, that's the worst thing for someone recovering from two stent procedures."

Her mother turned toward her, her left eyebrow arched. "I'm allowed to make my daughter's favorite breakfast, am I not?" She pointed to the kitchen table. "I've been up for two hours, and I started my day with oatmeal and fresh fruit, so sit and enjoy."

Warmth flooded over Georgie's cheeks, having nothing to do with the heat of the kitchen. "Sorry to jump to conclusions." Georgie lowered her gaze and shuffled her feet. Her mother knew French toast was her favorite? A surprise to start the day.

"Thank you for making me breakfast."

Her mother raised her hand and patted Georgie's cheek. "You don't let me do much for you, so I'm happy to do this." She smoothed Georgie's hair. "If only you'd let me schedule you an appointment with my hairdresser."

No one turned a compliment into a barb quite like her mother.

"I'll grab something for breakfast at the Biscuit Barn. Beau's in the garage apartment, since Heidi and Travis have a repair scheduled today. I'll be home at lunch to let him out."

As Georgie swiveled on her steel-toed boot to leave, her mother reached out and caught Georgie's wrist. "Now it's my turn to apologize." Beverly lifted her chin before letting go and plating the finished toast. She smiled and handed the dish to Georgie. "I guess you're old enough to wear your hair the way you like it."

That was enough of a concession. Mike had asked her for a fresh start. Maybe the first one should be with her mother. Besides, her mother might actually release her from that stupid promise.

"Thank you."

They sat at the Chippendale table, an antique handed down from her mother's family. As Georgie cut up the bread and poured syrup, her stomach clenched. Best to get the elephant out of the room. Big and gray, it would do much better elsewhere.

"Mike was called away, and I watched Rachel while he worked." Her mother's clenched jaw gave her pause, but Georgie forged forward. "I don't want to work for cousin Odalie. I love engines. I love their smell, fixing them, rebuilding them. That's who I am."

"Just like your father." Beverly shook her head, her hazel eyes briefly clouding over.

"I hope that's a compliment."

Beverly rose from the table and went over to her Keurig. Selecting a pod, she pressed buttons before returning. "No matter what people thought, Stephen and I were in love. We were polar opposites from two different worlds, but I loved him all the more for knowing what he wanted, in this case me, and going after it."

"Why don't you talk about him more?" Most of the stories Georgie learned about Stephen George Bennett came from Max or online articles.

Beverly rubbed her hand over her face before she glanced at the coffee maker. Rising, she went over for her cup of coffee. "Don't fuss. It's decaf." She gave a weak grin and then glanced with regret at the cream resting on the table. "It's hard to explain."

"I'll be thirty in a couple of months. Please."

That single word had worked last night when Mike tried it.

Gulping, Beverly raised her eyes and looked off as if she were miles away. "That morning, your father and I had our first fight. I wanted to buy a house with my trust fund. He wanted us to earn the money. When I went to apologize, he was already out on the track."

Georgie covered her mother's hand. Despite cupping the hot mug, her mother's fingers were chilled to the bone.

"I know the next part." Softness laced Georgie's words.

The newspaper articles had gone into detail about the twenty-six-year-old driver. He'd lost control in the last turn of the final lap at Pine Hill Speedway. His pregnant wife had watched horrified when his car crashed into the wall and burst into flames. Each word had been a searing brand. Yet Georgie had read every article multiple times.

A single tear slipped from Beverly's eye. "They said he died on impact. That's never been a consolation."

Georgie walked over and hugged her mother tight, the familiar scent of Chanel No. 5 comforting instead of smothering. Her mother's stiffness sent a shiver of sadness down Georgie's spine. She remained silent until her mother relaxed. Whether it was seconds or minutes, it didn't matter. Georgie had waited forever for this moment. If she stayed in Hollydale, more moments like this might be in the offering.

And maybe more moments with Mike and Rachel.

Maybe she should accept Max's offer and move past the notion of working at the track where her father had died.

Georgie caught her breath. "I'd like for us to have a normal mother-daughter relationship."

"Normal?" Mom shrugged and shuddered. "I don't do that well. Besides, it's hard to have such a relationship when you're gallivanting all over the country."

"We could try. One day at a time, and figure it out together."

Her mother nodded. "I like having you here."

A thump came from the doorway. How did Beau get out? He entered the room and trotted over to Georgie. Mom sighed.

"Even with that dog around." Her mom smiled.

Georgie gave Beau a pat on the head for added confidence. "I'm waiting to hear about a pit crew position at Pine Hill Speedway. As of now, I don't have it." She shrugged and leaned back. "I'll admit Hollydale is growing on me. Beau is, too, but he's not mine. Mr. Reedy wants him back once he leaves rehab. And—"

"Georgie, that dog adores you. Even I can

see that," Mom interrupted and then blew on her coffee, steam rising to her lips. "Surgery and recovery take a lot out of a person." Mom placed her mug back on the table. "It's taken me a month to work up to walking two blocks every morning."

"Beau loves walks. Maybe you could walk him and bond with him." Georgie glanced over her shoulder. Caffeine could wait no longer, and she excused herself and found the perfect pod for this morning. She returned, the expectant look still in Mom's eyes, and Georgie nodded. "Spit out the real reason you made me French toast."

"On my walk, I ran into Melanie Donahue, Sheriff Donahue's wife."

"And?"

Mom rubbed her thumb along Georgie's hand. "There was an attempted burglary last night."

Relief washed over her, and a big smile broke out. "That's great."

Her mother lifted her glasses higher onto the bridge of her nose.

Georgie winced. "Not great for the owner, of course."

"I never thought I'd hear myself defending Michael Harrison, but he's standing up for you."

Mike had told her the truth. Georgie furrowed her brows and gave Beau a scratch behind his ears. "But I wasn't in town for the first burglaries, and I was at his house last night."

"The sheriff wants you to take a lie detector test about the comic books."

"What?" The word exploded out of her, and she jumped up, knocking her coffee over. "I'm innocent."

"I've never doubted that." Her mother retrieved some paper towels and started wiping.

Georgie got more paper towels and helped while Beau settled back at her feet.

Mom's chest rose heavily. "Georgie. There's something I must tell you."

Georgie held up her hand. "Me, first." Her mouth went as dry as her mother's Thanksgiving turkey. "About Mike."

Mom lowered her gaze and tapped the side of her mug. "What about him? He hurt you once."

"Good grief. Eleven years ago." Georgie blew a stray strand of hair off her forehead. "I'm so past that. We're adults now." And he was an attractive adult with brown eyes the color of dark chocolate. "If I stay in Hollydale, he'll be a part of my life."

"If you stay? You've always wanted to see the world and experience life. So much like the old me. After Stephen died, I gave up on adventure."

She took after her mother? Who had once

dreamed of adventure? Wonders never ceased this morning. "Like what?"

Shrugging, Mom played with the handle on her mug. "Owning a small shop. Going back to college. Riding a gondola in Venice."

Striding over, Georgie kissed her mother's cheek. "You're not old at all. Fifty-four is the new thirty-four. Do all of that."

"Don't give up your dreams. Even for me. Promise me you'll never let a man get in the way of doing what's best for you."

"Kevin cured me of that."

"I never liked Kevin, either."

They glanced at each other and laughed, the tension easing away.

"Right now, I have an adventure waiting for me at Max's. The adventure of fixing Miss Louise's sedan."

Mom wrapped her arm around Georgie's arm. So cold. Worry shot through Georgie.

"Promise me you won't let Mike get in the way of what's best for you."

"You've already made me promise to deal with Mike on a business level only." Georgie breathed in and went for it. "I want you to release me from that promise. It's up to me who I get involved with."

"Fine. I release you from that promise. You can decide what you do and when with Michael Harrison." She sat down, cupping her coffee.

"Just promise me you won't let anyone interfere with your dreams. Even me."

That was a different promise, one made with Georgie's welfare at heart. She could live with that.

"Fine." Georgie gestured at Beau, whose ears perked up. "Right now, though, my biggest dream is fixing a whole fleet of cars."

After returning Beau to her garage apartment, Georgie grabbed her purse and headed to her Prius. From the driver's seat, she glanced around. The sun's rays accentuated the reds and oranges of the trees flaming around her. Peak season in the Smokies, and the tourists would continue flocking to Hollydale this weekend.

Her phone buzzed. No doubt Heidi was wondering where she was. Georgie rooted her phone out of her purse.

She blinked. The text wasn't from Heidi but from the pit chief, Brett Cullinan. Her stomach clenched, the taste of syrup now acidic rather than sweet. Taking a deep breath, she opened the text. Her eyes widened.

Congrats on being one of our three finalists for the position. We are conducting interviews and drills next week in Charlotte, NC. What works better for you: next Tuesday afternoon at four or Wednesday afternoon at five? Respond ASAP. Thx, Cullinan.

This was the text she'd been waiting for. Her heart lifted before it crashed back to earth. For so long, meeting Pine Hill Speedway in Charlotte head-on and having a Bennett create a happily-ever-after there by becoming a female pit member had been her dream. Now? Sure, her customers were coming around to her as their mechanic. Every week had seen an uptick in business. Natalie and Lucie seemed to like the car care class. And her mother had opened up to her. Moving would potentially destroy all of that.

Then there were Mike and Rachel. The gangly teenager turned hunky responsible adult who adored his daughter. The bond between father and daughter was strong, the love Mike had evident. Somehow that confidence made him all the more attractive.

Georgie wanted a chance to explore the chemistry between her and Mike. Two kisses, with the promise of more, were worth something. She banged her head against the steering wheel. This was not a decision that should have to be made so early in the morning.

Dreams changed. Maybe her destination had been Hollydale all along.

There was only one answer for Brett Cullinan. *No.* Already her shoulders felt lighter. Her fingers flew across the screen before she stilled, remembering what her mother said not even five minutes ago. Was Georgie using Mike as an excuse not to try? One in three wasn't a sure thing.

She had to know if she was good enough.

She changed the text and asked for the Wednesday slot. Within seconds a reply confirming her choice pinged on the screen.

Even while touring the country, she'd yearned for a chance to work at the same track as her father.

She'd never dreamed, though, about the emptiness spreading through her limbs when she was so close to that reality.

MIKE SCRUBBED HIS face with his hand and peered up at the repair shop. With the cooler crisp autumn air, smells of brake fluid and oil carried out to the parking area. Breathing it in and taking in the fall scenery were all classic signs of stalling, and he knew it. Darn it, if Donahue wanted to keep harping about a polygraph, then the sheriff should ask Georgie to take one. Then when she passed, that would be the end of that.

He felt weighted to the spot. He hoped Georgie would understand that it was Donahue asking him to carry out the order.

Because he'd sure like another chance to kiss her.

Summoning his courage, he entered the repair shop.

"Officer Harrison." Heidi Crowe raised her hand in greeting. "Caught the bad guys yet?"

"Getting closer every day." He removed his sunglasses and smiled. "Georgie around?"

"Working on a Honda Civic. Can I help you or give her a message?"

"See if she has a minute, will you?" He kept his grin as casual as possible.

Her eyebrows quirked downward as if she read him anyway. "Be right back."

Mike skimmed the announcements on the bulletin board. Babysitting, school play, Georgie's car care class. Standard stuff.

"You wanted to see me?" Georgie's husky voice sent quivers through him.

He steeled himself for what he had to do. "We need to talk."

"Let's go into my office."

Hmm, interesting.

Georgie no longer referred to the office as Max's. Was she staying in Hollydale instead of leaving when times became rough? Her eyes shone, and his gut tightened. She believed this was a personal call instead of business.

He shut the door behind him and let out a slow, deep breath. "Are you free tonight?" What a great idea. Get everything with the investigation out in the open and then maybe kiss Georgie again. She was worth the risk of rejection.

She turned, a frown replacing her sweet smile. "Who's asking? Mike or Officer Harrison?" Those emeralds sparkled with a different glint, more dangerous and hard. "My mother told me the sheriff wants me to take a lie detector test."

"Yeah, he does."

Huffing, she shook her head. "I don't know what Sheriff Donahue has against me. My mother couldn't even go for a two-block walk without being told her daughter was still being investigated."

The time to unload everything was now.

"Let's talk." Sighing, he pulled the small aluminum chair out from the corner and unfolded it.

"What's to talk about?" She plopped down in the office chair. "I wasn't here when the thefts began. I was with you last night when you were called in." She ticked off the points on her fingers. "I didn't steal the comic books, and I don't appreciate the sheriff talking about this so freely with his wife."

This time the sharp intake of breath came out of him. He was shocked. Donahue shouldn't be expressing his opinions about the case to his wife, who sure shouldn't be going around confronting anyone's mother about the crimes.

"I'll talk to Sheriff Donahue. He's up for reelection, and the talk around town over the past few months is some people want a younger sheriff." Namely himself. "He's feeling the heat, but that's no excuse not to follow protocol."

Georgie's chin lifted. "I can understand that type of fear, the fear you're not wanted in a place you consider your home."

A jolt hit him right in the chest. "Georgie."

"I know that tone. But you and I are good. Besides, nothing compared to my ex-fiancé telling me I wasn't pretty enough, frilly enough, woman enough for him." Her shoulders slumped, and he stayed still, amazed some jerk couldn't see the treasure in front of him.

"That guy was even more of a fool than me."

"Thank you." The husky words pierced his heart deeper than any arrow. She glanced up, and a faint whisper of a smile broke out. "For the record, I'm innocent."

"I'm doing my best to prove that. I believe you, and I believe in you."

"I know."

"I have a duty to my job, to Donahue and to the community. Without a court order, though, the department can't compel you to go through with the test." The pain in her eyes, even with his softest tone, was evident. "Can you come over tonight? Rachel and Ginger would like to see you." He paused. He couldn't hide behind the women in his family anymore. "Me, too."

Georgie winced, sending his gut down to the floor. "I have a car care class tonight. I moved them to Tuesdays. Here's the reason I came over last night, though. I'd like you and Rachel to go to the Smoky Mountains Car Show with me. It's at the Timber River Park this coming Saturday. You both might be interested in seeing what the Thunderbird will look like once it's reassembled."

Mike rose and couldn't remember the last time the air tasted this sweet.

"It's a date."

CHAPTER FIFTEEN

RACHEL POINTED TO a vintage restored Packard. "Daddy, is that the type of car Grandma and Grandpa drove when you were my age?"

Mike bit back his laughter. "No, kiddo." He glanced at Georgie, that wink meant for him alone. His spirits lifted. A sense of family, long missing, washed over him. "That was before my day. These are all classic cars."

Rachel commandeered the spot between them. Even with the slight disappointment of not walking next to Georgie and holding her hand, he couldn't remember the last time he was this relaxed. Besides, checking Georgie out from a distance wasn't so bad. She'd foregone her usual black T-shirt for a free-flowing burgundy top. The loose style suited her and complemented her curves.

He had only one real complaint. With Georgie around, smelling like a lemon tree and looking so pretty, it was hard to notice the cars. When a guy couldn't concentrate on a Ferrari, its sleek lines the epitome of power, something was up. He blinked and tried to focus on the MGs, gleaming and proud under the bright October sunshine.

Rachel tugged him toward the area where the Mustang Club of Timber River grouped their convertibles together. He gave Rachel's uninjured hand a slight squeeze. "Which one's your favorite?"

"I like them all." Rachel grinned and released his hand, sprinting over to a group of convertibles. "I take that back. This one's really pretty."

She'd gone straight to a fully restored Thunderbird.

He glanced at Georgie, her face as excited as a kid in a toy store with an unlimited budget.

Holding her thumb up, she grinned. "That's your daughter, all right. Your grandfather would be downright proud."

Mike ignored the guilt. Grandpa Ted would have frowned and then said some choice words when Mike transferred the title out of the family for the first time in over fifty years.

Today he'd cut himself some slack. Above all, this was his first break after an intense work week. Community leaders were pressuring Donahue to step aside if he couldn't make an arrest and stop the break-ins. Mike's ribs were sore from all the not-so-subtle nudging to run for sheriff.

No matter where he turned, it was as if everyone were handing him a one-way ticket to the doghouse. Donahue glared at him, even though Mike made his position clear that he wasn't running. Mr. Garrity from the bank, along with members of his posse, sent a glare of disdain his way when Mike said thanks but no thanks.

That doghouse was cold.

All the more reason to enjoy today with his two favorite ladies. Mike caught his breath. Maybe it was the old-fashioned Packards and LaSalles, but he wanted to pull Georgie aside and ask if she'd be his girl.

"Rachel." Georgie's voice, husky and confident, brought him back to the show. She pointed to a red Thunderbird. "This is what your car will look like when it's done."

The sheer stupidity of coming here hit him like a Mack truck. Flaunting the finished product to Rachel courted trouble at its worst. After one final ride he'd be selling it to the highest bidder.

Another mistake notched in his fatherhood belt. Dad had made everything look so easy, taking everything in stride. Hadn't Mike learned anything from him?

"Did I hear you right? Are you restoring a Thunderbird?" A man in his midfifties came over, shorter than Mike's tall frame. His paunch hung over his belted jeans, and he extended a hand to Mike, then Georgie. "I'm Terry Russell, and this here's my beauty."

Georgie squinted while she took her time walking to the front, examining the minute details even he couldn't miss. The cherry trim, the whitewall tires, the bright chrome. Georgie peered into the open engine, the hood extended upward. "My guess is '65 hardtop model with rear-wheel drive, and a V-8."

"The lady knows her stuff." The man whistled. And Georgie nodded.

Mike stood behind her and placed his hand on Georgie's shoulder. "This lady," he stressed each syllable, conveying his deep pleasure, "is a top-notch mechanic. Best I've ever met."

Russell smiled and then pointed to the metal running beneath the driver's-side windows. "Who's doing the restoration on your Thunderbird? Hate to ruin a great car with an amateur effort."

Georgie bristled. "No chance of that. If you're ever in Hollydale, visit Max's Auto Repair and ask for Georgie Bennett."

Another man ventured their way. "Georgie Bennett?" A grin came over his lean face, and he snapped his fingers. "You worked on my Thunderbird in Salem. I never forget a first-rate mechanic."

Her shoulders relaxed enough so Mike could

step back and let her appreciate the compliment. "Thank you." Her surprise came through.

"Bert Quinn's the name." Quinn clapped Russell on his back. "Georgie knows what she's doing. Cut her some slack. She's the best."

Russell held up his hand and tipped his baseball cap toward her. "Sorry. If Bert vouches for you, you're good. Just gets my goat when someone watches a YouTube video and thinks they're an expert. No offense meant."

Georgie dipped her head, her hair bouncing with the motion. "None taken." She turned to Quinn. "Is your Thunderbird here?"

Quinn coughed and glanced at the ground. "Not long after the restoration, I drove her to a car show. On my way home a drunk driver totaled her. Thought she'd be a tank and last forever, but I never saw that Humvee coming."

"That's an absolute shame." Georgie frowned. "She was a beauty."

Quinn agreed. "Been looking for another one for quite some time. None of them bring back the beauty of my Big Red." He reached into his pocket and pulled out a business card. "If you hear of anyone wanting to sell their vintage Ford, whether Mustang or Thunderbird, give me a call. That card has my contact info."

"I've returned to the everyday mechanics of car repair, so I won't have any leads." She handed him the card, but he pushed it back.

"Keep it. You never know. What were you saying about renovating a Thunderbird?"

Rachel pulled on Mike's jacket, and he glanced down. "Daddy, I'm hungry, and you promised me funnel cake."

Bert Quinn. Salem, Oregon. Former Thunderbird owner. Mike filed away the mental note and reached for Rachel's hand. "I most certainly did." As much as he'd like to stay and talk to Quinn about his Thunderbird, this wasn't the right place. This was the fresh start he'd wanted, an owner who'd treasure Miss Brittany, and he was going to grab it.

"One funnel cake coming up." He bobbed his head at Quinn and Russell. "Nice to meet both of you."

Georgie shook Quinn's hand and moved closer to Mike. "His Thunderbird has been in the family forever. It's not for sale, but if I hear of anything, I'll let you know."

"Can I have your business phone number to follow up with that?"

Quinn handed her a pen and one of his business cards. Georgie scribbled something and gave the card and pen back.

Yanking on Mike's arm, Rachel turned to him and smiled. "You can pick out the topping, Daddy."

"Hey, Mike, are you going to buy me one for

bringing you?" Georgie flashed her own smile at him.

His insides took on the consistency of molten lava. She always had a sweet tooth that could match Rachel's.

"Not to mention the cut-rate deal I'm giving you on putting Humpty Dumpty together again."

Keeping his focus on the food tents, he refused to look back at Quinn, Russell or Russell's Thunderbird. Instead, Humpty Dumpty, falling off the wall and shattering to bits, played over and over at the back of his mind. Sure as heck, when she discovered he'd intended to sell the Thunderbird all along, she'd have the power to smash his heart into a million pieces.

Like the fabled egg, he might have no one able to make him whole again.

CHAPTER SIXTEEN

GEORGIE GUNNED THE engine of the Prius and reached for her travel mug of coffee but found only air. She must have left it on the kitchen counter. What a start to her Monday morning. Waking up late meant no breakfast; plus, she'd forgotten her morning infusion of caffeine. Maybe she could sweet-talk Heidi into running across the street to Holly Days Diner. Even better, the Busy Bean beckoned to her, and she lost no time pulling in to the parking lot.

Getting coffee for Heidi and Travis, too, was a bonus.

With an extra spring to her step, she hurried to the entryway, where a departing customer kept the door open for her. She smiled her thanks.

"I'm telling you. I love Hollydale, and I wouldn't say this if I didn't believe it. Georgie Bennett is no thief." Mike's voice boomed and her smile faded away.

"Mike." Connie, the owner of the Book

Nook, tapped Mike on his shoulder as Georgie met her gaze.

"Let me finish, Connie. This is important. Georgie is part of this town, and I'm happy she's moved back." His shoulders stiffened, stretching the navy blue of his starched uniform.

"So am I," Georgie announced. She loved that Mike was willing to stick up for her, but some battles were worth waging for herself, and this was one of them. "I didn't steal from Max or anyone else in Hollydale."

Mike turned around, his belief in her on full display. His radio crackled, and he grabbed the transceiver and listened.

Georgie approached as he sent a wistful glance in her direction. "I have to go. Later?"

Definitely. A whole week had passed too quickly since the car show what with his schedule and her trip to Charlotte. She nodded and watched him leave before facing everyone. Walk out or stay? Before she could make up her mind, Connie Witherspoon stepped toward her.

"Georgie, I haven't stopped by Max's to say hello."

Just a minute ago Mike had defended her to Connie. What had changed? "For the record, I am not a thief."

"I should have realized that when I talked to Donahue. When you were a kid, you brought back that twenty I'd given you as change by mistake. That, along with the great work you did on my mom's car. She's still talking about how quiet her car is running now and she's recommending you to her friends. Come by the bookstore soon. Don't be a stranger, and we'll get to know you all over again." Connie patted Georgie on the shoulder before leaving with her coffee.

At the counter, Georgie ordered for herself and the Crowes. She reached for her wallet, and Deb, the owner, held up her hand. "How about a trade? No charge, and I'll throw in those cinnamon-sugar biscuits you love so much, if you'll change my oil for free this afternoon."

This was what Georgie had missed about Hollydale. People looking out for one another. Georgie extended her hand. "It's a deal."

Deb smiled. "Welcome home, Georgie."

WITH A FLOURISH, Georgie dabbed the finishing touches to the new coat of paint on the primed idler parts. The renovation was coming along faster than anticipated. Too fast for her liking.

After Miss Brittany was reassembled, there'd be no excuses for Mike to drop by the repair shop. That part stunk worse than the solvent for removing the rust and grime.

Running the bristles under water, Georgie shifted her feet. Her evenings with Mike, Rachel and Beau had changed from a way to count down the weeks until she left Hollydale to her favorite time of day.

Now she dreaded countdowns. In a mere twenty-four hours, Mr. Reedy would pick up Beau. If that wasn't hard enough, the day after that, Brett Cullinan was narrowing the candidate field from three to two now that the pit crew tests were complete. And excitement fought with concern over Max's imminent return. He'd expect a decision about whether or not she intended to purchase the business.

Did she want to settle down?

What had begun as five weeks of torture had turned into the best five weeks of her life.

She wasn't ready for it to end.

She didn't want her time with Mike to end.

Whenever she had wanted a new adventure, she'd packed her bags and moved on. New customers and a renovation project for a friend of Miss Louise's, warm greetings on her walks with Beau, and Mike. If those cues to stay were any closer to her face, they'd bite her nose. More than ever, she wasn't ready to retrieve her suitcases from the storage room. It might even be time to put them away for good.

"Georgie. Do you want the good or bad news first?" Heidi's voice broke through her reverie.

"I'm an optimist, so let's get the bad out of the way."

"A friend of Sheriff Donahue canceled their

hundred-thousand-mile service for tomorrow," said Heidi. "On the bright side, Natalie and Lucie are here. Wish I could stay—"

"But you and Travis are off to Baltimore this weekend." Georgie finished the sentence for her. She'd have to talk to the sheriff soon. His misguided notion she had something to do with the theft had to end.

Heidi tilted her head toward the reception area. "I'll serve your cookies before I leave, okay?"

Georgie wriggled out of her gloves and used the bathroom for a quick washup and to change out of her coveralls.

In the reception area Natalie jumped up and squealed, her bright pink boots standing out in the dimness of the room. She ran over and hugged Georgie. "I did it. I changed my oil this weekend."

"Great job." Georgie gave her a high five.

Before she settled next to Lucie, she snatched an oatmeal raisin cookie and savored the first bite. "How was your weekend?" she asked, the words a bit garbled but still comprehensible.

Lucie grabbed a chocolate chip cookie and nibbled on it. "Let's talk about batteries instead."

"What's wrong?"

Lucie lowered the hand with her cookie to her lap. "Nothing for you to worry about."

Georgie's chest throbbed with hurt. Guess she'd been wrong about the past couple of weeks. Here she'd believed she was building friendships with them—sweet Natalie, with her frilly dresses and cowboy boots, and hard-bitten but optimistic Lucie, whose floral shirts were always smudged or spotted with something. Until now, staying aloof had served her and her independence well, or so she'd thought. Friendship wasn't overrated, but it was harder than replacing the brake booster on a pickup truck.

Maybe she'd been wrong about Natalie and Lucie. What if they thought of her as just a teacher and not as a friend?

If she'd been wrong about that, what else had she been wrong about since her return to Hollydale?

Georgie retreated to her end of the couch and rubbed her temples before shoving the rest of the cookie into her mouth. Tasteless.

"Hey, you hurt Georgie's feelings." Natalie defended her, and Georgie loved her for it.

The emptiness still remained.

Mortification crossed Lucie's face as her hand flew to her mouth. "I'm so sorry, Georgie. I just didn't think you'd want to hear the latest. I lost another job."

And here she'd been thinking about herself. Wow. Friendship was a two-way street.

"Next time call me right away to tell me bad news. I'll be over with a pint of ice cream and two spoons."

Lucie's laugh came out as more of a sob. "A pint would do Mattie and Ethan."

"Okay, a gallon and four spoons."

"Five spoons." Natalie inserted herself between them. "I'm part of this little group, too. Growing up, everyone always thought Becks and I were bookends. I love my twin. We'll always have a bond that can't be broken, but she lives in California, and I don't. I need y'all, too."

So many misconceptions based on appearances. Georgie glanced at Lucie. "Will you be okay? Which job?"

"The temporary one. The owner's daughter decided to come back from maternity leave after all. I still have your mom keeping me busy, although she's getting better every day."

There was strength inside Lucie that many had underestimated. Georgie switched her gaze to Natalie. For years Mike's sisters had always been known as Becks-and-Natalie, the syllables all running together. But Natalie, while a wee bit flaky, possessed a deep caring side that matched her intellect.

As for herself?

They accepted her. Could Mike accept the real Georgie? He'd defended her today, so the answer must be yes.

Georgie cleared her throat. "The best way I can show how I feel about you two is to make sure nothing bad happens to either of you on the road. Batteries provide current to the motor. Without your battery, you can't start your car."

Georgie reached for her water bottle, the truth of what she'd said crashing into her. Without her friends, without Rachel and Mike, did she want a new start in Charlotte?

Had what she wanted been here in Hollydale all along?

"ON THREE, WE LIFT." Mike's gaze met Georgie's, and she arched her eyebrows. "One, two, three."

Together they lifted the dashboard. His grunt joined with hers, a herd of elephants in action. The dash weighed a ton. Nothing felt half as good as dropping that sucker into place. Already the Thunderbird seemed to preen from the attention and detail going into her restoration.

Georgie tightened a screw and stepped back. Mike checked out their handiwork with a satisfied smile. He and Georgie made a pretty good team. The car show from a couple of weeks ago had confirmed what he'd seemed to know forever.

Sweat dripped off his forehead, and he swiped at it with his shirtsleeve. With his parents back in town and taking care of Rachel, he'd run out of excuses to continue spending more time with Georgie.

"Break?" In the past month the shop had become as familiar to him as Georgie's husky voice. As special, too.

"I'd like to finish the wiring…" Georgie glanced at him, and the left side of her mouth quirked up. "Sure."

They walked past the auto bays, the first with a diesel truck, before passing a Kia. The whiff of oil and gasoline fumes used to make him lightheaded, but they no longer fazed him. On the other hand, Rachel still pinched her nose, refusing to hug him until he took a long, hot shower.

"How's business?" He held the door open for her. Even with her independent streak, she allowed him this small courtesy. He loved anything he could do to make her life easier.

"It's picking up. More people are asking for me. Today was our first Wednesday senior citizen discount day, and our business increased quite a bit." Pride tinged her words. He smiled at the change steady business could make in a person's outlook.

Georgie led him to the new minifridge behind the reception desk and handed him a bottle of cold water. He unscrewed the cap and swigged a long sip. The coolness quenched that parched spot in his throat.

"Thank you for what you said at the Busy Bean. How's business on your end? Have the burglaries stopped altogether?"

"No new break-ins. Edwards and I are following up some promising leads. With the deadline to register to run for sheriff in thirteen days, Donahue is happy he's running unopposed, and the atmosphere at work is lighter."

Relief broke out on her face. "That's good. Maybe we'll see more of each other."

Mike laid his hand over hers, warmth from the sheer presence of Georgie filling all the spots empty over the past years.

Empty since Caitlyn left? Or empty since he'd written that stupid letter to Georgie, choosing the sure thing over the right thing?

It didn't matter. What mattered was Georgie was here, in Hollydale, and the car was bringing them together.

Best to find out if it had the power to drive them apart.

"Sheriff Donahue hired Jonathan Maxwell for one of the two vacant positions yesterday, so my schedule should start improving soon." He smiled, the assurance more for him than her. "He's new to the area but experienced in law enforcement."

"I like your update." She wrinkled her forehead and approached him until she was close enough to tap her finger on his shoulder.

"Last time you said you wouldn't wait so long for our next kiss."

He smiled, wanting that more than anything. Georgie always put all of herself into whatever she set her mind to. Losing himself in a swirl of lemon meringue pie for a few seconds was all he could allow before he broke off.

"Georgie."

Mere appreciation for all she was doing for him didn't even begin to scratch the surface. This intensity of what was developing between them almost scared him, but he'd lost her once. He wouldn't lose her again.

He caressed the softness of her cheek.

She leaned into his touch and then jerked away. "Is Caitlyn back?"

"Never. She relinquished all rights to me a long time ago." He blinked, shaking his head. "Rachel and I have that in common. Neither of us having our biological mothers in our lives. I'm so thankful for the Harrisons. They made sure I always felt wanted, and I'm making sure Rachel knows how much I love her."

"Hmm. Growing up with one parent? It just hit me Rachel and I are alike that way."

"Your mother produced one heck of a daughter."

His breath whooshed out. Unlike Georgie, though, he hoped Rachel wouldn't always live with only one parent. But for now, he alone made the choices about what was best for Rachel's financial welfare.

That was why he had to give up Miss Brittany.

"You're doing a great job with Rachel." Georgie gave the tiniest hint of a smile and reached for his hand, squeezing it with a lightness that surprised him. "She loves you, and you're so supportive of her. She's clever and super bright. She certainly doesn't think inside the box. My type of girl."

"Since Caitlyn left, it's up to me to make sure Rachel has everything she needs." He sat on the couch, and Georgie settled next to him, her lemon scent and sweet smile distracting, to say the least. He fought to get back on track. "And a little of what she wants as well."

A phone buzzed. It wasn't his.

"Sorry. Heidi's not here so I have to get that." Georgie ran over to the desk and scooped up the portable handset, returning to his side with an aggravated growl. "It's Bert Quinn. This is the third time this week he's called."

"Go ahead and answer."

She shot him a warning look but went ahead and pressed the accept button. "Hello, Mr. Quinn. Okay, then, Bert. No, I haven't heard of any new Thunderbirds in need of repair." She rolled her eyes, along with her hand, in a sweeping circular motion. "Yes, I'm sure Mike

Harrison has no intention of selling his grandfather's Thunderbird."

The hairs on the back of his neck prickled. He stood and reached out for the phone.

"Mr. Quinn, this is Mike Harrison. Can you give me specifics about what you want and what you're willing to pay?"

Mike listened, the blood draining away from his face. Thirty-five thousand dollars for a restored Thunderbird, one in mint condition. "I'll get back to you."

Before he could say anything else, Georgie snatched the phone back. "Talk to you later, Bert." She crossed her arms. "Why'd you ask him those questions?"

"I'm a single father." Blowing out a deep breath, Mike stood next to her. "Right now, I can't give Rachel any of the things she deserves. Her friends stay after school for dance lessons. I can't afford that."

Georgie held up her hand and waved him off. "She doesn't want that. She wants time with you. You're raising a lovely kid. She's independent and smart and caring. Being with you and your family means the world to her. The Thunderbird is your family's past. Isn't that the legacy you want for her?"

"I want her to experience life, and some things in life require money."

"The best things in life don't."

Their gazes met; electricity sizzled in the air. Deep down, Mike knew Georgie was right, yet Carl and Diane Harrison sacrificed for him. He'd do no less for his child.

"I'm selling the Thunderbird."

Georgie had no reaction apart from staring at him. His heart shattered. What he'd feared all along was true. Georgie wouldn't be able to get past this. Turning his back on Miss Brittany was the same as turning his back on Georgie.

"You've made up your mind, haven't you?" Her voice cracked, and she clenched her jaw. "Rachel needs you, not lessons. She needs what that car represents. Tradition, family, love."

Who needed those most? Rachel? Or Georgie?

He wouldn't lie anymore. If he didn't accept himself, warts and all, he couldn't ask anyone else to do so. Son, cop, single father. Pride surged through him.

"Rachel deserves more. She burned herself because I wasn't watching her." His breath caught. "This is the least I can do for her."

"And who looks out for you? I'm asking as your friend." The pleading was there, yet he couldn't meet her gaze, not now. "Selling the Thunderbird would be a huge mistake. Kids grow up so fast, but you have this treasure underneath your nose. Don't sell for the wrong reasons."

"When I sell, it will be for the right reasons."

Mike watched as the bay door swung open and then closed behind her. As much as he wanted to, he didn't follow. She had called herself his friend. Nothing more, nothing less.

He didn't like it, but he respected her.

He walked out.

CHAPTER SEVENTEEN

THE SINGLE-STORY brick police station was more imposing today than ever. Georgie paused and glanced at the pink cake box in her hands. Chocolate cupcakes from the Night Owl Bakery couldn't be considered a bribe, could they? Okay, so she was trying to bribe her way back into Mike's good graces. Nothing else. His weakness for sweets was well documented in the Harrison household, and cupcakes tasted much better than crow.

Her stomach roiled at how she'd bolted when Mike was only trying to explain. Her mother made it sound as if parenthood were only a duty, whereas Mike loved Rachel. Duty with love behind it was a powerful motivator.

For her to walk out on Mike last night? Even if she didn't agree with his decision about the Thunderbird, she shouldn't have lost her temper.

Relationships deserved more. The unsettled air between them sizzled for a reason. Mere friends didn't feel the way she felt inside whenever he was around—all quivery, as if there weren't enough oxygen in the atmosphere. Mere friends didn't share amazing kisses that made her legs go weaker than a race car after a lap around the track at two hundred miles per hour.

She entered the station and shored herself up. The first person she encountered would have to be Sheriff Donahue, the man who wouldn't let up about the burglary at Max's.

"Well, Miss Bennett." His dry tone didn't escape her. "What brings you here on this fine fall day? Don't suppose you're here to schedule a lie detector test about those comic books?"

"When you catch the burglars, ask them to take a polygraph test."

"Did the burglar sell the comic books online direct? Or did she fence them?"

If he thought his piercing gaze would make her waffle, when she'd done nothing wrong and had lived with Beverly Bennett most of her life, he was sadly mistaken.

"Since I didn't take them, I wouldn't know. I'd appreciate it if you stopped blaming me for something I didn't do." She refused to let him bait her. Instead, she pasted a smile on her face and asked, "Is Officer Harrison here?"

"In the back." Donahue jerked his finger to the hallway and frowned. "The department disapproves of visits of a personal nature."

At that moment, Melanie Donahue swept inside. "Hello, Georgie." She walked over and grazed the sheriff's cheek with her lips. "Hello, you."

"As you were saying…" Georgie kept her smirk to herself.

"Take as long as you need." His words came out as mottled as the red blotches spreading over his cheeks.

Georgie held her head high until she found Mike in the back. Then her confidence wavered.

He noticed her and blinked, giving a quick shake of his head. "Georgie?"

She thrust the box forward. "I come bearing gifts."

But he stayed where he was. "I'm the one who should be throwing out the olive branch. I should have told you sooner. Once the car was in pieces, I lost my courage. I thought you'd leave, the same as Caitlyn."

Georgie wasn't happy at the comparison before the truth washed over her like a soft blanket of rain. She relaxed her shoulders and her voice. "Only I came back." With her nerves finally getting to her, she shirked her thumb toward the entrance. "Can we talk outside for a couple of minutes? I won't keep you long."

She couldn't get over how proud he looked in his navy uniform. Sure, the road home had some potholes, but she was here. There was nowhere else she cared to be.

He hesitated, and her stomach started sinking toward her ankles. The box in her hands felt as heavy as an anchor, and she started toward the nearest table. "I'll go ahead and leave these here. They're for you and Rachel." She swiveled on her heel, intent he wouldn't see her upset.

"Wait." The honesty in his voice compelled her to stop, even though it took effort.

She turned around, the pleading in his gaze heartrending.

"Thanks for whatever's in the box. You're right. It's best we go somewhere private."

He opened the back door, extending his arm for her to go first. With a quick nod, she hurried past him, the smell of soap, shampoo and Mike overcoming the strong bleachy scent of the station. The crisp air enveloped her in welcome coolness.

The wind picked up, and a scurry of leaves scattered into mounds beneath the shade trees lining the street. All around her change was happening as fall surrounded them in all its glory. What changes lay in store for her and Mike? She wasn't the type to stand by and watch everything happen around her. Taking charge was more her style.

The zing in her chest stopped her forward progress. She ran her gaze over him, chills overtaking her. This was Mike. Her high school buddy. All grown up with broad shoulders and a kind heart.

She more than liked everything about him.
In fact… *Whoa.* She loved Mike Harrison.

For too long they'd counted on friendship to express any unspoken words, both too scared of change that might wrench another loved one from their midst. The flutters in her chest quit. This time there was no going back. They'd lost each other once. She didn't want to lose him again. Shivers ran through her.

"Georgie. You have the funniest expression on your face." He reached up and touched her forehead.

The world spun all around her.

"How many fingers am I holding up?"

"Three, you dolt."

Then he flashed two fingers before switching to four, then one.

She laughed in spite of herself. "I'm fine. Why didn't you tell me about the Thunderbird sooner?"

"Most of the time I try to dwell on the positives." He shrugged and leaned against the brick building. "Lately it's been one thing after another. I've just tried my best to weather every storm."

"Aye aye, skipper."

He smiled and shook his head. "Just what I want to hear from the prettiest woman in Hollydale. I have dog eyes."

"Wait a minute." She jammed her hands into

her pockets and met his gaze. "You think I'm pretty?"

"I know you're pretty. You just don't see yourself like I see you."

Her mother had always told her she'd be prettier if she wore clothes that fit properly and let her hair grow out. But it didn't matter what her mother had ever said. What mattered was how Georgie viewed herself. So she sometimes had grease and grime under her fingernails? She liked who she was. Who she is.

If Mike liked her, too, that was a bonus beyond compare.

"Thanks." The left corner of her mouth quirked up as a wry chuckle squirmed out. "You're not bad looking yourself."

"What are we doing, Georgie?"

"What do you mean? I'm here to bring you a peace offering. I already feel bad. Earlier today Mr. Reedy picked up Beau." She stopped, her voice giving out. She hadn't wanted to make this about herself.

"Oh, Georgie." He came over and rubbed her cheek.

"He wasn't mine to begin with. And Miss Brittany is your car. If you need to sell it to provide for Rachel..." Her throat clogged worse than a rusty fuel line.

"The Hollydale Hoedown is coming up in two weeks."

"The what?" Shrugging, she rubbed her right ear as that sure sounded like a dance. They didn't have a good track record with dances. "What's that?"

"About five years ago, the mayor started a yearly dance as a fund-raiser for our town's community center. People buy tickets, dress up and have fun." He smiled and reached for her hands. "I stood you up eleven years ago. Will you give me another chance?"

His brown eyes twinkled. They danced and dared, waiting for her answer.

"But yesterday…" She shifted her weight and left other words unsaid.

"We disagreed and you walked out. Today you came and we talked. You could call it our first fight and make-up session." He grinned that devilish grin she'd always loved. "I have a feeling it won't be our last."

"But a dance…" She gulped and checked out her jeans, already smudged with a wipe of oil, grease and some other unidentified sticky substance. Her breaths came out fast and unsteady. Of all the first dates, he wanted to take her someplace where she'd have to dress up?

"I can read you like a book right now." He stroked her cheek. "I don't care if you want to wear a gunnysack or jeans or whatever. I want to show up at your door," he stopped, sighed and stared up at the sky, "announce myself to your mother and dance with you. Once we're there, it's up to you how long we stay. Our first date."

A date with Mike?

"A dance is outside of my comfort zone, but as your daughter said, there's no such thing as a box. The answer is yes."

MIKE HAD INSISTED on tonight's hush-hush stake-out after noticing a pattern in the timing of the other burglaries. He yawned and positioned his binoculars toward a block of buildings that hadn't been burglarized.

Cramped into his mom's hatchback with no one for company—not a perfect way to spend an evening.

Disgusted with the lack of success on this case, he grabbed the last cupcake from the Night Owl Bakery box and wolfed it down. The sweetness of the icing appeased him, and he thought again about how much he appreciated having Edwards as backup, stationed nearby, rather than the sheriff. Donahue was asleep in bed, so Mike's plan for a cloak of secrecy was now in motion.

Pouring a cup of coffee, Mike breathed in the rich aroma, then set it to cool. He rubbed the sleepiness out of his eyes. He'd been focusing so much on the burglaries themselves he hadn't considered the lives of locals. Had any Hollydale residents showed significant financial gains in the past three months?

He picked up his thermos lid full of coffee and blew, dissipating the steam hovering there.

Max's Auto Repair. Mike's breath caught. Heidi and Travis Crowe. According to Georgie, they'd been traveling all over the place. Traveling cost money.

Could they be behind the robberies?

Out of the corner of his eye, Mike caught sight of an older model white Ford Explorer rolling to a stop in front of the bakery. The hair on the back of his neck stood up. What sane driver at night didn't use headlights? *Drivers up to no good, that's who.*

Mike reached for his walkie-talkie and pressed the button. "Edwards?"

Two figures, one stocky and short, the other taller and lean, jumped out of the car and pulled black ski caps over their faces. *Payday.*

"Ten-Four. Over."

"Suspects on premises." He recounted the details and then ran through a mental checklist of his utility belt. Blood pounded in his ears. Even though this was Hollydale, apprehending perps always held an element of risk. He waited for the sense of calm before proceeding. "I'm alerting dispatch and then going in. Ready?"

Mike approached the bakery with the stealth of a panther ready to pounce. He caught sight of

Edwards and nodded. They neared the back entrance, the scratched door and broken lock clear signs of forced entry. With a nod of his head, he and Edwards both readied their weapons.

Mike took the lead, adrenaline charging through him. "I'll go first."

Elbowing his way in, Mike lunged, his weapon drawn. "Police!"

The two perps raised their hands.

"Don't shoot. We're not armed." One cried out, genuine fear in his voice.

"Oh, man. My grandfather's gonna kill me." The other perp moaned.

Mike recognized that voice and gave an inward groan. Edwards checked the rest of the bakery. "All clear."

Stepping toward the second suspect, Mike lowered his gun, patted him down and snapped handcuffs on him while Edwards did the same to the other one. With a deep breath, Mike removed the guy's ski cap, revealing Sheriff Donahue's teenage grandson, tears already running down the youth's face.

"We're in big trouble, aren't we?"

Mike merely nodded and read Zachary Donahue his rights.

CHAPTER EIGHTEEN

No sooner had Georgie set out the usual boxes
of cookies than the front door of the repair shop
flew open, bringing in a gust of cool air and
Natalie.

"Why didn't you tell me?" Natalie rushed
over and hugged her before stepping back.

"Because everyone in town hasn't been talking about anything else except the robbers'
identities over the weekend?" Georgie shrugged
with a smile. Then her gaze flittered down to
Natalie's red cowboy boots. They might be a
little conspicuous in Hollydale, but they suited
her friend.

Natalie reached for a chocolate chip cookie and
scarfed it down. "Sorry, didn't get a chance to
eat lunch today. My planning period was crazy."
She closed her eyes and licked the crumbs off her
lips. Then she opened her eyes again. "I wasn't
talking about Zach Donahue. Why didn't you
tell me about your date?"

Georgie's jaw dropped. The room grew

twenty degrees hotter as a rush of warmth flooded her cheeks. "Um…"

Yeah, friends confided stuff like that. She was still learning. Just then Lucie entered, and Georgie sent her a silent thank you.

"Sorry I'm late. Twin trouble." She bit her lip and hung her purse on the coat rack.

Natalie kept her gaze steady, and Georgie knew she wouldn't give up without an answer. "I thought it would be weird to talk about going to a dance with your brother."

Dating Mike. Both of their rather rocky roads led to this point. His road looped around Hollydale, and while hers wound around the whole Eastern Seaboard with a short hop to the West Coast, the detours had been necessary. They hadn't been ready for each other when they were younger.

Lucie chose an oatmeal raisin cookie. "If it works out with Mike, you can have my wedding dress. If it doesn't, I'm learning karate with the twins, and you can come with us to the studio. This new job still lets me help your mom, who's getting better every time I see her. Soon she won't need me. Then I'll work at the dress shop during the day and work at the karate studio after school. Lessons come with the job so I can bring the twins with me."

Georgie frowned. "Are you okay? You always go for chocolate chip."

"I wanted a change. Sometimes it's nice to break out of the same-old, same-old and reach for the stars." Lucie sat on the closest aluminum chair and bit into her cookie.

And sometimes it was right to come back home and return to the familiar. Was it Hollydale that had changed, or her? No matter. The time was right to stay here for good.

The fact Mike Harrison believed in her was a bonus. If that belief came with love attached, settling down wasn't settling at all. The only remaining question was whether to contact Brett Cullinan and withdraw her name or wait until she found out if she'd be offered the position, which she would then refuse. She'd lost her heart, not her pride. A few days wouldn't change what she felt for Mike.

"Speaking of changes." Natalie glanced at Lucie, who smiled in a Cheshire-cat sort of way.

"Go ahead and tell her."

Georgie narrowed her eyes. When had these two developed telepathic powers? This wasn't going to be good. She released that pent-up breath.

"Care to let me in on the secret?"

"Let's get this car care class started. Afterward we're going shopping." Lucie sat back and sighed. "I miss shopping." She gave a shy smile before glancing at her phone. "Odalie is letting me open the shop just for you. It'll be fun, but we need to hurry. I have only two hours of babysitting arranged, and I can't afford to pay overtime."

"Whoa!" Georgie held up her hands. "No one said anything about shopping."

She shuddered at the *s* word.

"Besides," Georgie blustered, "I have you all to myself on Tuesday nights, and today we're talking exterior maintenance. That shouldn't be rushed."

Natalie sighed and reached for another cookie. "I elect Lucie to be in charge of shopping."

Lucie opened her mouth, but Natalie cut her off.

"Rachel and I are finishing her science fair project tomorrow night. I'll watch Ethan and Mattie for you."

Lucie gasped, her blond ponytail swaying back and forth. "They'd destroy her project."

"No, they won't." Natalie arched her eyebrow, a determined gleam in her eye. "I won't let them. How quickly you forget I'm a twin. I know the tricks of the trade. This is my brother's first date in years. I haven't seen him this happy in a long time."

Georgie's insides twisted up. She made Mike happy? "Okay, I'll go shopping." Her tongue grew thick and heavy at the word. "But if we don't find anything, we don't buy anything."

Her gaze roved over Natalie's sundress with a denim jacket and Lucie's frilly top with a smear of ketchup at one cuff and a mustard stain on the other. "And nothing that isn't me."

"Agreed." Lucie stuck her hand out and they shook.

THE NEXT NIGHT, Georgie entered Odalie's small boutique with Lucie at her side. The smell of roses and honeysuckle filled the rarified air, and Georgie panicked, already counting the minutes until it would be polite to leave.

After locking the door behind her, Lucie smiled as if a weight had lifted from her shoulders. She was enjoying an evening out. For Lucie, Georgie would endure shopping.

Georgie hustled forward. "Let's get this over with."

A bull in a china shop stood out less than she did right now. Beautiful fabrics, chunky jewelry and soft music gave her the creeps. Give her grunge, flannel and good ol' grease any day of the week.

"Come here." Lucie waved her over, and Georgie's stomach roiled at the frilly lace decorating the overlay of the dress. "I see that face. Just listen to me for a minute." Lucie held up the dress to her frame. "This is what I'd wear if I was going to the hoedown, and an eclectic print with cowboy boots would suit Natalie. You, however, are not meant for frills and furbelows."

"Fur-what?" Thank goodness she didn't see anything with fur linings. She'd have left in a second.

"Furbelows. Anything that looks overly girly, like this." Lucie held up a pink ruffled confection of a dress before she placed it back on the rack. "Avoid it like the plague."

They were in total agreement on that. Georgie eyed a dress with a plain top and a leopard print as if it were a V-8 engine in a Honda Civic.

"Good grief. This isn't torture, you know." Lucie shook her head. "Didn't your mother ever take you shopping?"

"We made a deal. She picked out my dress for cotillion—" Georgie shivered at the memory "—and I got to wear jeans and T-shirts the rest of the time."

Maybe it was time she and Beverly went on a mother-daughter outing. Retail therapy always helped Mom.

"Shopping isn't a four-letter word, Georgie." Lucie glared and then concentrated on the racks.

"If frilly is out and prints are out, what's left?" Georgie tapped her foot and crossed her arms. She gave up an evening with Miss Brittany for this? Then again, it kept her mind off Beau. Forty-eight hours and counting since Mr.

Reedy had picked him up. Loneliness filled her heart.

"Something like this." Lucie held up a red dress made of some sort of clingy material with a V-neck that would reveal some cleavage but not all.

"I'd stick out like a sore thumb in that."

"You know what your problem is?" Lucie leaned in, her whisper fierce and for Georgie's ears only. "You don't think you deserve pretty things. You won't stop being tough if you wear a dress. Your true self, the caring tomboy you that we all love, will always shine through, but it's okay to treat yourself to something beautiful."

Georgie fingered the fabric. The soft silk caressed her rough calluses. Biting her lip, she searched Lucie's face.

As if answering her, Lucie held out the dress. "Try it on."

Minutes later the knock on the dressing room door alerted Georgie to Lucie's presence. Hesitating, Georgie glanced at the mirror one more time. The short sleeves showcased her arms, muscular from her work but not overly so. The smooth fabric clung to her curves, stopping just past her knees.

Catching sight of the tag, she winced and stepped out of the dressing room.

"Lucie, this dress would feed me for a month." She folded her arms and frowned.

Her friend's staggered breath said too much. Georgie should have known she'd look ridiculous in this. She turned toward the stall.

"If you don't buy that dress, I'll call your mother, and she'll buy it for you. You're gorgeous."

If Lucie had that type of reaction, would Mike?

Less than a week until she'd find out. While not the prom, this evening held so much more promise, as sure as the promise in Mike's chocolate-brown eyes. This dance was the beginning of their future.

And this dress might set her back a day's salary, but it was the one for her.

"THE PARTS FINALLY came today!" Excitement broke out on Georgie's face. She ran her hand over the Thunderbird's fin. Now she could get back to restoring the classic car.

Mike couldn't help but smile at her enthusiasm.

"You're keeping a list, right? Once the car sells, I'm paying you what you would have charged, plus parts and labor." Mike regretted the words as soon as they left his mouth. They made this sound like a business arrangement and nothing more.

When Georgie meant so much more to him.

Her nostrils flared for a brief second, and

she shook her head. "As the *friend*," she said, putting enough stress on the word for him to step back clear to Asheville, "who is going with you to the hoedown, I'm going to ignore that. This isn't about money to me, Mike. It's about spending time with the people closest to you. Remember how we'd drive with your grandfather for the fun of it? You and your grandfather accepted me and included me. Those adventures to Sully Creek and Timber River kept me going. They were my lifeline."

Rachel ran in, and some of the tension in the air dissipated. "Miss Georgie, I don't have to wear my dressing on my hand at night anymore."

Georgie clapped and reached for Rachel's good hand, swinging her around in a wide circle. "That is great news."

Rachel giggled and plopped her backpack at Georgie's feet. "How's Miss Brittany?"

"Come and see." Georgie pulled her over toward the Thunderbird. "Tonight we're going to finish rebuilding the engine. That's why I'm so happy the parts arrived. We won't fall behind schedule this way."

Schedule? There was a schedule for this? He liked puttering around, putting the car back together bit by bit. Same as they were rebuilding their friendship, a friendship he didn't mean to test so often, a friendship he hoped would become more at the Hollydale Hoedown two nights from now. He took a good long look, the not-so-subtle changes in the Thunderbird quite astounding. Georgie wasn't just restoring her. She was making her shine, with Miss Brittany's character emerging stronger and prouder than ever.

This car was their past, their present. If only it could be part of their future.

Wishing never solved anything. Hard work and duty did.

While Georgie pointed out the progress to Rachel, Mike drank in the sight of his two favorite ladies getting along so well. The slow hum that had attacked his brain when he responded to the B&E call was now a full buzz.

"How can I help, Miss Georgie?" Rachel's sweetness snapped him out of another reverie. But he stayed silent, not wanting to disrupt the interaction between Georgie and Rachel.

Of course, if Rachel weren't here, he'd…what would he do? Work on the Thunderbird? Kiss Georgie? She was more than he deserved. As she brought Miss Brittany back to life, so, too, had she brought his rusty heart back to life. Fun and caring, she reminded him of the side of himself he'd lost touch with. Everything swirled together, and he couldn't imagine her leaving Hollydale again.

"How can we help, Miss Georgie?" He stepped

forward and echoed his daughter's words. "Use me any way you like. I'm yours."

Georgie threw him a look, part exasperation, part mirth. "Michael Harrison, I don't know what to do with you."

"More like you don't want to know what you'd do without me anymore, either." He winked. Sunshine, lemon trees and pie. Those were what Georgie deserved.

"Hello? Anyone here?" His father's voice came from the reception area.

Georgie went toward the voice, shaking her head all the while. He smiled to himself, swearing he heard a small chuckle.

"In here, Mr. Harrison," Georgie called to his dad. "Come join the party."

"Grandpa!" Rachel ran over to her grandfather as he appeared in the doorway. "Come see Miss Brittany. She's growing prettier every day."

"Same as you, my darlin' girl." Dad reached over and ruffled Rachel's hair. Rachel pulled him into a hug, and he glanced over Rachel's head. "Georgie Bennett, it's been too long, and I'm Carl, not Mr. Harrison."

Rachel released her grandfather. He walked over and extended his hand. Georgie wiped her hand on her coveralls before offering hers in return. "Sorry to hear about your father passing away. He was a good man."

"The best." Dad walked toward the Thunderbird and whistled. "After she'd been in the barn for so long, I never thought she'd be in this good of condition again."

And this without the doors and bumpers yet.

"Dad, how'd you know I was here?" Changing the subject to something more neutral seemed safe, dependable. Much like how he'd been living life the past couple of years.

Until Georgie had returned.

"Little Miss Sunshine told Natalie, who told your mother, who decided dinner at Holly Days would hit the spot after a hard day's work. Besides, we're still recovering from visiting Becks. Chocolate-cream-pie night every Thursday, you know. My favorite." Dad rubbed his stomach and licked his lips.

"That's my favorite, too, Grandpa." Rachel jumped up and down, her brown ponytail keeping time with her bounces.

"That's why I stopped by. Your grandmother insisted on inviting all of you." He glanced over Georgie's way and nodded. "You're more than welcome, Georgie. It'll be like old times."

"Thanks, Mr.—" she grinned and rolled her eyes "—Carl. I'm going to pass, though. I'm almost done with the engine, and I don't want to mess with progress."

Dad looked at him. Mike shrugged. Sure, he hated disappointing Mom, but there was no way he'd go out for dinner while Georgie stayed behind and worked. "Can you take Rachel? I'll pick her up as soon as I'm done here."

"Once Georgie declined, I expected nothing less." Dad grinned and reached for Rachel's hand.

"Aw, I don't want to miss out on anything here." Rachel jutted out her bottom lip and scuffled the cement with the tip of her hot-pink sneaker.

"Go ahead and have fun with your grandparents." Mike went over, hugged Rachel and nudged her toward the door.

"Come on, squirt." Dad reached out his hand to Rachel, a gleam in his blue eyes, the same as Becks's and Natalie's. "You know your grandma will have one bite of her chocolate cream pie before she declares she's full and gives you the rest."

The door closed behind the pair, the hinges squeaking a last goodbye. His breath caught as he realized he was alone with Georgie. Actually alone. No pets, no Heidi or Travis, no Rachel.

Messing with progress? Did he chance it? The last time he believed he was making progress with a relationship, he woke up to a "Dear Mike" note attached to the refrigerator door. More than anything else in his life, he'd vowed right then and there never to send bad news by a letter ever again.

Georgie was examining socket wrenches on the back pegboard. If he messed this up—and he didn't have the best track record for successful relationships—he might lose Georgie, both as a friend and as a partner.

If he didn't try, though, he'd definitely lose her.

Yet he hesitated. Would this sound better under the stars with a band in the background and twinkling lights sending a soft glow of romance around the evening?

To most women, perhaps. But Georgie Bennett wasn't most women. The sweetness in hearing a broken engine running once more always trumped traditional romance for her. This repair shop, with its pungent odor of brake fluid and gasoline, would be a better backdrop for a serious discussion about relationships for them.

He arrived at her side and bent down. "How can I help?"

"It's okay if you want to have dinner with your family. I can handle this by myself."

"I wouldn't be anywhere else right now." And he meant it. He removed his jacket and placed it on a hook. Returning, he ran his hand over the cool metal of the work table, clear of unnecessary clutter. So like Georgie.

"You can still catch up with them. I don't mind." She picked up the wrench before shaking her head and swapping it out for another.

Walking toward the Thunderbird, she dropped the wrench again, and he picked it up. They reached for it together, her hand trembling. So the nervousness rocking his insides wasn't limited to him.

"Georgie." Crouching on the hard cement floor wasn't comfortable, but he didn't dare straighten for fear of breaking the connection between them, a connection growing stronger every day they spent together. "Are you trying to get rid of me?"

"I can do this myself." If it weren't for the pleading in those green eyes, searching him, forcing him to dig deep into himself to his core, he'd almost believe her.

He covered her hand with his. "We work well as a team."

They always had. Even way back when they were doing something silly like toilet papering the principal's yard on Halloween, they'd always complemented each other's strengths. Her fire to his ice.

She straightened, and he scrambled to his feet, as well. To heck with it. Why wait? He leaned down and kissed those red lips, plump and full. Lemon broke through the gasoline smells and permeated all of his senses. Bringing his hand to her face, he caressed her cheek, her smooth skin soft under his rougher fingertips. Metal rattled on concrete. She must have dropped the wrench again. He didn't care. Instead, he pulled her closer. His heart soared with Georgie here, with him.

Seconds passed before she stepped away. "You're right. Teamwork has its advantages."

He grinned. "Yep."

She bent down and grabbed the wrench. Thrusting it at him, she returned his smile. "Work first. Then fun."

"Aye aye, skipper." He gave a mock salute, his chest thrust out. "Lead the way."

They settled into a comfortable rhythm, car therapy good for his morale. The sound of his smartphone buzzing brought his head up. With the burglars caught, he hadn't anticipated any work calls tonight. Must be his parents or Rachel. He hurried over to his jacket, where he'd left his phone. The screen was blank.

"It's my phone, not yours." Georgie waved hers in front of him. "We must have the same alert sound."

Her hand flew over her mouth, and her eyes widened.

"Is it your mother? Is she okay?" Considering how Beverly Bennett felt about him, he'd have to find some way to convince Georgie's mother he wasn't half-bad. Georgie remained still. Chills shimmered through every inch of his body. "What's wrong?"

She shook her head and performed a jig. "Nothing's wrong. Everything's right."

A perfect summary of his world, as well.

"Care to share the good news?"

With a sigh, she reached for his hand and didn't let go until they settled on the couch in the reception area, the bright LED lights hurting his eyes. His stomach clenched tighter with every passing second. "Georgie?"

"You caught the burglars, right?"

"Yeah. They're juveniles, so I can't speak about the case, though."

Releasing her, he rubbed his forehead, where a slight pressure was building. If he thought people were pushing him to run for sheriff before the arrest, that was nothing compared to now. The arrest had hurt so many, in more ways than one. Donahue was on a leave of absence. Some were calling for his resignation, while others defended him.

The truth stared him in the face, though. If Donahue resigned, no one else was as qualified for the position as he was. The deadline for declaring for the election was next Tuesday.

"So I'm in the clear."

"Of course. I never doubted you." He shrugged and lifted the left side of his mouth. "Maybe I did in the beginning. For all of five minutes."

As much as he'd wanted to hide himself from

her, there was something about her that let him lower his guard, let her see the real him hidden in the depths.

"What's this all about?"

"Before I came back, I applied for a job on a pit crew. Actually, the job's as good as mine. The text is from the team manager giving me a heads-up in case I wanted to look for a place to live."

"Where?"

"Charlotte."

"What? Georgie?" He jumped up, and for once he didn't care about staying calm. For years he'd thought if he was the dutiful son, the Harrisons wouldn't get rid of him. For months he thought marrying Caitlyn would help them bond over time, a shared link with Rachel. No more. "You never said anything about moving."

"Now you're the one making assumptions."

Assumptions? Sounded like a done deal to him.

"How long have you known about this?" He couldn't even remember the last time he'd raised his voice. Blood rushed through his veins. For the third time in his life, the carpet was being yanked out from under him. Looking at Georgie's calm expression, there wasn't a thing he could do about this time, either.

"Since my mother's stent operation."

Stunned, he fell into the armchair. Not once

had she told him. Not once had she even given a hint about it. Just like Caitlyn.

How could she be so calm? Didn't he mean anything to her? Georgie was always fire to his ice. Now that the positions were reversed...

"Sort of ironic. The first time I find something worth fighting for, worth reaching for the stars, I crash to the ground." He hadn't had any say when his biological mother gave him up for adoption. Then again, that decision had changed his life for the better.

When push came to shove, Caitlyn's actions also helped him.

He couldn't see how Georgie's decision would make his life better. Not with her three hours away.

Reason restored his vision. This wasn't about making his life better. This was about her dreams. Growing up, she'd idolized her father, gone in a blink of an eye before she was even born. If Mike truly cared for Georgie, he'd have to let her go.

His heart broke.

He didn't just care for her. He loved Georgie Bennett.

"I've been going back and forth. I thought saying no would be so easy." Her voice was thick with emotion, which he understood. "Actually, I didn't think I'd get the job. Female pit crew members aren't a dime a dozen. When I came to Hollydale, this was my dream."

He couldn't stand in her way.

"You'll be great." He found his legs, no longer rubbery, and stood. "I should check on Rachel. I don't like her out of my sight for too long. Not since the burns."

He walked to the door and reached for the handle.

"Mike, dreams change…"

"You'll be terrific. They're lucky to have you."

Wanting one more kiss, he paused for a second. Georgie was so caring, so generous, so everything he'd always wanted but never felt like he deserved. Sunshine, lemon pie and dreams. Could Georgie have everything she deserved if she stayed in Hollydale?

He wouldn't hold her back.

He walked away.

"Rachel's asleep. Let's give her five more minutes and sit on the front porch together." His dad grabbed a mason jar of tea and headed outside.

Mike sighed and followed. Best to get this over with. Two beatdowns in one night? Still nothing compared to the four he'd received on prom night from Mom, Dad and the twins all those years ago.

The front door creaked behind him, and Mike

made a note to bring over some WD-40 for repairs.

"I haven't fixed it because I like knowing when your mother comes home from her errands."

How did his father read his mind like that?

"I didn't say a word."

"Didn't have to. It was all over your face." Carl pointed to the rocking chair next to him. "Your mother and I like sitting out here in the evenings, sipping tea and watching the sunset. Might not sound exciting, but it's home."

If Georgie were sitting next to him, Mike couldn't imagine anything better. Not much chance of that if she lived in Charlotte.

"What's bothering you, son?"

Mike searched the horizon for a quick and easy answer. The night sky stared back, twinkling stars reminding him of the enormity of the universe. His problems seemed small in comparison. Still, his father cared, and that made all the difference.

"Georgie's leaving."

"Saw Beverly and Kitty at Holly Days Diner. Beverly didn't mention that. Asked about you. Even called you Mike. Strangest part of all? She said she was going to talk to Georgie about getting a pet." Dad chuckled, shook his head and sipped his tea. "Beverly misses Beau, it seems."

Mike blinked. Beverly Bennett had changed? Would wonders never cease?

Then again, he thought Georgie had changed. He thought she had settled down and would be staying for good. Mike clenched the armrest of the chair, his knuckles turning white. "Not surprising Georgie didn't tell Beverly."

Once independent, always independent.

"Did Georgie say how much longer she'll stay? What exactly did she say?"

Mike struggled to remember her exact words. "She's going to be offered her dream job."

His father drew in a deep breath, a sound Mike knew only too well. Growing up, Mike learned to listen whenever he heard that sigh. His father gave the best advice. Mike leaned forward.

"Did she say she's been offered the job or did she say she's accepted it?"

"What's the difference?" Mike leaned back and rocked, the motion and his father's taking the time to listen most reassuring. "You know Georgie. Once she sets her heart on something, it gets done."

"Same as you." Dad placed the mason jar on the cement and kept time with Mike's pace. "But you're jumping to conclusions. If she hasn't packed her bags and left, she's wavering. Maybe she's realizing she has other dreams, that something better might be out there. It might even be right here in Hollydale."

Mike started. He stopped rocking. "It sounds like you learned that from experience."

Dad huffed out a breath and rose from the rocker. He tilted his head toward the street. "I think better on the move." He opened the door a crack. "Diane, I'm talking Mike for a walk. We'll be right back."

That was his father through and through. Always one to do something or get his hands dirty rather than stay still. Mike let him lead the way.

Halfway down the block, Dad shoved his hands into his pockets. "I don't often talk about the past. Can't change it."

"But you can learn from it." Mike surprised even himself with that as he kept up with his father's long strides.

"Your mother had four miscarriages before we decided to adopt." His father stared straight ahead, not meeting Mike's gaze. "We both grieved, but your mother…"

Mike understood why Dad couldn't say anything else, his love for Diane a shining example for him, Becks and Natalie. "Why haven't you talked about them?"

"Your mom has told Becks and Natalie in the recent past, but we didn't want you feeling you were an afterthought, like we didn't want you. But the time is right to tell you about this now.

Your mother and I changed our dream about biological children and consulted an adoption agency. Twice we got a phone call that a young woman chose us. Twice we got a phone call that the mother decided to keep her baby."

Shaking his head, Mike reeled at the revelation. "You should have mentioned this before now."

"When? When you were a kid? When you were a teenager? After Caitlyn left you?" Carl shrugged and sighed. "You're right. We should have talked about it. The fact we are now means something."

"How could you keep going?"

Dad stopped and stared at him. "I didn't want to. I wanted to take your mother to Europe and give up on parenthood. After six lost chances, I was spent. I wanted us to look to our future together, without children."

Mike blinked at the thought of Diane Harrison never being a mother. How different his life would have been. And Becks and Natalie? They wouldn't even be here.

"Mom's not the type to give up."

"You've got that right." Dad laughed and grinned. "Somehow she found out I consulted a travel agent. I had a great trip to Spain all planned out when the adoption agency called. Your mother convinced me to try one more time. Best thing that ever happened to me. We're both proud of the man you've become."

"I've done some pretty stupid things in my life."

"They're called mistakes. We all make them. I thought traveling the world would replace my dream of having children. I even gave your mother an ultimatum. She had one week to change my mind or we'd take that trip."

Hmm. Georgie hadn't accepted the offer. One week. If he could persuade her to give him one week…

Her decision had to be hers alone, though. "Georgie's pretty stubborn."

"Like you aren't?"

Wait. Dad's right. Mike nodded. "Just a little." He exhaled. "What if Georgie's my dream, but I'm not hers?"

"I saw the way she looked at you tonight." Dad turned and walked in the direction of the house. "Besides, if she didn't want to stay, she'd have accepted the job outright."

"You only saw us together for two minutes."

Dad shrugged and picked up his pace. "That's all it takes. It's time for you to stop dwelling on the past and move forward."

"My mistakes…"

"We always make mistakes. You'll make more in the future. It's easier when someone's at your side. Duty without love?" Dad picked up the pace. "It's worthless."

Dad walked inside. Mike fell onto the rocking chair. *Duty without love.* Had he been running on cruise control so much since Caitlyn left he focused on duty more than love? Sure, he loved Rachel, but he'd been so concerned about being both parents it was easy to get caught up in the day to day and miss the big picture. He loved his job, but he performed his duties as a way of eking out a living rather than seeing the people he served and loving why he wore the uniform every day.

He glanced at the house and thanked his lucky stars. There weren't many role models that came better than Carl Harrison. How easy it would have been for Mom to go to Spain. His mother, however, didn't take anything lying down.

Neither would Georgie.

If she wanted that job, she'd have already been packed, one foot out the door.

One week. He had to convince her to give him that long to show her why love was the best reason to stay in Hollydale.

CHAPTER NINETEEN

GEORGIE TIGHTENED THE last bolt on the passenger door and then jumped up, wrench in hand. She'd imagined big, but nothing prepared her for the reality in front of her. Miss Brittany in her prime again, restored and proud.

She ran her hand over the Thunderbird's turquoise frame, gleaming to perfection. For some reason a vision of the Thunderbird delivering her and Mike to the hoedown on Friday night had popped into her head. Ever since, she'd worked overtime, and then some, to make this happen. With a whole lot of help from Travis and Heidi, that was. It was all worth it. Miss Brittany would be beautiful gliding down the open road.

She sighed. Now she wasn't sure if Mike was still taking her to the hoedown. Not after last night.

The lights flickered overhead, and Georgie turned toward the door.

Heidi waved, her other hand on the switch. "You have a visitor, but I kept him in the reception area so you could show him the progress yourself."

"Mike's here?" Georgie's heart soared, sending away the tiredness seeping into her bones.

She paused. What if Mike jumped to the conclusion she only put her heart and soul into this in order to start her new job with a clean slate? Not that the job was hers. Not yet. Not officially. Everything was on hold until Cullinan cleared his choice with the racer.

Why she hadn't pulled out of the running still confounded her. Every time she tightened a bolt or performed an emissions test, she'd told herself she'd text Cullinan next chance she got. Something had always held her back. Her simple and stupid pride.

She wanted to be someone's number one choice.

Then another, more chilling thought came to mind. What if Mike had come to collect the Thunderbird?

Best find out why he was here. Pushing all her assumptions aside, she rushed toward Heidi, wrench still in hand. Huffing, she returned to the workbench and stored the tool before hurrying into the reception area. Sure enough, Mike was there, and he'd never looked better, his uniform molding to his shoulders, tapering to a flat waist. It had taken her some time, at first, to reconcile this new Mike with the Mike of her youth. Duty suited him well.

Even if that duty was leading him to the conclusion he had to sell the Thunderbird.

"I should have listened to all you had to say. One of these days, maybe even starting today, I'll get that right." He ran over. "You should know right off the bat—I've done some serious thinking over the past twenty-four hours."

Her eyes widened. Seriousness lurked in his brown depths. Those stiff shoulders told a story unto themselves. *No way*. He wasn't going to ditch her before another dance. Even though the dance wasn't scheduled until Friday night and it was only Thursday, her stomach roiled. She clenched her fists at her side.

"No matter what happened yesterday, you're not getting off the hook this time." She unclenched one fist and poked him in the chest. "You mean too much to me to ditch me. I mean too much to me to keep quiet."

Mike closed the distance. "Georgie, I came to apologize." He paused, brought her hand up to his lips and kissed the back. "I want to take you to the dance as much as you want me to. Even more."

She willed herself to concentrate on anything except how he made her knees so weak she was afraid they'd buckle right here.

"Oh." A wisp of hair fell across her forehead.

Before she could push it back into place, he beat her to it, his long fingers brushing away the wayward strand. Their gazes locked as if nothing else in the world existed.

Memories flooded back. His comforting her after a group of girls laughed at her greased-stained fingernails. His laughing with her about cotillion. His casual arm around her shoulders after she bombed a history test. If they'd gone to prom, they'd have laughed and shared a few jokes. Then what? They'd have gone home and continued on with their friendship. She'd have left Hollydale anyway, left while he stayed behind.

"I came here for this."

Before she could move or say anything else, he kissed her, strong and emphatic, as if he had something to prove. He didn't have to prove anything to her. His true character came through. His love for his daughter, his love for the town, his love of duty. It was so Mike.

Enough thinking, Georgie. She let the kiss enthrall her, and the world fell away. There was her and Mike, nothing else. Stubble tickled her cheek while sandalwood tickled her nose.

He broke away and shot her a smile as calm as an idling engine. "I have to warn you. I play dirty."

"Huh?" Dizziness still consumed her.

"Have you been offered the job yet?"

She shook her head, the movement only making her feel even fuzzier. Darn Mike Harrison. Before him, she'd always had both feet planted on the ground. She couldn't decide if she liked feeling dizzy and flustered or not.

"No." Letting out the breath pent up in her, she willed everything to return to normal. But it didn't. She'd never be the same again. Licking her lips, she owed him honesty. "There's been a holdup. They won't announce anything before tomorrow or even next week, at the earliest."

"One week, Georgie. Give me one week."

"One week for what?" Confusion rocketed through her. Part of it came from how close he was, but part of it came out of the fact they weren't on the same page. "Could you start at the beginning?"

"Give me a chance to show you why you belong in Hollydale." He caressed her face, and she leaned into him before her breath caught in her chest. Secrets were never her strong suit. "Here with Rachel and me."

She opened her mouth. Telling him she wouldn't accept the job would provide some relief to those shoulders with the weight of the world upon them.

Still, that part of her would always wonder if she was good enough, when she hadn't been good enough growing up with a mother who kept trying to change her, when she hadn't been good enough for a fiancé who wanted to mold her into someone she wasn't.

Even if she knew she wasn't going to accept the job, Mike didn't have to know. Yet. Besides, it might be fun finding out how he intended to change her mind. She'd reveal all once she knew the answer.

She gasped, and her eyes grew wide. His kisses had made her forget the big reveal.

"I have to show you something." She led him toward the garage. "The car. Come on."

Georgie pulled him to the auto bay where Miss Brittany sat, finished and proud. His eyes grew wide as he circled the Thunderbird. No words escaped him. Happiness and awe escaped every pore.

"But we just installed the dash the other day…"

"Without Beau, I've been able to stay late, especially since Mom got the all clear from her cardiologist and Lucie's been great with her. Since then I've spent every spare minute with her. Even with a lot of customers returning, and Travis and Heidi helped."

Her father's dream involved the racetrack. Growing up, she believed she had something to prove to him and the world that a Bennett belonged there.

Yet Max's Auto Repair and Hollydale were where she belonged. She'd never stayed up all night souping up a race car, yet she'd burned the midnight oil here, where she learned the ropes. Her first oil change happened in the far bay. Her first brake flush in the middle one. She'd performed her first engine rebuild in the bay occupied by Miss Brittany. All here.

Hmm. Would Max consider bending his offer? He could handle the everyday repairs while she specialized in auto restoration and body work. That was what she loved doing, what she was made for.

"Georgie." The reverence in Mike's voice caught her off guard. "You've done all this for me?"

Why was he so surprised? Almost as though he wasn't worth it? He came over, and she dropped another kiss on his lips.

Someone cleared her throat behind them. Georgie turned around.

Beaming, Heidi stood there, bemusement in her eyes. "Well, this is a welcome sight, I do declare."

With reluctance Georgie stepped back. All of this was happening so fast.

"Guess we're going public before the dance?" Mike whispered in her ear.

"I—" Her voice faded.

His gaze caught hers as if he was searching deep into her soul, searching for affirmation of something. What? Her feelings for him?

They'd always been there. She'd hidden them well. Even from herself.

Or was it something else? Maybe a sign she'd stay.

"I agree, Heidi," he reached for her hand and squeezed. "I'm taking her to the hoedown on Friday night. Better late than never."

"About time." The older woman fingered her purse strap. "Sorry we'll miss it, but after his shift is over on Friday, Travis and I are leaving for Baltimore to see Missy. She wants us to visit, and I'm hoping for some good news."

"Have fun."

Fun. She'd missed out on that over the past couple of days, all work and no relaxation. It might be fun finding out how Mike would convince her to stay. One thing about Mike. He never backed down from a challenge.

Yes, the next week would be fun. Then once she knew Cullinan's decision, she'd tell Mike everything.

Holding back the truth wasn't all that bad. Not if something good came out of it.

"Shut the door behind you." The sheriff's voice held resignation and more. Today, a Friday of all days, was his first back on the job after a week's leave of absence, which had only put the station on edge.

Skittish, Mike kept his back to the sheriff for

a minute. Everywhere he went this week, from the grocery store to Holly Days Diner, people stepped up their efforts to get him to register his name for the ballot before next Tuesday's deadline. Mike breathed in and set his expression to stone before facing Donahue.

The sheriff had earned his respect. He'd spent his entire life upholding the law. No matter what, Donahue still wore the badge.

"How are you doing, Rick?" Mike settled in the hard wooden chair.

Donahue removed his glasses and set them on his desk. He rubbed a spot on his forehead, where the wrinkles had seemed to multiply over the past week.

"You want to know the real problem?"

Mike's own forehead creased. "Of course."

A big sigh ruffled the papers at the edge of the desk. Donahue leaned forward, propping his elbows on the edge. "Zach and Randy are juveniles. In a big city the case would be sealed and their identities would remain a secret so the mess they've gotten themselves into might not dog them the rest of their lives." He leaned back, shook his head and held up his hands. "I know. This is bigger than a mess. They're looking at serious charges. Only thing in their favor is their ages."

"They seem remorseful, too."

Mike's heart went out to Donahue. How easily their situations could be reversed. What if Rachel had committed a burglary like that, thinking it was easy money that wouldn't be missed? At least that was the story Zach and Randy used. Mike knew the truth, though. It wasn't just the money and electronics that hard-working business owners would miss.

It was peace of mind.

Donahue gritted his teeth. "Too little too late for me."

Mike squirmed in his chair. "What do you mean?"

"Election's coming up soon. Some have suggested I hand over the reins to someone else in the department." Donahue's shoulders slumped. "Namely you."

"I don't want the job." The growl that came out of him was most unlike him. It was all he could do most days to get out of here on time and be with Rachel. He'd counted on Donahue to have one more good term in him before Mike ran. His knuckles stiffened from the pressure from grasping the sides of the chair. "You didn't force Zach or Randy to commit those crimes."

Donahue leapt out of the chair. With one stride he made it to the window, his back to Mike. "Turns out Melanie was talking about the earlier stakeouts and the issues with the security company to our daughter-in-law, Sylvia, while Zach was in the room."

Mike cringed. So that was how Zach and his buddy had kept one step ahead of them.

"Did they admit this?"

"They did. Randy had counted on going into the military someday. Won't happen with this on his record. He won't be considered trustworthy."

The frustration in Donahue's voice conveyed his fear he'd no longer hold the same weight or have the same level of trustworthiness.

"They're young. If they complete their sentences and learn from this, there's enough time for them to turn their lives around." Mike hated sounding like Pollyanna, but the sheriff was reaching for some kind of encouragement. While life held no promises, a little solace never hurt.

"Sylvia and Rob are talking about moving to Asheville after Zach's trial and sentence is completed. Maybe even farther away. Fresh start."

"The fresh start we need is new blood filling the vacant positions, not throwing away the ones that are already filled. Hire people who'll actually stay, and that'll increase morale more than new leadership." Mike rose and headed for the door. As far as he was concerned, this conversation was over.

"I haven't told you the reason I called you in here."

There was more? The election seemed like

enough news for one conversation. Returning to the chair, he huffed out the breath he'd been holding. "Go ahead."

"Zach and Randy admitted to all the B&Es— all but one. Max's Auto Repair. They insist they didn't pull that job."

Donahue moved away from the window and back to his seat.

Flutters of doubt about Zach's statement filled Mike's lungs. "How could they keep them all straight?"

"They were very specific. They went in, took small electronics they could sell online and left. No messes, no scattering stuff everywhere. Seems Zach hung on everything I've said about robberies over the years." Bitterness entered his voice as his lips screwed into a big O. "That kid had such a bright future. Straight-A student. All that down the drain."

Mike had made a mess of it with Georgie in high school, but that didn't compare to the trouble these kids were in. Since Hollydale was so small, the trouble wasn't limited to them, either. Their families were bearing the brunt of it, as well.

"Your career's not down the drain, Rick."

"Sure feels like it right about now." Donahue steepled his fingers, almost like he couldn't contain the energy massing inside his heavy frame.

"I'm closing the files on all but the repair shop. The MO was different on that one."

How could he conclusively convince Donahue of Georgie's innocence? Mike clenched his jaw. "It's been two months. The chance of anything else cropping up is slim to none. No trace of those comic books online, and no sign of them or that folder anywhere else. For all we know, they're rotting in a landfill."

"Was it a coincidence that burglary happened between the others? Or was the burglar deliberate, knowing two other B&Es had occurred?" Donahue speculated.

Mike almost grew dizzy from the constant pendulum motion.

"Georgie Bennett had something to gain. If Max lost customers, she wouldn't have to pay him as much for the shop. Selling those comic books would help cover the cost of it."

Time to play his trump card.

"Georgie's waiting to hear back about a pit crew job in Charlotte. She's been in the running for it all this time."

"I want to solve this before I step down. Show I still can do my job."

Setting up Georgie as the fall guy gnawed at his gut. For some reason Donahue seemed intent on arresting Georgie when everything pointed away from her.

"In my opinion, it is solved. If this was a

deliberate B&E done by someone other than Randy and Zach—and I stick to my opinion those boys committed the job at Max's as well," Mike said, stopping short, as did Donahue, his face expressionless, "then it wasn't Georgie. For one thing, money's no object. Not with Beverly Bennett's funds. Besides, Georgie's not the only person who works at Max's. Heidi and Travis Crowe have been taking a lot of trips lately."

"I've known Travis Crowe since grade school." Donahue's chest puffed out, and anger flared out of him. In a way, Mike preferred that to the pity on display.

"You met Zach the day he was born." Mike's quiet tone understated his point.

Judging from Donahue's glare, the arrow struck home.

Donahue settled back in his chair and sorted papers into piles. "Outside the box. Ever since you used that phrase to me, I've been trying to think outside the norm so Hollydale can get back to its radar gun and occasional shoplifter."

Seemed like they were at an impasse, with Donahue in the Crowes' corner and him in Georgie's.

Mike rose and shrugged. "The trail on this is stone-cold."

Donahue extended his arms, linked his hands together and cracked his knuckles. "I want to find those comics and that folder for Max. I'm going to do what I should have done in the first place. Ask for search warrants for both the Crowes' residence and Georgie's."

At the Hollydale Hoedown, after he asked Georgie to reconsider her decision to move away, he'd warn the DA, Stuart Everson, of Donahue's misguided suspicion. By next week Donahue might listen to reason. Until then? "I respectfully request to be removed from this case."

"Denied. You responded to the original call." Donahue shook his head and reached for the phone. "I'm calling the judge now."

"There's no probable cause. How can you get a warrant on a cold case with no evidence against any of them?"

Maybe it was time for Donahue to retire. Fixating on something like this when they needed to repair the damage done from the B&Es? Unacceptable.

"The judge owes me a favor. If people want me out, I might as well collect while I still can. As far as probable cause, there's plenty. No sign of forced entry. Valuable comic books worth the same as Max was asking for the shop taken along with a proprietary folder containing customers' addresses and credit card numbers. No electronics or small valuables were touched. Everything points to an inside job. Don't tell anyone about this, Harrison. I'm not saying a word to Melanie or anyone. Once we receive the warrants, we execute them."

Mike nodded and left the room, his fists clenched at his side.

Problem was he didn't want to be sheriff, but when this goose chase ended without any evidence, he wouldn't have a choice but to get on the ballot or mount a write-in campaign. Besides, Georgie was innocent, so he had no reason to worry.

He only hoped she wouldn't think he'd doubted her again.

His gut told him otherwise.

CHAPTER TWENTY

"Max!" Georgie ran over and threw her arms around him. "You're back."

"Of course. Turns out I can't stay away. I'll finish my treatment in Hollydale. This is my home." He released her and surveyed the auto bays. Time in Florida suited Max. His tanned skin set off his white teeth, flashing his ready grin below his bushy mustache. After the surgery he'd lost a couple of pounds. Hard to judge with that bright Hawaiian shirt that almost blinded her. "The bays are full up. Looks like you're winning people over after all."

Her cheeks flushed. "I wouldn't quite put it like that, but..."

"Where are Travis and Heidi?" Max doffed his Panthers ball cap and scratched his bald dome.

"On their way to Baltimore to visit Missy. I let them leave early."

Max smiled. "Winning that scratch-off ticket sure made a difference."

"What scratch off?"

He shrugged and replaced his cap. "They won about ten thousand with a lottery ticket. Enough to send half to Missy and have fun with the other half. Splurge on a couple of nice hotels but not enough to buy me out, even if they wanted to, which they didn't." Max whistled and walked over to the Thunderbird. "Beautiful."

"She sure is. Want to know something?" She checked out the bays. Even with no one around, she lowered her voice to a whisper. "I'm hoping Mike won't sell once he drives her on the open road."

"I always credited the man with more smarts. Letting something this special get away?" Max's appreciation for the restoration was clear in his eyes. He met Georgie's gaze, and she almost burst with pride. "Twice. I knew you were good, Georgie, but this…" He strode to the grille, pulled up the metal handle and popped the hood, peering in at the engine. "It's a work of art."

Georgie shifted her weight and took a deep breath. Now or never. "I'm glad you think so. I'd like to propose a change to your offer."

Shaking his head, he lowered the hood, the clash of metal against metal almost jarring. "You should be doing this full-time. I can't hold you back. Have you contacted Foreman's in Asheville?"

"Max O'Hara, will you listen to me?" Had

that loud voice come out of her? For years her mother emphasized not talking back to her elders, about how Georgie should speak with respect. And of all the men in the world, her mentor was one she respected above all. But, she reminded herself, she was Max's equal, and he needed to listen to her.

The gleam in his eyes was unmistakable. "I knew my leaving you in charge would do you good. Problem is I can't accept a penny less now. Not with those comic books gone. Last time I talked to Mike, he said there was no sign of them."

Her stomach sank. Her negligence led to Max's nest egg being stolen. Of course, the burglar was mainly responsible, but still…

As it was, she'd have to use every cent of her savings to buy him out. Living with her mother wasn't how she envisioned turning thirty. But she'd own her business. That was something.

There was one better alternative. Would Max go for it? She crossed her fingers.

"I have another solution. I want to buy in, but I want to use my bay for auto restoration until we can add another building. Travis and I have worked out a system over the past couple of months, and it's going well. I work on maintenance during the morning, and then in the afternoon I've been restoring Miss Brittany here."

She outlined the rest of the details and a payment plan.

He folded his arms and shook his head. "No can do."

"But Max, where else are you going to get such an offer?" And how else could she stay in Hollydale?

She couldn't afford to open her own repair shop, and she didn't want to work in Asheville. Georgie held her chin high, determined to find some way to wear him down. This was a good compromise, and she'd stay until he accepted it. Good riddance. She was Georgie Bennett and she was a tomboy mechanic who liked the feel of a silk dress against her skin every once in a while. If Max rejected her idea…

She'd prosper and grow here. Same as she'd been doing the past couple of months, coming into her own.

Max let loose with a huge grin. "You're doing body work full-time. We'll be partners. When you want to help or if we get backed up, you work on the repair side. You can't buy me out since I'm staying. I convinced Rosie to move here." Max stared straight at her and winked. "You needed time away from Hollydale. Your dad would be so proud of you. Welcome home."

This was Max's plan all along, and she'd fallen for it, hook, line and sinker. He extended his hand, and the grin curling her insides came out, extending all the way to the tips of her toes. "You've got a deal." She tilted her head toward the Thunderbird. "I'm going to take her for her first test drive and give the keys to Mike tonight. Thought this would be a great way to arrive at the hoedown."

"That's tonight?" Max sighed and glanced at the cars in the bay. "These cars repaired or waiting their turn?"

"I was going to come in tomorrow and work on them."

"I'll repair them. You have fun tonight and don't worry about tomorrow."

Her grin grew even wider. "Thanks, Max."

No cares at all except having fun at the dance tonight. With Mike.

Floating on cloud nine, she waved goodbye to Max. This dance would go off without a hitch after all.

THIS DANCE MIGHT be the shortest date Mike had ever had, considering he was serving a search warrant at Georgie's residence two hours before he was set to pick her up. He wouldn't blame her if she canceled.

With paper in hand, he and Donahue approached the door of Beverly Bennett's house and glanced at the bevy of cars in the driveway. Three cars, and not one of them Georgie's. If she wasn't home, that might be best.

Donahue knocked, the forcefulness catching Mike off guard. Mike had wanted to search Travis and Heidi Crowe's house first. Donahue insisted on stopping here first.

Beverly Bennett answered and arched her eyebrow. "Mike Harrison, why on earth are you in your uniform? Shouldn't you be in a suit?" She inhaled a swift breath, her rare smile turning into a frown. "If you stand up my daughter again…"

Donahue doffed his cap and stepped inside. "This isn't a social call, Mrs. Bennett." He extended his hand out to Mike. Without a word Mike handed him the warrant. "This is official police business. I have a search warrant to look for evidence relating to the burglary at Max's Auto Repair."

Beverly's friend Kitty came over, her forehead knit into a mass of wrinkles. "I'm going to call my husband. He's an attorney and can advise us if they can do this."

"What's going on?" Georgie's husky voice came from the top of the stairs.

Mike glanced up, fighting to hold back his sudden laughter, a welcome relief from the tension reeling around him. Green gunk covered her face, and that ratty robe was probably a relic from high school. In jeans Georgie was beautiful. In a robe? His gut clenched, and he fisted his hands resting at his sides.

Lucie Decker appeared. "Don't furrow your eyebrows, Georgie. It will crack the mask."

His sister Natalie appeared. Groaning, he bet his parents would hear all about this before he arrived home to change. If Georgie would still go to the dance with him, that was.

"Michael, what are you doing here?" Natalie stopped halfway down the staircase. "Do Mom and Dad know you're here?"

Swallowing hard, he rubbed the spot on his forehead where the pounding was intensifying. "No one outside of this house knows I'm here."

"This isn't a social call. Officer Harrison," Donahue said as he looked over his shoulder, his lips pursed into a straight line, "you search down here while I search upstairs."

Georgie held up her hands. "Mike, what's going on? Make it fast, please."

"It's been ascertained the burglaries around Hollydale weren't related to the B&E at Max's. Donahue asked the judge for a search warrant regarding the comic books and Max's folder."

"Here. At my house?" Her voice grew even huskier as the betrayal deep in his stomach burned fiery hot.

He nodded, the facial mask hiding her expressions but not the hurt in the depths of her green eyes. While he longed to wrap his arms around Georgie and comfort her, he had this one formality to go through before he could explain.

With some luck, and a whole lot of pleading, the weight of his job might balance the scales in his favor, along with the explanation of how duty was part of him, had been all along. Duty was ingrained in him as much as Dad's ability to say the right thing or Mom's ability to hold Becks's hand. As much as he wished Edwards could have executed the warrant with Donahue, Mike couldn't, and wouldn't, foist his job onto someone else. When he went against himself, the results were disastrous.

He took the stairs two at a time, wanting some connection with Georgie, hard enough under the circumstances, even harder with all these people surrounding them. Natalie scurried back to the top while Georgie met him halfway.

Grasping her hands, he lowered his voice for her ears only. "I know you're innocent, Georgie. Trust me."

Two little words, but he meant them with all his heart. For Georgie, who'd grappled with a mother who wanted her to be someone she wasn't growing up and a fiancé who wanted someone feminine and demure, what he was asking was almost downright impossible. Breath couldn't get into his lungs as the seconds ticked by with no answer coming from her lips.

"I love you, Mike."

Oxygen filled his lungs along with the sweetness of those words. He squeezed her hands.

He didn't deserve her. He would thank his lucky stars every day for the gift of Georgie in his life, for the roads that led her back to Hollydale.

"Let's go." Donahue swept past him.

When they didn't find anything at either house, Mike would agree to formally add his name to the ballot.

After twenty minutes of upturned furniture and emptied drawers with everyone glaring at him, Mike was ready to throw in the towel. There were no binders or comic books anywhere in sight.

Mike approached Donahue. "I have somewhere to be in less than two hours. I'd like a private word before we leave."

Donahue straightened, the grim expression from before gone. He'd seemed to age ten years in the short time they'd been here. He shrugged and blinked. "I figured if I could solve the robbery at Max's, people might trust me again."

Mike scrubbed his face and threw a glance over at Georgie, the green gunk now off hers. She must have heard the sheriff, as the smile she sent him absolved him of all wrongdoing.

The weight lifted from his shoulders. One by one, everyone started leaving her bedroom, rather the worse for wear. Natalie glared at him, and Mike threw up his palms. He'd hated any doubt cast over Georgie, but now it was out in the open. Any shadow was gone. Perfect timing for the dance.

"What's that room?" Donahue turned to Georgie, his forehead lined with resignation. "Officer Harrison and I would like a consult prior to our departure."

"It's the laundry room. Just a washer, dryer and my suitcases. Haven't touched them since I arrived. Go ahead and talk away." Georgie sent a smile in Mike's direction. She didn't need words. Her understanding gaze said everything.

Did he dare hope? Could he convince her tonight that her road to Hollydale wasn't in vain? That love here would last her a lifetime?

"We'll talk in here."

Opening the door, Donahue switched on the light, tripping over Georgie's three suitcases on the floor opposite the stainless steel washer and dryer.

Mike strode into the room, his arms folded. "Enough. You've turned this into a joke. Georgie's innocent, and it's time to move on."

"She is, is she?" Donahue straightened, comic books and a bright yellow binder in his hands. Property of Max's Auto Repair.

Mike's world shattered around him. He reached for the handcuffs on his utility belt. "Georgianna Victoria Bennett, you have the right to remain silent. Anything you say can and will be used against you in a court of law."

CHAPTER TWENTY-ONE

"I didn't steal anything."

Mike put her hands to her back. She winced and tried to breathe, rather hard with her rights being read to her. No, this wasn't happening. Tonight was supposed to be the happiest night of her life. They were supposed to drive to the Hollydale Hoedown in the Thunderbird, the proverbial riding off into the sunset. Instead, she'd be escorted to jail.

"I'm not a thief." Georgie screwed her eyes shut, willing those tears not to flow.

"I am." Her mother's voice tore through her.

Georgie opened her eyes, her hands now manacled behind her back. How ironic. Her mother was finally defending her. Couldn't argue with cold, hard evidence. In her suitcase, no less. If she weren't in utter despair, her heart might have leaped at how Mom was fighting for her.

In a way, it was sweet for her mother to come to her defense.

"No offense, Mrs. Bennett." Donahue tipped

his hat. "Everyone knows you were recovering from stent surgery when this happened."

"She planned it. I'm the one who took Georgie's keys and committed the burglary." Kitty came up, her face in tears, her hands extended. "Lock me up. Throw away the key." She sniffled. "But if you can do this without telling my husband about it, I'd be a mite grateful. Being the DA and all, he might not understand."

A sharp breath came from behind her. Mike. Despite his earlier protests, he had no problem reading Georgie her Miranda rights. These weren't even Donahue's handcuffs around her wrists. They were Mike's.

All around people were shouting. Natalie was yelling about the Harrisons, Lucie was protesting something about a good lawyer who'd have her bail set before she knew it and Kitty was continuing the charade.

Chills ran down Georgie's spine. What if Kitty wasn't lying?

"Quiet!" Mike shouted, and everyone, including Georgie, turned toward him. Mike didn't lose it often, but with the way he clenched his jaw, Georgie could tell he was near his boiling point. "One at a time."

Still, he didn't uncuff her.

Everyone erupted again, except for Georgie. Mike hadn't hesitated, believing the worst about her. Sure, the evidence was right there in Donahue's hands, but Mike could have given her the benefit of the doubt.

Couldn't he?

"Hush." Mike slashed the air with his hands as if to emphasize his point. "Beverly, you go first."

Georgie kept herself from laughing. Good grief, the idea that her mother was a criminal mastermind was preposterous. The woman was known far and wide for Southern charm, her hair always perfectly coiffed, her nails perfectly manicured, her manner always polite, and also for her unswerving resolve to get her own way. She turned to her mother, wishing she could reach out to reassure her. Little hard to do that with her hands handcuffed behind her.

"Mom, thanks for the good thoughts, but, at this point, I need you to call a lawyer, not make up some spur-of-the-minute story."

"Georgie," Mike whispered in her ear, "let your mother talk."

She should have known something would come up so they couldn't have tonight's dance. She just didn't imagine that the something was a small cell with her name on it. Or that Mike would be the one holding the key locking her in.

She nodded at her mother. Was it too much to hope that one good attorney would be willing to skip tonight's hoedown to bail her out?

"I don't know where to begin." The color drained from her mother's face.

"This isn't good for her. She's had two stent procedures in the past couple of months." Georgie stepped toward her mother and glared back at Mike. "Are these necessary? I won't run."

Mike said nothing, just unlocked the cuffs. Something deep in his eyes struck her. She'd seen that look before, when she told her mother she wasn't going to college. Disappointment. Georgie rubbed her wrists before hugging her mother. "Do I need to call your doctor? Have you taken your medication today?"

Tears were welling in her mom's eyes. "Georgie, I did this. Working as a mechanic? Right here in our very own town?" She shuddered. "Around engines and cars that can lose control." She lowered her gaze. "I lost Stephen that way."

Georgie's breath caught. If her mother and Kitty pulled this caper, she'd lose Georgie, too.

"I don't understand."

"I thought if Max believed you stole his comic books, he'd have to fire you. Since you'd promised to stay, I was hoping you'd have to work away from cars and maybe find something you like better. Something safer."

Georgie leaned against the wall for support. "No, Mom. And I wished you'd talked to me first."

"No one got hurt." Kitty stepped forward.

"Georgie, you were asleep. It was quite easy really. Once I had the keys, I drove over to the repair shop, scattered everything around and found the folder. The comics were below it, and I thought my grandsons might like them for a Christmas present. I hid everything in your suitcase." She shot a guilty look in Beverly's direction. "You and Georgie always fight, and Georgie always runs, so I thought she'd find them eventually, when she packed, and she'd return everything to Max."

More words tumbled out, yet Georgie wasn't listening, the buzz surrounding her growing louder with each second. Her mother hated her choices this much? Enough to have Kitty steal her keys and break into the repair shop? Lucie and Natalie accepted who she was. And for a while, Mike had, too.

But now?

Everything crashed in around her. He'd arrested her. Sure, the evidence was overwhelming, but he hadn't even said he'd stand by her as her friends were yelling at her about bail and lawyers.

He believed the worst of her. He believed she'd betray everything she held dear.

A doorbell chime momentarily interrupted the chaos. Georgie jerked her hand toward the hall. "Can someone answer the front door?" She glared at Mike. "Or would that be used against me in a court of law?"

"I'll get it." Natalie scurried away.

Everyone resumed arguing.

Georgie held Mike's gaze, emotions flowing out of her all at once. The shock, the disbelief, the anger.

Still he stood there, his sudden calmness rattling her even more. How could he be stoic when her world was collapsing around her?

Max appeared at the doorway, out of breath. "Someone texted me to get here on the double." He waved a piece of paper in the air. "Georgie, I brought the amended contract over."

Georgie couldn't meet his gaze. Even though her mother and Kitty had committed the actual robbery, embarrassment still gripped her like tires to pavement.

Sheriff Donahue stepped forward and handed Max the folder. "This is yours, isn't it?"

"Actually, it's Georgie's and mine. As of this afternoon, she's half partner in Max's Auto Repair and Body Shop." Max's grin stretched from ear to ear.

Mike cleared his throat. "Mr. O'Hara, I'd like to ask you a few questions."

"Are you asking as Mike or Officer Harrison?" The disappearance of Max's smile sank Georgie's heart again. Max was staring at Mike's uniform.

The truth was Mike was both. They were both facets of his true personality that had emerged after she left Hollydale. The one who rescued a kitten. The one who prized family. The Mike who loved deeply. While she'd been the one protecting him the day they met, he'd always had this sense of duty deep in him. After all, he'd played lookout while she climbed the tree and toilet papered Mr. Reedy's yard. He'd hugged her and lent her ten bucks when her mother cut off her allowance when Georgie announced she wasn't going to college. After she protected him that first day, he protected her.

That was why that letter had shocked her. Because it was so unlike Mike.

This part of him in the laundry room? The sense of duty and honor above all? It was ingrained in him.

"The police are here investigating the burglary at your shop." Lucie started talking, all the while glaring at Mike.

"Kitty and I broke in, Max." Mom sighed and held out her wrists. "Arrest me, Officer Harrison."

"I'm telling Mom." Natalie narrowed her eyes.

"No one's arresting anyone." Max boomed and stepped toward Georgie. "Georgie, what did I walk into? Everyone else, stay quiet."

An appalling mess that all centered around

her was what he'd walked into. Georgie shrugged and recapped everything. As soon as she'd finished, everyone seemed intent on adding their two cents.

"Officer Harrison, I insist you do what's right." Her mother patted a stray hair into place.

"Should I call my husband now?" Kitty asked.

"Georgie, make sure you bring my medicine with you when you come to the police station." Her mom fake-coughed a little.

Max whistled. Silence swept over the room, still crowded with too many people. Would they have this many people over for Thanksgiving?

"I'm not pressing any burglary charges," Max announced. "Kitty borrowed this for my partner, and it's back. So are the comic books. I'm sure they'll volunteer their time for a worthy cause, helping others to show their remorse. Enough already."

Enough was right. Enough with people trying to run her life. Enough with people being disappointed in her.

Enough.

"Are you sure, Max? Breaking and entering. That's a serious offense." The sheriff grunted and wiggled his thumbs into his utility belt.

"I'm not pressing any charges." Max enunciated every word, his mustache quivering with anger.

"Let's go, Donahue." Mike placed his hand on the sheriff's back and pushed him forward. "We have a report to fill out, and then some of us have to try to salvage the rest of our evening."

Max turned his gaze to Mike. "What did you think of the Thunderbird? Isn't she a beauty?"

"I can't keep the car, Max." Mike's frown deepened, although that didn't quite seem possible as all he'd been doing was frown for the past half hour.

"Georgie." Her mother pleaded with her eyes as well as her voice. "We need to talk."

With a couple of conversations going on at once, Georgie stepped back and glanced at Mike. His calmness usually strengthened her. She knew how he regretted the times he'd given into impulse, rather than thinking matters over. Sure, she was fighting mad at her mother right now. So much so Georgie couldn't form words. All the more reason to wait to speak to anyone until she was capable of listening.

Uh-oh. Mike Harrison really was rubbing off on her. Keeping a level head and thinking before she spoke? Mike traits, for sure. No wonder she loved him, but she couldn't deal with that yet.

"We will, Mom, but not now. I need time. Okay?"

Her mother had betrayed her, and her heart

told her Mike hadn't trusted her, either, even if her brain did understand his commitment to duty. She was so confused.

And then her gaze landed on her suitcases. Running sounded good right about now. So many cities left to explore. Maybe Georgie would head south to Florida. A warm winter might be a nice change of pace.

She leaned against the wall, grateful for the support. Running away never solved anything. Look at what was crammed into this room. Her friends, Max, her future. If she left, she'd be saying goodbye to all of them, even her mother.

Mike walked out into the hallway, looking over his shoulder. She met his gaze and nodded. There'd be no dance tonight, and this time she'd be the one canceling.

Her heart shattered into a million pieces. The Thunderbird, Rachel, him. Her dreams lay at her feet, scattered like the leaves of the season.

Her stay at Hollydale was nearing its end. She'd listen, say her goodbyes and stay away for good this time.

NOT MUCH HAD changed in Beverly Bennett's living room. Same curtains. Same cabinet of fancy china dolls. Same picture of Stephen Bennett in the middle of the mantel. This was where he should have been eleven years ago on prom night. Would the time ever be right for him and Georgie?

He rubbed that pounding spot on his forehead. No sooner had he come to terms with the role that duty played in his life, then *wham*. The overwhelming evidence blindsided him. If only he'd given Georgie some clue that he'd stand by her. Lucie had promised her an attorney. Natalie promised support before glaring at him in a way that let him know Mom and Dad might not invite him for Thanksgiving dinner for the next ten years. And he?

He gave Georgie handcuffs.

At the least he should have let Donahue arrest her.

No. He plunged right in and did the deed, hoping it'd be easier being arrested by someone who loved her. He fought back the chuckle at how stupid that sounded. Was it ever easy to be arrested, even when the arrest lasted all of five minutes?

Most of all, Georgie couldn't know how he felt. He'd slapped those handcuffs on faster than Rachel devoured pink birthday cake.

And now?

It might be too late. He'd seen the steel lurking in those green depths earlier, before he left the laundry room and headed down here.

The sheriff appeared. "I expect the report on

my desk tomorrow by noon. I'll review it, and then it'll become public record."

"I'll be in bright and early to write it."

Donahue pursed his lips. "Along with a decision, I suppose, about running for sheriff?"

More people came downstairs.

"Yeah, I'll be opposing you," Mike answered.

Donahue slipped away. Mike searched for Georgie, her face the only one not in the crowd.

Natalie glared at him as though he'd chopped the head off her favorite Barbie. Her sigh only added an anvil to the anchor already around his neck. "The path to good intentions is often rocky, but you brought along boulders tonight, big brother."

He invoked his right to remain silent, letting her pass without comment.

Lucie gave him a wry smile and patted his shoulder. "Hang in there. She went through a lot tonight, but she'll come around. True love is rare, but it exists. For you guys, that is."

Lucie walked away, and Mike shook his head. He hadn't missed the way Georgie looked longingly at those suitcases.

The parade didn't stop. Natalie's bluntness had nothing on Max's, whose glare was downright blinding. "She didn't sign the contract. You'll make this up to her, or so help me..."

Without completing the rest of that threat, Max swept out of the house. Mike had all he could take. Running for the stairs, he stopped when Georgie came front and center. A sweatshirt and jeans had replaced her robe. Dismayed, he knew. She wasn't coming tonight.

"The Thunderbird is this way." Her cold tone was unmistakable. Georgie headed past him, and he followed her. "I'll return the keys to you."

She opened a door, and he braced himself. The feeling he was losing more than the Thunderbird broke his heart. There was so much he wanted to say, to explain. He entered the garage and was amazed.

This had been not a job for Georgie but a passion. A job was one thing. What he'd chosen for himself was more than a job, too. He was upholding the law, serving all the citizens of Hollydale. So much so he'd accepted running for sheriff. He and Rachel would work together to make the new reality better than the old. He'd protect his baby and the community.

He'd learned from the best. His parents, Georgie, his own mistakes. Whenever he turned his back on duty or performing his duty with love in his heart? Disaster. He couldn't, and wouldn't, do that any longer.

Sure was easier to have a support system in place. Was Georgie still part of his support system?

"Do you want me to wait for you to change

and then we can show Rachel the Thunderbird before the hoedown starts?" He tried to sound casual. Inside, though, his heart thundered, and his chest clenched, a far cry from the calmness he showed on the outside.

"I'm not changing."

"I don't want you to change. You're wonderful just the way you are. You're strong," he stopped as the words jumbled together and wouldn't come out right. Her lemon scent didn't make it any easier, either, only confusing him even more.

"I'm also angry and hurt." Her green eyes flashed fire, and he stepped toward her. She held up her hands, and he stopped. "But since I've been home, you've taught me how important it is to weigh everything and make a decision once all the facts are in. I know I need to retreat, even if I have to leave town to do exactly that."

His shoulders slumped. She'd learned from him but didn't want to be with him. He steeled himself and closed the gap between them. He lifted her chin. Even the sadness and hurt couldn't get in the way of their chemistry.

Yet that hurt was shutting him out. He'd seen that look before, the moment she discovered him with Wendy, that note in her hand. The connection they'd rebuilt had taken a beating when they'd disagreed about the sale of the Thunderbird. But now?

She was leaving. Most likely for good.

"Hear me out." His voice cracked, his wanting her to stay making his bones ache. "Even while I was snapping on the cuffs, I knew I'd stand by you, bail you out, defend you."

"You didn't say that out loud."

His chest heaved, and he tried again. "We make each other better. I love you, Georgie Bennett."

That said it all. Either she'd believe him or not. When only silence filled the air between them, he had his answer. They were over before they had even begun.

He walked away.

"Wait."

Turning, he looked for any sign she was going to approach him, kiss him, love him back. Nothing. At least Rachel would hug him, and Ginger would climb onto his lap as he tried to figure out how to rebuild his world.

"Georgie?" Exhaustion swept over him.

"The Thunderbird." She reached inside the open driver's window and then threw him the keys. "It's yours. You can drive it now. Rachel—" she paused and a wistful look came over her "—wants a ride in it. Maybe then the two of you will decide to keep it."

Running his hand over the fin, he remembered all the drives with Grandpa Ted. It wasn't the car that mattered. It was his grandfather spending time with him, talking to him, loving him. That was what counted. He'd spend time with Rachel, listen to her, treasure her. His heart wouldn't allow him to do anything else.

"No chance of that."

She flinched, but he wouldn't back down.

"Grandpa Ted's legacy isn't in things. You were right. It's how he made time for me. It's not the car that counts. It's the people around me. It's loving Rachel when she hurts or when she's happy. Just like Grandpa Ted loved me. Just like my mom and dad love me. That's Grandpa Ted's real legacy."

He reached out for Georgie's hand and placed it over his heart. "That's what I want to build with you, do for you. I want to live with you, love you, be there for you."

Her silence said everything. He released her hand and let his fall by his side.

"Goodbye, Georgie."

"Wait."

For what? She wouldn't change her mind. She knew herself, and the confidence from that was one of the reasons he loved her so much. He kept walking.

"What about the Thunderbird?" Her plea hit him like an arrow to his heart.

That car represented dreams that would never

come true for him. Maybe it would for some-one else.

"Make sure the new buyer gives it a good home. Rachel and I will find our own way to make new memories together."

For the second time in Georgie's life, her dream night had ended in ruins. Once more, Mike had walked away. And once more, she'd be leaving Hollydale. This time for good.

A hand patted her shoulder. "Georgianna? Why don't you come inside where it's warm?"

Georgie heard the tremor in her mother's voice, but it dulled compared to the Grand Can-yon–sized crevice in Georgie's heart.

"I prefer Georgie." Turning, Georgie let the anger sweep over her. "How could you? How could you frame me like that?"

Her mother blanched. "I didn't think it would get this far. Forgive me?"

"You didn't think, period. It was bad enough growing up with someone who never accepted the real me. Now I've lost my best friend. The man I love." Georgie took a long, slow breath, then released it. "There's no way I can forgive you in the blink of an eye."

Beverly pointed at the Thunderbird. "You fixed the car. You'll fix this."

"You can't fix someone thinking the worst of you, thinking you're everything he stands against." Georgie opened the door to the house, her heart broken. "I can't stay here like this."

"I did this for you, Georgie."

"You did this for yourself."

Georgie didn't look back, but kept walking all the way to her suitcases.

CHAPTER TWENTY-TWO

GEORGIE GRIPPED THE steering wheel of her Prius and stared at the road ahead. From the moment she'd arrived in Hollydale, she'd been counting down the minutes until she could leave again. After accepting Cullinan's offer yesterday, this should be the happiest day of her life.

Saying goodbye to so many people was proving harder than she'd ever imagined. Max had shaken his head and told her she'd be back. Her mother had insisted the second stent procedure had been a true wake-up call for her. The subject of counseling had even broached Beverly's lips. As much as Georgie appreciated the effort, the betrayal was too fresh. She'd packed up her bags and soon she'd be on her way.

In the middle of all that, Mr. Reedy had called, explaining Beau had missed her and wanted to see her. That was one invitation she couldn't refuse.

Considering she had her dream job in her pocket, her heart shouldn't ache this much. The one goodbye left unsaid hurt the most, she admitted.

Ringing Mr. Reedy's doorbell, she straightened her shoulders. So she was lying to herself. So she wasn't okay with leaving. There was no reason to stay. Her mom was on the mend. Mike would have more responsibility at work, and there was Rachel to look after, too.

A dog barked, and a scattering of paws clipped the floor. Nearly a minute passed with the barking growing more insistent. The hair on the back of her neck curled, and Georgie rapped on the door. No answer. She rattled the knob.

"Mr. Reedy?"

Georgie started banging on the door with her fist. Only more barking. She pressed her right ear against the door. She strained, waiting to hear something, anything, even the rolling oxygen canister. Nothing other than Beau's barking.

She stepped away from the door and rummaged through her purse. Her smartphone in hand, she'd just pressed nine when the door opened. Relief stilled her pounding heart until she caught sight of Mr. Reedy leaning against the frame, breathing hard, his oxygen tube askew and his face ashen.

"Mr. Reedy!" She reached for his arm and held him up.

Beau barked and ran circles around them.

"I'm fine. I'm fine." He batted her hand away.

"The shuttle's coming to take me to my doctor's appointment."

"You're not fine." Stressing the last word, she clenched her jaw. "Let me drive you to the hospital." One little detour wouldn't hurt. Cullinan wasn't expecting her until tomorrow anyway.

Beau jumped on her and whined as if he wanted her to make Mr. Reedy all better. If only she could.

"No, Georgie." Mr. Reedy stopped and waved her inside. His wheezing broke her heart, the spry teacher of her high school days struggling for every breath. "I want you to do something for me."

"Anything." For one of the people in Hollydale whose faith in her never wavered? She'd go to the moon and back. "Name it."

"Take my Beau as your own. Love him. Keep me updated about him." His voice cracked, and Beau must have sensed something as he nudged Mr. Reedy's hand. "One of my neighbors, Hannah, she's in high school, has been walking him and playing with him. Her father's allergic, and she can't take him. Besides, he loves you."

Georgie bit back the tears threatening to fall. A couple of deep breaths later, she found her voice. "I'll watch him until you get better."

He pursed his almost blue lips and waggled his finger in her face. "We're not playing the lying game. My doctor's been after me to go into assisted living permanently. Hate giving up my independence." He paused and drew in gulps of air. Standing helpless when the world collapsed around you stank.

Georgie longed to do something, anything for him.

"Hate giving up my Beau." He gave a slight chuckle and lifted a shoulder. "Having someone else do the cooking and cleaning, though? That won't be bad."

Georgie scrubbed her face. Beau trotted over, his head nudging her hand as if that would get her to agree. "I'm moving, though."

"Stuff and nonsense. You belong here." He shuffled over to a faded orange armchair, which had seen better days, and collapsed as if all the exertion was catching up to him. His rheumy gaze met hers. "You come visit and tell me about Beau. Sneak him in every once in a while if they'll let you."

The very thought of trying to sneak the massive dog anywhere made her smile. Beau would never fit in anyone's purse.

"Okay, no lying game, Mr. Reedy." She petted Beau, trying to wrest some courage with every stroke. "I'd love for Beau to come with me, but I won't be in Hollydale."

He squinted and shook his head. "You're still here, aren't you? I'll take my chances I'm right."

When a rumbling sound grew stronger, Georgie moved to the window, Beau at her side. The county shuttle parked in the driveway behind her Prius. Gulping, Georgie turned to Mr. Reedy. "The shuttle's here. Do you want me to take Beau?"

With a quick jerk of his head, Mr. Reedy placed his hands on the armchair and pushed himself up. Beau whined.

"His leash is on the kitchen table, and his kibble and bowl are all there, too." He pressed his head to Beau's coat. "You be good for Georgie."

Beep. A loud honk issued from the shuttle. Mr. Reedy scuttled along with his oxygen tank. Beau followed Mr. Reedy to the door.

"Key's on the back table. Just leave it under the mat."

With that, Mr. Reedy left. Beau wandered over to Georgie.

"Goodbyes are never easy, are they, Beau?" She stroked him, taking comfort in his soft fur.

After Georgie loaded Beau's gear into the Prius, she clicked on Beau's leash. He wouldn't budge. "Sorry, Beau, but I have a schedule to keep." Beau tilted his head to one side as if trying to understand her. She chuckled. "Car ride."

Magic words for a dog, if she did say so herself. He jumped in, settling to rest on the seat.

She patted his head. "Good boy." She readied herself and pulled out of the driveway. "This will be fun, Beau. A new adventure."

She glanced in the rearview mirror, the guilt

rising. She lied to a dog. Her dog. Sharing an adventure wouldn't be nearly as fun as if Mike were along for the ride.

No, but she could have a permanent reminder of Mike. The Thunderbird. Beau would have much more room to stretch out in the Thunderbird's back seat.

It would be tight, but she had enough money. She was the person to give Miss Brittany the best home. After a slight detour, she installed Beau in the back seat. The flick of Beau's tongue against her cheek was thanks enough.

The Thunderbird rode like a dream.

Breaking at the stop sign, she flinched. That twinge in her heart caught her off guard. Sure, Mike hadn't had a choice. He'd done his job, but he didn't have to like it so much.

Georgie pressed the accelerator. The sooner she left the city limits, the sooner the next chapter of her life would begin. A chapter without her friends, Max's Auto Repair, Rachel and Mike.

At least she had Beau.

She squinted at the old clunker on the side of the road. Not just any clunker, a white PT Cruiser. Groaning, she rubbed her forehead and pulled the Thunderbird over. She should have known she wouldn't get out of Hollydale without saying one final farewell. And, of course, it would have to be Lucie. Appearances could be deceiving. Coming back to Hollydale had taught her that and more.

"Stay here, Beau." She rolled down the windows enough for Beau to get fresh air but not enough to wriggle out and get hurt.

She eased out of the Thunderbird and headed over to Lucie's ancient Cruiser just as Lucie slammed shut the open trunk.

"Georgie!" Lucie scooted over and hugged her. To her own surprise, Georgie didn't even flinch at the contact.

Because it's real and genuine. Just like everything about Hollydale.

"What can I do to help?" Georgie waved to Ethan and Mattie, who waved back. "If you pop the hood, I can take a look."

"No need." Lucie wiped her hands, a smudge of dirt on her cheek and mud on the knees of her jeans. "I changed the tire myself. I was just getting ready to leave."

Pride shone in Lucie's eyes, and Georgie stepped back. "Good for you."

Was it her imagination or did her voice sound even huskier than usual?

Lucie came over and gave her another hug. "No, good for you. You taught me so much, especially how to take care of my car so I can be more independent."

Was that what everyone thought? That she had

taught the car repair classes to preach independence? Well, that might have been part of it, but...

"You've got a support network, you know." Georgie bit her lip. Independence had served her well, too well perhaps.

Lucie laughed, a light, whimsical, feminine laugh. "They're called friends." She glanced at the Thunderbird. "Are you taking that to Mike?" Her face lightened, and a genuine smile lit up her perky features. "Have you two made up? Are you staying?"

"No." Georgie hesitated. She had her dream job waiting for her, a fresh start. Why did everything feel so wrong? "Mike sold the Thunderbird. The new owner's taking possession."

The smile left Lucie's face. "I was hoping..."

"What? What were you hoping?"

"That you'd forgive Mike." Lucie shrugged and fretted with her hands. "He's one of the good ones. After the feds arrested Justin, our bank accounts were frozen. I didn't know how I was going to feed Mattie and Ethan. I couldn't rub two cents together. Then someone started leaving groceries on my porch. They even packed Oreos, the real ones, not the generic ones. I caught sight of the Good Samaritan's back once. It was Mike. Good guys don't come along every day. Might be worth a second thought."

Or a third or a fourth... Mike was one of a kind. Her heart slammed into her chest with a thud. *Mike is one of a kind.* She was throwing away his love like an empty package of Oreos.

Georgie looked at her jeans and flannel shirt, now flecked with brown fur. Mike accepted her, loved her. The real her, the tomboy who loved motors and oil and cars. Love like that did not come along every day.

Love like that would provide a new adventure every day.

"I love him, but that's not enough. He arrested me, for crying out loud."

"Love is always more than enough, if you let it. You have to believe in it, Georgie. Believe." Lucie leveled a stern gaze in Georgie's direction. "When will you realize Hollydale is your home?"

Suddenly, Georgie had realized it as everyone, once hazy, came into perfect focus. She could see giving Mr. Reedy updates at the assisted living home. She could see partnering with Max. And if it wasn't too late, she'd be counting her lucky stars that someone accepted her, just the way she was.

Friends. Acceptance. Home. "Now."

The weight lifted off her shoulders. The sun glinted off the metal on the back of a sign. No, it couldn't be. Georgie walked over and read the words.

Welcome to Hollydale, City Limits.

She had never even left.

"DADDY?" RACHEL ENTERED the living room, her nose scrunched up and a scowl marring her pretty features.

A scowl that matched the gray covering Mike's world. Mike hadn't a choice about the Thunderbird, or had he? Losing the car wasn't causing the hurt, though. The real pain came from missing Georgie.

He had to hold it together for Rachel's sake.

He drew a deep breath. Although he loved his daughter and would do anything that would help her, even selling the Thunderbird, he had to be himself while he did that. If he could, he'd thank Georgie for that hard lesson. He'd had to dig deep, but no longer would he be the shadow of the person he'd been when Caitlyn left him. Now he was whole again.

Whole, and without Georgie.

His throat clogged at how he wanted her at his side, wanted her to know he accepted her and would fight for her. How he was better with her beside him. Even though only a day had passed since she left, this Sunday had a dull and dreary fog all around it.

Rachel tapped her foot. "I have a confession."

Mike sat up at the insistence in her voice. Ginger yowled her displeasure and scattered off his lap. He glanced at his daughter, hiding something behind her back. He waved her over.

"What's wrong?" he asked.

"I failed a test." She threw the paper at him, and it fell onto the floor. Then she crumpled against his side, strong sobs taking over. "I should have told you on Friday. I didn't want you to think less of me, Daddy."

His chest heaved, and he retrieved the test. A sixty-nine was circled in red ink next to Rachel's name. Her first failure. He brought her close and comforted her. "I'd never think less of you." Did Georgie believe he thought less of her? He pushed away the thought and focused on his daughter, her spasms lessening. "Let's look at what you did right, then look at what you did wrong and see what you can do differently next time."

Sniffling, she sat up straight beside him. "I thought you'd be mad at me."

"Disappointed you didn't tell me right away, but I'm not angry." He studied the paper as if it was a lifeline. He wasn't spotless in forthright disclosures. "I also have a confession to make."

She rubbed her nose on her sleeve and glanced at him, her huge brown eyes wide. "You did something wrong? But adults are supposed to get things right."

Yeah, he hadn't gotten that memo, but he was trying his best. That was all he could do.

"I gave the Thunderbird to Georgie so she could take it, Rache, to the person I've sold it to." He could go into specifics and try to justify himself, but he left it at that.

Rachel pushed up her other sleeve, the red skin raw but healing, although there'd always be a scar. "Is it because of me?" More tears streaked down her cheeks. "I'm sorry, Daddy."

Mike brought her closer, shaking his head. "No, kiddo. You have nothing to be sorry about. Accidents happen. This was my decision."

"What did Miss Georgie say about it?" She wiped away her tears. If only it were that easy to wipe away the tears on the inside.

"Miss Georgie and I had a…" Fight seemed a strong word, one he'd rather not use in front of Rachel. "We had a falling out."

"Why?" Rachel fingered the edge of her pink shirt. "I think she likes you."

Heat flooded his cheeks, a ridiculous reaction for a man his age, but not unwelcome. Balling the paper, he longed to call Georgie, talk to her, see her.

"Daddy!" Rachel cried out.

"What?" Mike stilled his fingers.

"You have to sign that, and I have to take it back to the teacher tomorrow morning."

Mike smoothed the paper and searched for the right words. None came. Since Caitlyn left, he'd sat on the sidelines and gone through the motions. Of course, that had been easy enough with a daughter and a full-time career. Still,

Georgie had opened his eyes to how love and duty combined could make life richer, fuller.

How did he repay her? By walking away. That mistake ate at his insides like acid on metal.

Rachel had faced up to him and admitted her failure. Thirty was old enough to fix his shortcomings.

First he'd bring Miss Brittany home. Dreams, memories, family. He and Rachel would manage fine without the extra money. Nothing wrong with peanut butter and jelly. Miss Brittany was worth it. Mike jumped off the couch and ran to the kitchen, where he grabbed a pen and his phone. Returning, he scribbled his name on the top of the test.

"After I make a phone call, we'll go over this together. You'll do better next time, kiddo."

Putting work into a relationship was new to him, but he was up to the challenge.

Was Georgie?

He found Georgie's name in his list of contacts and pressed the red button. Four, five, six. No answer. A text would have to suffice.

Have changed mind. Don't sell Thunderbird. Will u change yr mind & come back 2 Hollydale? I love U. Mike.

The return ping came back almost instantly.

Not possible. Thunderbird is already in hands of new owner.

So Georgie couldn't even bear to hear his voice and had ignored his call. The full impact of what he'd done hit him hard. Georgie always did everything with her whole heart. Even staying mad. But underneath it all? She loved him. He was sure of that. His fingers flew across the screen.

Call me. Let's talk. You name the subject, and I'll listen.

A return ping came less than a minute later.

Subject is Thunderbird. Already sold. Have cashier's check in hand. Will mail tomorrow.

His reply was quick and sure.

Tear up check and bring car back.

Her reply arrived.

Not possible.

Was she so upset with him she wouldn't talk to him? Then again, he did arrest her and handcuff her. Guess she needed more time to get past that.

Rachel left and bounced back into the room, purse in hand. "Daddy?" He put down his phone, something obviously on Rachel's mind. "Miss Georgie came over when I asked her to make a house call and offered her money. I think you need to ask her to make a house call. Money talks. I have eighteen dollars left. How much money do you have?"

He closed his mouth, anything to stop from laughing. One of these days he was going to have to have a long talk with his daughter about how money didn't buy everything. Of course, he didn't know whether to throw his arms around her or head for the hills. Either way, life with Rachel would never be boring.

Rachel was right about one thing, though. Convincing Georgie to stay would involve more than a mere apology. That great big gaping hole in his heart grew even bigger.

"Um. Love doesn't work like that. When you love someone, your pocketbook doesn't matter. You want to spend time with them, do something special for them, be with them."

Something special. What could he do to show Georgie he loved her just the way she was? A plan came together. It would take work and some convincing and help. Lots of help. Georgie was worth it.

Want u to deliver check in person. Don't trust mail.

Her reply was almost instantaneous.

I have to return on Friday. There's something you should know.

Three dots indicated she was still typing. He'd be faster.

See you Friday. Face-to-face.

He held his breath as he waited for her reply.

OK.

He sighed and pushed the phone away. He had one shot to convince her to stay. At least that was more than he had five minutes ago. With any luck, they'd make this work. Together.

CHAPTER TWENTY-THREE

GEORGIE CLUTCHED THE keys to her new home in her hand. Moving to Hollydale and partnering with Max was now a reality. She didn't want to go through another week like this one again. Packing up her apartment in Nashville had taken longer than she'd expected. She glanced at the moving trailer, now detached from the Thunderbird. Unloading her possessions would have to wait until after she met with Mike.

Beau barked from the back seat of the Thunderbird, and she hurried over. Clasping his leash in one hand, she let him sniff his new yard before unlocking her front door. This was her new home.

An image of Mike's home with Ginger and Rachel popped into her mind. Mike. The hardest part about this week was not texting him everything, from her relocation to her buying the Thunderbird. He'd seemed insistent on a face-to-face meeting. That alone was the only reason she didn't spill everything to him. She wanted to see his face when she told him her plans.

She unclasped Beau from his leash, and he ran circles around her. She chuckled, and her phone pinged.

I'm running late. Pls meet me in high school parking lot. MH.

"Okay, Beau. Change of plans. We're not meeting Mike at his house." Her phone alerted her to another text. "Hold on."

Still mad at you for not hearing my brother out but heard you're in town. Meet me at high school, and we'll talk.

Groaning, she hadn't even considered how Natalie would be feeling about her right now. A sister bear defending her kin bested the friend card every time.

Another text pinged, this one from Lucie. Natalie would have to wait as Georgie opened Lucie's note.

Had interview at high school. Twins are at a friend's house. How about you pick me up and we'll go to dinner?

Wait a minute? Three texts about the high school in three minutes?

"Beau, methinks there's something rotten in Denmark."

Her phone chirped again. Another message from Mike.

Am late. Meet me in high school parking lot. I have eighteen dollars. LOVE, Michael. XXXXXOOOOO.

"Now I know something's up." Biting back her chuckle, she grabbed her keys and waited for Beau to calm down enough before clasping his leash back on. She might as well try to persuade Natalie and Lucie to help her unpack.

As for Mike? Had Rachel sent that last text? She rubbed Beau's head for luck before grabbing the check for the Thunderbird. Whatever was going on, she intended to get to the bottom of it.

"RELAX, SHE'LL BE HERE." Natalie came over and grinned. "I sent her a text, and who can resist me? Besides, I went all grizzly bear, and Georgie hates conflict. She'll be here."

"You sent her a text?" Mike groaned and taped the final streamer in place. "I did, too, asking her to meet me here."

The third cohort in his scheme cleared her throat. "Great minds think alike. I lied and told her the twins were at a friend's house." Lucie's gaze met Mike's. She shrugged before pointing to Mattie and Ethan. "I haven't lied since Justin lied to everyone, but it's for a good cause, so Georgie will forgive me, right?"

Mike gave a slight nod, his stomach sinking. At least Rachel didn't have a phone. He patted his back pocket. His phone? Where was it?

He trotted over to Rachel. Sure enough, his phone was in her hands. "What's going on, kiddo?"

She handed the phone back, her bright smile scaring him to the pits of his stomach. "I'm a great helper. Miss Georgie's on her way." Her wink catapulted his stomach down to the floor. "She not only does house calls—she does gym calls, too. It was my eighteen dollars that did the trick, Daddy."

Life without Georgie wouldn't be as bad as it'd been all week, would it? With his helpers, he might find out. Glancing around the gym, Mike hoped Georgie would forgive their clumsy efforts to get her here. And forgive him.

Natalie ran back from the door and held up her thumb. "Showtime! She's here."

Mike sprinted to the cooler and brought out the pale pink wrist corsage, better late than never. Nerves took over, and his mind blanked for a second. What if Georgie didn't want to stay in Hollydale?

He closed his eyes. Then they'd have their

first and last dance. He made his way to the entrance of the gym, corsage in hand. Natalie leaned over and kissed his cheek. "We have the gym for two hours. We all love you. Don't screw it up this time."

Natalie left, her duty to guide Georgie to the gym well in hand. Lucie, holding one child's hand in each of hers, shot him a hopeful glance and followed Natalie. Deep breathing helped little to calm his agitated nerves.

Within minutes, the entrance opened, and Georgie stood there. A week only magnified her beauty. Without her, his mornings wouldn't be filled with light, and his evenings would seem all the duller.

"What's going…" Her mouth fell open as her gaze swept over the gym.

His crew went beyond his wildest expectations in just a few hours. Twinkling lights covered the basketball posts. Silver and white balloons stood on either side of cutouts dotted all around. The Eiffel Tower, Big Ben, the Pyramids. All places he'd love to explore with Georgie and Rachel at his side.

"Oh." Her last word slipped out as her gaze landed on him, surprise and shock in the depths of her eyes.

"Welcome to your senior prom, Georgie." He stepped forward, corsage in hand, absorbing all of Georgie. If she chose to leave Hollydale for good, accepting her choice would be the hardest thing he'd ever done, even harder than saying goodbye to Grandpa Ted, harder than signing the divorce papers, harder than changing Rachel's dressings. "The theme was A Night to Remember. Better late than never, right?"

Because some things in life were worth the wait.

"I'm underdressed."

She'd never looked more beautiful standing there. Her jeans and old sweatshirt, while not a typical outfit for a dance, suited her and them. He wouldn't have cared if she'd shown up in rags or a designer dress. She was here. Mike closed the gap. "You're you. You're beautiful, inside and out. That's all I've ever wanted." He grinned and shrugged. "Once I was old enough to know my own mind."

She squinted at him, that old Georgie gleam back. "And when, pray tell, did this happen?"

"When I saw a dog pulling my old best friend along on a blue leash. But it wasn't until this past weekend Rachel made me realize it's never too late to make a wrong right." Emotion choked his words, and he held out the corsage. "For you."

"I warn you. I sometimes lead." Her words came out sweeter than honey on his mother's biscuits.

He bit back a smile. Somehow, in spite of everything, he sensed she was on the way to forgiving him, all of him. The boy who stood her up all those years ago, the man who let go of the Thunderbird she lovingly restored and the man who arrested her.

"We'll take turns leading." He winked and removed the corsage from the box. "Equals, Georgie. We'll talk, we'll fight, we'll make up."

Rachel ran over, inserting herself between them. "Miss Georgie, I finished the book about Princess Alixandra. The end was the best. She and the dragon lived happily ever after."

Wait a minute. Was he the dragon here?

Rachel turned to Mike, and she nudged his ribs. "Tell her how pretty she is. And remember what we talked about. Offer her money. Then maybe she'll stay in Hollydale."

A confused look came over Georgie's beautiful face. "Did Rachel have your phone this afternoon? Is she the one who offered me eighteen dollars for a house call to the gym?"

He raised his eyebrows but chuckled anyway. "Let's just say Rachel gave me some interesting pointers on what I should say to convince you to move back to Hollydale. I decided to go a different route." Mike touched Rachel's shoulder.

Natalie scooted over and reached for her niece's hand. "Hey, Rachel. Let's give them a couple of minutes." Natalie pulled on Rachel's hand.

His daughter was having none of it. "Miss Georgie, are you staying in Hollydale?"

His heart fluttered.

"Yes." That might be the sweetest word he'd ever heard.

Beaming, Rachel made a fist and brought it toward her in a victory motion. "Will you come to my house? I spent a couple of dollars, so I only have eighteen dollars left, but this time I need you to fix my daddy. He's been awful cranky since Saturday."

"Rachel!" He and Natalie shouted at the same time.

"Come on, my little matchmaking niece. We shall return." Natalie pushed Rachel toward the girls' locker room. "Later. Much later."

"What's matchmaking? I want to stay." Rachel's protests could be heard until a door slammed in the background.

The gym faded away, and there was only Georgie and him. He drank in the sight of her, her cheeks pink and her eyes twinkling.

"You're staying," said Mike.

She gave a single nod, and he lowered his lips to hers and tasted lemons and Georgie and love. She was in his arms, and he wouldn't let go again.

She deepened the kiss before breaking away and resting her head on his shoulder. Music began playing in the background, and they fell into a slow dance. "This week I went and packed up my old apartment and settled the lease. I also contacted Brett Cullinan, thanked him and made the other finalist for that job very happy. Max and I have agreed to terms. When I have a project I believe in, I'll take it. Otherwise I'll work with Max and Travis."

"You did all of this in one week?"

"I could say the same." She pointed at the gym, her wrist graced by the corsage.

"Keeping a secret in Hollydale is rather difficult." He pulled her back into his arms, their dance a reassurance she was really here and not going anywhere. "When I wasn't planning this or at work, I've been swamped with election details. That was how I stayed relatively together this week. No more police or election talk."

"No, we have to get this out in the open. We have to learn to communicate. I was rather—" she paused and shrugged "—upset at your arresting me."

His heart constricted, and his hand stilled on her back. "Georgie, that's part of me. Duty and protection and love. Everything my parents and you taught me over the years that I needed three kicks in the pants to understand."

She raised her finger to his lips and made a soft shushing sound. "I know, and that's why I love the man you've become, Mike Harrison."

She still loved him. The world came back

into focus. With Georgie at his side, sharing his life, loving him, everything would be all right. "I love you. That's why I didn't give you any notice about this. I wanted you to show up in the clothes you're most comfortable in. To be yourself."

"A little notice would have been nice, though. I would have at least brushed my hair. And Lucie—I wonder where she went to—helped me pick out a beautiful dress for the Hollydale Hoedown."

He couldn't help the goofy grin coming over him. "Tell you what. You can wear that dress to a special dinner one evening, and I'll propose. How's that sound?"

A stunned look crossed her face, and the corners of her mouth lifted up. "You've got yourself a deal."

There'd be ups and downs, storms and sunshine, lemons and lemon meringue pie. But they'd weathered the storm, and his heart was whole again. She was home, and he'd hold her tight as they faced the road ahead together.

"You weren't kidding. You like to lead, don't you?" Mike brought Georgie back to their moment.

She glanced at her feet, her sneakers having seen better days. "Old habits die hard. We're equals. Sometimes you'll lead, and sometimes I will. Sound good to you?"

"Always." He grinned, and how his smile lightened his face sent shivers down her spine.

She'd made the right choice. This was the dream of her heart.

A loud bark came from the entrance. The doors flew open, and Mattie, Lucie's daughter, was holding on for dear life to Beau's leash, her twin brother at her heels, arguing it was his turn. Lucie hurried behind as the flash of brown fur hurdled toward Georgie and Mike.

"Beau!" Her dog jumped up, and she waggled her finger. "No jumping."

Beau swiped his tongue out and licked her finger before turning his attention toward Mike. She saw obedience lessons in this dog's future, whether the dog liked it or not.

"Beau? What are you doing here?" A note of puzzled amusement laced Mike's words.

"Mr. Reedy had to go into assisted living, so he asked me to take care of Beau." Georgie knelt on the gym floor and petted the dog.

Mike knelt beside her, his fingers bumping into hers when they both stroked Beau's head. "That must have been hard on him. I know how much Mr. Reedy values his independence."

Their gazes met, the electricity heightened between them.

Independence was great, he even liked that

about her. But she'd realized she didn't have to change her nature to let someone share her life. Especially when it was the right someone.

"I visited Mr. Reedy today. He's already looking 100 percent better. Having someone else help with his load has been good for him."

Mike didn't waver, his penetrating gaze shrewd and discerning. "What about you, Georgie? Will you let me share your load?"

She smiled and nodded. "Beau's a big commitment. I do love him—though not as much as I love a single father and his daughter." Before anything else, he had to know the truth. "I have your cashier's check for the Thunderbird."

"Can we call Quinn right now? Maybe if you offer to restore the first Thunderbird he can find…" His shoulders stiffened. "No, don't. We'll make our own memories and work on restoring a new car together."

"Um, Mike." That quiver in her voice was too real, and his eyebrows knit into a V. "I cashed in the bonds my father left me, figuring I was accepting the pit crew job and wouldn't need the money for the repair shop."

"Well, then. Max is probably happy with the money now."

She gave a slow shake of her head. No more running away. She'd learned her lesson. Talking to Mike, no matter how hard, always came first.

"I bought the Thunderbird."

He blinked as if processing the information.

She rushed onward. "I wanted it to stay with someone who knew your grandfather, someone who loved the car and his family as much as he did."

Mike rubbed his index finger along her cheek. "You did that for me?" He moved forward, and Beau scooted out of the way. Mike's lips met hers in the sweetest kiss. It was as if Mike poured his thanks, his soul, himself into it. He broke away. "Your choice. Do you want me to tear up the check or do you want to be the proud owner of the best Thunderbird ever?"

The truth hit her smack in the face. "I want to keep the car in the family."

He chuckled, rose and reached out his hands to help her off the ground. "Did you just propose to me, Georgie Bennett, to get out of wearing a dress to dinner?"

She blinked before lifting her chin. "I might have."

"Georgie Harrison. I like the sound of that."

She groaned and hit her forehead with the bottom of her hand. "I'll have the same name as one of the Beatles, for crying out loud."

"But you'll have Rachel and Beau. I might be able to persuade Ginger to share me with you. Most likely." He tapped three of his fingers against his chin. "By the way, my answer is yes." He grinned and winked. "Don't make me wait too long."

He fluttered his eyelashes, and her laughter filled the air. The road to Hollydale had been long, but there was nowhere else she'd rather be. He wound his arms around her, pulling her close so she could smell sandalwood, shampoo and Mike. *Now* there was nowhere else she'd rather be.

EPILOGUE

GEORGIE AND MIKE bounced down the gazebo steps, where they'd just said their "I dos." She glanced over at the Thunderbird. Several strings with attached cans paraded behind its bumper. Shouts from the crowd surrounded them. One lone woof announced Beau's presence. Seeing her dog in a bow tie broadened her already wide smile.

Mr. Reedy, his oxygen canister in place, gave them two thumbs up. Natalie, a pregnant Becks, and the Harrisons beamed from Mike's side. Everywhere were faces she'd come to love since she'd moved back to Hollydale. Max flanked by his sister and Heidi and Travis; Lucie and her twins; her new stepdaughter, Rachel. Her heart filled with happiness at sharing this day with so many friends and family.

Her mother stepped forward, tears glittering in the winter sunlight gracing the afternoon. "Your father would be so proud of you." She wiped the corner of her eye with a lacy handkerchief. "Thank you for insisting on counseling and for including me. I'm proud of you."

The counselor had urged baby steps for their relationship. Mom's restraint today was a huge leap forward. "Thanks, Mom."

"Throw the bouquet!"

"Throw the garter first!"

Laughter poured out of her. She turned to Mike and waggled her eyebrows. "Hey, Sheriff, you up for throwing the garter first?"

"Bring it on."

From behind, Rachel snorted. "Everyone's crazy. The cake's the best part."

Mike leaned toward Georgie, a sly chuckle brushing the sensitive part of her skin near her ear. "Not the best part. That comes later."

Heat flushed her cheeks. Georgie yelled, "Garter, then bouquet."

She stepped over to a stone bench and pulled up her dress enough for the garter to show. White sneakers covered with hearts drawn in red marker graced her feet. Several people gasped, but Mike's smile grew even wider.

"The bride wore sneakers." He laughed, a rich, robust sound that sent her heart overflowing with more love. "Just when I didn't think I could love you any more, you surprise me by being totally Georgie. Don't ever stop being yourself. I'm the luckiest man in Hollydale."

"I helped. The red hearts were my idea." Rachel nodded her head for emphasis. "I'm glad you're my stepmother now, Miss Georgie."

"I couldn't be happier."

Lace and tennis shoes. Ginger and Beau. Engines and a sheriff's badge. She and Mike. Pairs that shouldn't go together but did captured her essence to a T. If she hadn't come back to Hollydale, she wouldn't have discovered any of that. She wouldn't have reconnected with herself.

She was home, and she was happy. The road here had been bumpy, but with Mike, the road ahead would be navigated with purpose, laughter and love. He squeezed her hand. She'd made the right choice, the only choice, living her dreams with Mike and love at her side.

* * * * *

For more Harlequin Heartwarming romances, please visit www.Harlequin.com today!

Get 4 FREE REWARDS!

We'll send you 2 FREE Books plus 2 FREE Mystery Gifts.

Love Inspired® books feature contemporary inspirational romances with Christian characters facing the challenges of life and love.

FREE Value Over **$20**

Get 4 FREE REWARDS!

We'll send you 2 FREE Books plus 2 FREE Mystery Gifts.

Love Inspired® Suspense books feature Christian characters facing challenges to their faith... and lives.

FREE Value Over **$20**

THE FORTUNES OF TEXAS COLLECTION!

18 FREE BOOKS in all!

Treat yourself to the rich legacy of the Fortune and Mendoza clans in this remarkable 50-book collection. This collection is packed with cowboys, tycoons and Texas-sized romances!

Get 4 FREE REWARDS!

We'll send you 2 FREE Books <u>plus</u> 2 FREE Mystery Gifts.

FREE
Value Over
$20

Both the **Romance** and **Suspense** collections feature compelling novels written by many of today's bestselling authors.

YES! Please send me 2 FREE novels from the Essential Romance or Essential Suspense Collection and my 2 FREE gifts (gifts are worth about $10 retail). After receiving them, if I don't wish to receive any more books, I can return the shipping statement marked "cancel." If I don't cancel, I will receive 4 brand-new novels every month and be billed just $6.99 each in the U.S. or $7.24 each in Canada. That's a savings of at least 13% off the cover price. It's quite a bargain! Shipping and handling is just 50¢ per book in the U.S. and $1.25 per book in Canada.* I understand that accepting the 2 free books and gifts places me under no obligation to buy anything. I can always return a shipment and cancel at any time. The free books and gifts are mine to keep no matter what I decide.

Choose one: ☐ **Essential Romance**
(194/394 MDN GNNP)

☐ **Essential Suspense**
(191/391 MDN GNNP)

Name (please print)

Address   Apt. #

City   State/Province   Zip/Postal Code

Mail to the **Reader Service**:
IN U.S.A.: P.O. Box 1341, Buffalo, NY 14240-8531
IN CANADA: P.O. Box 603, Fort Erie, Ontario L2A 5X3

Want to try 2 free books from another series? Call 1-800-873-8635 or visit www.ReaderService.com.

ReaderService.com has a new look!

We have refreshed our website and we want to share our new look with you. Head over to ReaderService.com and check it out!

On ReaderService.com, you can:

- Try 2 free books from any series
- Access risk-free special offers
- View your account history & manage payments
- Browse the latest Bonus Bucks catalog

Don't miss out!

If you want to stay up-to-date on the latest at the Reader Service and enjoy more Harlequin content, make sure you've signed up for our monthly News & Notes email newsletter. Sign up online at ReaderService.com.

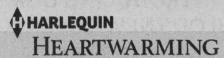
#315 ALWAYS THE ONE
Meet Me at the Altar • by Tara Randel
Torn apart years ago, FBI agent Derrick Matthews has the chance to reunite with the love of his life and solve a cold case involving her family. Can Hannah Rawlings accept his solution—and him—after all this time?

#316 THE FIREFIGHTER'S VOW
Cape Pursuit Firefighters • by Amie Denman
Laura Wheeler lost her brother in a fire, so fire chief Tony Ruggles is shocked when she volunteers for the fire service. He wants to help her find the answers she needs—but will she let him into her heart?

#317 MONTANA DAD
Sweet Home, Montana • by Jeannie Watt
Alex Ryan is hiding from her past, and with the help of Nick Callahan, her handsome, single-dad neighbor, she tries to blend in in small-town Montana. But as Alex and Nick grow closer, will her secrets tear them apart?

#318 SOLDIER OF HER HEART
by Syndi Powell
While renovating a vintage home, Lawrence Beckett discovers a cracked stained glass window. Art expert Andie Lowman is able to come to the troubled military vet's rescue...in more ways than one.

HWCNM0120

INTRODUCING OUR
FABULOUS NEW COVER LOOK!

COMING FEBRUARY 2020

Find your favorite series in-store, online or subscribe to the Reader Service!

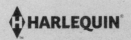